In My Father's House

and Related Readings

McDougal Littell

A HOUGHTON MIFFLIN COMPANY

Evanston, Illinois • Boston • Dallas

Acknowledgments

Scholastic Inc.: *In My Father's House* by Ann Rinaldi. Copyright © 1993 by Ann Rinaldi. Reprinted by permission of Scholastic Inc.

Doubleday: "A Dark Indefinite Shore," from *Reflections on the Civil War* by Bruce Catton. Copyright © 1981 by Gerald Dickler as the executor of the estate of Bruce Catton and John Leckley.
"When Freedom Came," from *Long Journey Home: Stories From Black History* by Julius Lester. Copyright © 1972 by Julius Lester.
Used by permission of Doubleday, a division of Bantam Doubleday Dell Publishing Group, Inc.

Harold Ober Associates Incorporated: "Southern Mansion" by Arna Bontemps. Copyright © 1963 by Arna Bontemps. Reprinted by permission of Harold Ober Associates Incorporated.

Gwendolyn Brooks: "In Honor of David Anderson Brooks, My Father," from *Blacks* by Gwendolyn Brooks. Copyright © 1991 by Gwendolyn Brooks. Published by Third World Press, Chicago, 1991. Reprinted by permission of the author.

Dell Books: "She" by Rosa Guy, from *Sixteen: Short Stories*, edited by Donald R. Gallo. Copyright © 1984 by Rosa Guy. Used by permission of Dell Books, a division of Bantam Doubleday Dell Publishing Group, Inc.

Cover central photograph: Corbis-Bettman.
Background calligraphy by Holly Dickens Designs Inc.
Background photo by Alexander Gardner.
Author image by Bart Ehrenberg.

Printed in the United States of America.

ISBN 0-395-88933-2

4567—QNT—03 02 01

Contents

In My Father's House

Ann Rinaldi

Chapter 1

Christmas 1852

Before the war they called the area where I lived in northern Virginia, Tudor Hall. When the war started in 1861, it became known as Manassas. And I suppose that name will forever after conjure up the first battle of that war, which took place on our front lawn.

I wasn't there for that event. Daddy Will had sent us away by then. But in the days before we left, when there was so much confusion and mayhem, worse than a hog-killing, we didn't have any clever notions about first battles. It all just happened.

When I was growing up at Yorkshire, my home, nobody ever dreamed the North and the South would pick our front lawn to start their old war on. Although I suppose armies have to commence killing each other someplace. In those days Tudor Hall was a quiet place, a land of small plantations where people raised cattle and hogs. A land of secret dark woods, crystal clear streams, gently rolling hills, wheat fields that went on forever, and corn standing high in the sun.

Nothing much ever happened. We had our frolics, our church suppers, our barbecues. Every Christmas Mama and Doctor John, my real daddy, gave a ball. Mrs. Judith Henry, the widow, lived as an invalid on Henry Hill, face as stiff as a preacher's collar, but nice as can be. Lucinda Dogan's cattle grazed five miles northwest of us near the Warrenton Pike. Her brother John raised corn and peaches at Rosefield. The Matthews gave refreshments to the teamsters going to and from the markets in Alexandria, because the Matthews lived along Warrenton Pike.

The Carters owned Carters Green; Benjamin Chinn toiled in the fields right alongside his nigras at Hazel Plain; the Van Pells ran Avon. People gave their plantations fancy names like Liberia and Mayfield, though nobody had more than twenty nigras. We had fourteen. The Stratton-Wilchers called their place Lang Syne.

Manassas Junction was the cause of all the fuss in 1861 because two railroads met there, the Orange and Alexandria and the Manassas Gap. The South needed its rail lines to defend northern Virginia. And the Yankees wanted the junction too, being it was only twenty-five miles from Washington. Myself, I couldn't see why anybody would want it. All that was there were some warehouses, a tallow factory, and the station with the telegraph office. We got the train there to go to Alexandria.

So the war came to Manassas. But for me the confusion and mayhem came before that, when Will McLean came into our lives. Which should tell a person how I felt about him when he first came to us.

Mama said that McLean and my daddy knew each other, because Doctor John used to go into McLean's store in Centreville. Mama said sometimes my daddy took me with him into the store. But I don't remember that, or McLean. Perhaps I just chose not to. The first time I had a real conversation with the man was two days before Christmas in 1852, the evening of the party the Stratton-Wilchers gave for him and my mama. And he'd been courting Mama since August. Up until then I managed to stay clear of the man whenever he was around.

He knew I was steering clear of him, too. "We're going to have to talk someday soon, Oscie," he'd said several times that fall. "I *am* going to be your new stepdaddy. Maria and I have had many quiet chats."

I'd rather talk to his hound dogs. They were the only decent thing the man had going for him far as I could see. Daddy John always said you could tell the mettle of a man by his dogs. McLean had fine dogs, all right. They'd sit for hours and wait for him while he was out taking Mama for a drive. Or follow him around the place and obey hand signals.

I suppose that's how he wanted me and Maria to be. Well, Maria was just one step away from it, simpering over him the moment he stepped on the place.

"Oh, he's so tall and dashing!" And she'd swoon like a drunken hooty owl. Maria never did have the sense God gave a goose. McLean was tall, yes. And he sported a mustache, so I suppose that qualified him for dashing. He knew how to use his voice, too. Why I never saw such a man for having people jump when he spoke just above a whisper. You knew he was there when he walked into a room. And he could dance, I'll give him that. Maria said he had dimples. I said no decent self-respecting man had dimples. They had creases in their faces. I may have hated

McLean on sight, but I knew he was decent and self-respecting because Mama was nobody's fool and she sure loved him.

We finally had our little talk, before the party that night, in the barn. Mirabella was giving birth. I was determined not to leave for the party until it happened, because Mirabella was my Daddy John's horse. The only reason I agreed to go to the party was because Julia Stratton-Wilcher said she had a secret to tell me. I was seven that year, but thanks to my Daddy John's unofficial schooling, more like twelve. Julia was eight, like Maria, and more like fifteen. But if Julia had a secret, I'd go. Not because she was a friend. She was a weasel, a snake in the grass, and a prig. But Daddy John always said that we learn more from our enemies than from our friends.

Steam seemed to rise from the straw beneath Mirabella. She lay very still, her large wonderful eyes glistening with acceptance. "Do you think Mama will let me name the foal, Allie?" I asked.

"Doan see why not." He and his twin brother, Billie, were attending Mirabella. I trusted them. My Daddy John had taught them all about horses when they were twelve and they were now in their twenties.

"Will McLean won't let me name it," I said dismally.

"Mister Will's a good man," Allie said loyally. "He done promised to buy my Mary Ann."

"He's going to *buy* her?" Mary Ann was the Stratton-Wilcher's house girl and Allie was smitten with her. But this news was not good. It meant McLean was bringing his own servants to Yorkshire.

We had no need for them. The plantation had gotten on just fine in the two-and-a-half years since my daddy had died. I ought to know. I'd ridden out with him since I was four, learning everything. And I rode out now with Hiram, my daddy's personal man who had taken charge, seeing that the fences and farm implements were in good repair, the wheat and corn harvested on time. We were out at first light, inspecting the stables, the spring house. Why Hiram had even allowed me to name the day for hog killing this year; the first good cold day in December.

The servants all came to me with their complaints and with the help of Hiram I settled them so they wouldn't bother Mama.

"If'n Mister Will doan buy Mary Ann, Mister Wilcher sell her," Allie said. "He has debts. Bad luck at cards."

"That doesn't surprise me, Allie. Mr. Wilcher drinks and gambles. What does surprise me is McLean's buying Mary Ann. He's an abolitionist. He goes around boasting he's never bought a darkie in his life."

"You can't never tell what a person will do," Allie said. "Did you ever think your mama wud marry again?"

"No, and I hate that she is. More than I hate going to this party tonight."

"You're gonna hate Will McLean even more if you don't get up to the house right quick, little lady, and get yourself pretty for that party."

McLean approached to lean on the stall. He wore an old woolen greatcoat, open in front. Under it I could see he was all fancied up for the ball. His eyes, under bushy brows, shone like black jewels.

We glared at each other. Always when I saw him about the place, his appearance startled me. Was it that he was too dapper? That he was a merchant? I didn't know. But he stuck out on the landscape where my daddy had blended in. He brought some of the outside world with him, something that did not belong.

"I'm staying until Mirabella delivers," I said.

"Look here, Oscie, I don't give a cobbler's boot if you come to the party tonight. But I've commissioned an artist to do a portrait of you and Maria and little Sarah. It's a wedding present for your mother. He's waiting for us at Lang Syne."

He knew how to please Mama, all right. She had often spoken of wanting such a portrait. Now he looked to Billie and Allie. "How are things going with the little lady?"

"'Jus fine, Suh," Allie said. "Things is movin' along."

"Will you two be able to handle it alone?"

"Doctor John teached us long time ago," Billie said.

"Well, Doctor John seems to have done a good job." McLean drew his greatcoat about him. "This barn is a horseman's nightmare. I'll send Tom down to fill in some of those cracks in the chinking. And Meta, with some quilts for the mare and foal. And the first chance I get, I'm building a new barn. Come along, Oscie. I promised your mother I'd fetch you. You don't want me to look incompetent in her eyes, do you?"

There was nothing I wanted more. But I knelt down to hug Mirabella and told Billie to send word to the Wilchers when the foal came. So McLean would know the servants obeyed me.

As we walked out, I looked up at him. "My daddy was going to build a new barn," I said.

"I know that, Oscie. Your mother told me."

He held up his lantern. "Your daddy's old doctor's gig," he said.

It sat in a corner. We both stared. "When Doctor John made calls in that, he was so fast nobody could outrun him," I said.

"I remember. But look, Oscie. Do you see the condition it's in? Covered with spiderwebs? Well, this plantation is fast becoming the same way. You think your father would want that?"

Tears filled my eyes. "I see to what needs doing. Me and Hiram."

"You've both been doing a fine job. But you're just a child and Hiram's getting old. The servants need better direction. I intend to buy a McCormick reaper to harvest the oats and wheat. Expand the crop yield and eliminate the need for more darkies. Then maybe the ones we have won't always be too busy when I ask them to do something."

"I speculate they just don't like you," I said.

"I speculate you've had a hand in that. Which is why Maum Hanna serves me cold coffee and Meta and Tom and Tyron won't give me reports on the field work."

"They've been too busy for that."

"In the middle of winter? And why won't Paula and Fanny feed my dogs? And why, when I stay the night, does Hiram put me in that godforsaken downstairs bedroom where it's cold as a witch's ear?"

"I speculate he's not used to you."

"And I speculate you had something to do with Mathilda's giving me back a shirt with no buttons the other day after she laundered it."

"I'm grievous hurt that you think such things of me, Mister Will."

"The name is *Daddy Will,* Missy. And if you

continue to turn the servants against me . . . well, just don't, that's all."

His tone brooked no argument.

"Yes, sir." I knew I was beaten temporarily. I was no fool. "I'll tell the servants to pay you mind. You don't have to buy Mary Ann. I know how that would worry you, being you're an abolitionist."

We were walking on the path up to my daddy's house, which sat on a large knoll in the midst of the pasture lands. He stopped short in front of me and whirled around so his greatcoat swung wide. His shadow, cast by his lantern, was larger than life against the two-story brick house, like a great winged bird come to hover over it.

"I'm a *what*? What do you know of abolitionists?"

"Mama read us Harriet Beecher Stowe's book."

He sighed. "I'm not an abolitionist, Oscie. But I am a realist. I was cared for by nigra servants as a child. And I love the South. But I hate the slave system. And as a merchant, I know our cotton makes a long journey to the North to be manufactured into goods that come back to us at terrible prices."

"My daddy explained that to me."

"Did he now?" His tone was one of rich amusement.

"Yes, sir. He said he rode on a Northern saddle, read Northern books, wrote on Northern paper with a Northern pen. He said all our money is tied up in land and nigras, .that we sell cotton to buy more nigras to make more cotton."

He was no longer amused. "Go on."

"He said someday the music would end for us and the piper would have to be paid. But we could write our own music, if we had a mind to. I think he was talking about the waltzes they played at Mama's balls. He always liked the country tunes better."

"Your daddy meant that the South must learn to rely on itself. I go one step further. I say that when the piper asks for his money, we're going to have disaster. And I intend to provide for my family when that happens."

I nodded. But I was disinterested. Grown-ups had been talking about things like slave states and free states, Yankee money and the Missouri Compromise for as long as I could remember.

"Is that creek always that high?" McLean asked.

I looked to the bottom of the slope. "It gets high when the rains are bad. Mama worries about Sarah playing down there more than about the price of wheat."

"Can Sarah swim?"

I eyed him as if he'd taken leave of his senses. "None of us can."

He said nothing, but I sensed his brooding disapproval. And I wanted to defend my mother and father for what he obviously considered a serious lapse in our education. My anger toward him returned.

"If you buy Mary Ann, you'll be a slaver," I said.

"Go and get ready for the party," he ordered. "I want to see you looking like a charming Southern belle in that Northern dress I bought in New York. Sarah and Maria already have theirs on. And behave tonight or you'll answer to me."

I walked around him on the path. "You'll be no different from the rest of the slavers around here."

"That may be." His attention was on the creek again. "But I hear tell that Mary Ann is the best there is at laundering a man's shirt. And if I buy her, it's my business."

Chapter 2

What happened that night at the Stratton-Wilchers' set the tone for the way of things between me and Will McLean for the next thirteen years. Only I was so miserable that evening, I wouldn't have believed it if someone told me so.

My starched pantalettes scratched me and at supper Julia spilled gravy from the roast saddle of lamb on my blue watered taffeta. Blue was my favorite color. I had no notion of how Will McLean had known that. I only knew that Maum Hanna blamed me and scolded, saying I'd be the death of her yet. And that Julia smirked and when we were finally released from a long after-supper session with the artist, I was not only ready for a set-to with Julia, I was overdue.

Maria, Julia, little Sarah, and I were sitting on the curved stairway, watching the guests whirl around on the polished floors in the ballroom below, to the sweeping music of waltz after waltz. Then Julia asked us which man we thought was most handsome.

"Daddy Will," Maria said right off.

"You would say that," Julia snickered. "I heard he has a past. That he's a rake with women."

Both Maria and I stared at her. I know Maria didn't understand and I sure didn't, either.

"He's thirty-eight," Julia explained, "and well-traveled. He's never married. Of course, there's that business with Annabelle Hurst."

I faced Julia, that child-woman, knowing I had a lot of catching up to do with her. She listened behind closed doors all the time, which was why she knew so much. "Explain yourself," I said.

Julia tossed her head. "Her father is very wealthy. Your new stepdaddy courted her for at least three years."

I glared at her. "If that's your big secret, Julia, you can stuff it in an old pair of drawers!"

She waited until Maum Hanna, who had come to take away a sleepy Sarah, walked off with the child in her arms. Then she smiled wickedly.

"It isn't any secret. That's just it. Everybody knows how Will McLean ran after Annabelle Hurst, then turned his attentions to your mama when Annabelle wouldn't have him."

For a moment my world stopped. And the sound of tinkling glasses, the laughter, the waltz music, all froze in time. All that I saw was Julia's face, strained with her wickedness. Then I came to life.

"You take that back, Julia Stratton-Wilcher," I said.

"I will if you want, but half the people in both Prince William and Fairfax counties are talking about it and saying that when Will McLean couldn't get one wealthy woman he just went out and got himself another."

She smoothed the skirt of her green-and-white

striped taffeta. "Your mama is a woman of property. Why do you suppose men marry wealthy widows?"

I felt the rage boiling. Her simpering smile was like a knife in me. And so I did the only thing I could to defend my mama's honor. I slapped Julia in the face.

Well, there was some caterwauling then. She sounded like a hound pup caged up during coon season. I was getting some good fistfuls of hair when Maum Hanna came along and dragged me off.

"Actin' like a field hand! Actin' like white trash! My bones'll rust and I'll never see you wif any manners."

"You shouldn't have stopped me. I'll tear the eyes out of her head."

"Only tearin' 'round here is gonna be by me. Now you both git to bed."

No sense protesting. Maum Hanna's authority came directly from God, through Mama. As we passed Julia's room, the door was open. She rubbed her eyes and managed to smile. "Since you think he's so handsome, Maria, I don't suppose you'll mind knowing that he's adopting you all and you'll have to change your name to McLean."

"Do you think it's true?" Maria's voice floated in the dark across the room. We were both in bed. "Do you think he's marrying Mama for her money?"

"I don't know."

"Look at what Julia's stepdaddy is doing, going through all her mama's money. Should we tell Mama?"

"I don't know." I was starting to sound like the village idiot.

"Will Maum Hanna tell Daddy Will what happened?"

"She'll tell him, all right."

"What do you think he'll do?"

"I'll probably get whupped."

"It's cold in here. Can I get in bed with you?"

She was frightened, so I said yes and held her against me when she came into my bed.

"I don't think Daddy Will would whup you. He's so kind, Oscie. You don't know him like I do. He's so gentle with Sarah. And he knows a lot about books and learning."

I needed to think, but I couldn't with Maria around.

"Oscie, is Mama a woman of property?"

"Yes. She owns twelve hundred acres at our place, three hundred and thirty in Fairfax County, and five hundred more acres someplace else in Prince William County. Daddy told me before he died."

"Oh, I can't bear to think such about Daddy Will."

"Don't then. Let me worry about it."

"Oh, Oscie, you're so strong and you're a whole year younger."

"Before he died, Daddy told me I had to be strong and look after you and Mama and Sarah. I promised him I would."

"Why did our Daddy have to go and die, Oscie? It isn't fair."

"Because he was riding out all day in the pouring rain to take care of people in the yellow fever epidemic. He took a bad chill."

"I can barely recollect what he looked like, Oscie. Can you?"

"I'll never forget," I said. "Sometimes he comes to me in my dreams at night."

"He *does*? What does he say?"

"Don't you tell anybody I said that. They'd think I

was weak in the head or something. The dreams aren't much. Just some shapes that wouldn't stand up to the light of day. He doesn't say anything. But it's the feeling I get. That he's real close to me. And what was between us before comes alive, too. You go to sleep now, Maria. I need to think."

Before long I heard her even breathing. And then, finally, the sound I was waiting for. Footsteps, and the door of Mama's room opening and closing down the hall.

My daddy had always said that Mama was a strong woman. But with all women, he had told me, there is a breaking place.

Mama didn't look as if she'd reached her breaking place just yet. After I told her what Julia had said, she just paced up and down in her room in her blue silk robe de chambre, her arms folded against her.

"Oscie, you must stop this hysteria of yours. You've been seeing disaster everywhere since your daddy died." She said it sadly and she did not scold.

"It's true, Mama. Julia listens behind doors all the time. That's how she heard it."

She stopped pacing. "True."

"Yes, Mama."

"Are you telling me that all those people who congratulated us and gave us those lovely presents tonight are talking behind our backs?"

I stood my ground. "Yes, Mama."

She sank down on the dressing table bench. "I can't believe this."

She was beautiful, my mama. She was only thirty-four then, and she was slim as a young girl. Her face was so fine that I felt sore in my heart every time I looked on it, a kind of bittersweet pain. Her dark hair was lustrous, her eyes huge and luminous. I thought it the highest honor to be allowed in her bed chamber when Paula or Fanny helped her dress. I wanted nothing more than to be like her.

"Did Will McLean really court Annabelle Hurst?" I asked.

She smiled wanly. "Yes. The girl was sickly and wouldn't think of marriage. Oh, how can they make a fuss over that? His intentions were honest. As they are with me! How *can* people say such things about my Will! He's so good, so decent!"

Fear gripped me and I wished my daddy was here. He'd know what to do for her. Would she call off the wedding? Before now I'd have jumped for joy at the idea. But now I was frightened. She was so alone. She *needed* somebody. And I knew how she loved Will McLean. She said he was charming.

"What will you do, Mama?"

"I don't know what to do," she said. "But it will come to me by morning. I'll pray on it. Leave me now. I must think."

I went to hug her. She kissed the top of my head. "You are so often a plague to me," she said. "But you are always true."

I was flooded with happiness.

"You must explain to Will McLean why you hit Julia. First thing in the morning. He wants to see you in the library at seven. You've embarrassed him horribly with our hosts."

"Embarrassed *him!*"

"Yes."

"What about what he's done to us?"

She scowled. "*He* hasn't done anything to us, Oscie. The *gossips* have done it. Do you think for a moment that I believe their lies?"

"But . . . "

"What would your daddy have to say about holding with gossip about someone?"

She *would* go and bring my daddy into it. "He'd say to hear the person out," I recited dutifully.

"Exactly. Your daddy always said Will McLean was honest in his dealings. So you have my permission to ask Will if he's marrying me for my money. And decide for yourself." She got up. "I only ask you one thing. Be kind to my Will in the morning."

What about her Will being kind to me? But there was much pleading in her eyes, I said yes, I would.

"And I wish you'd call him Daddy Will, like Maria and Sarah do. It would mean much to me. Don't shame me, Oscie. Or your daddy who brought you up to know better."

There it was again. Mention my daddy and I'd walk over hot coals for her. What else could I do?

Chapter 3

Of course, the next morning Will McLean carried on as if I'd shamed not only my own family but his whole Scottish clan, including his grandfather Bethannath Hodgkinson who'd crossed the Delaware with George Washington.

·He didn't carry on outright. That wasn't his way. First he closed the library door and invited me to sit and have coffee with him.

"Mama doesn't allow us to have coffee," I said.

"I know that. But with plenty of milk, it won't harm you. I know your fondness for it."

How did he know I loved coffee? Or that my favorite color was blue? I watched him put cream and two spoons of sugar in the dark liquid, just as I would have done. And it came to me that this man was no one to shilly-shally with. He made it his business to know everything about me and Maria and probably even little Sarah!

I accepted the cup gratefully and drank down the sweet hot liquid.

"When I was about your age—how old are you now? Eight?"

He was playing now. "No, sir, I'm seven."

"You act older." He smiled his most engaging smile. "Except, of course, when you play the hooligan, like you did last night. And dishonor us all. Then I'd say you were three."

A chill came over me.

"Anyway, when I was eight, I was orphaned. My brothers and sisters and I were farmed out to different relatives. I went with Captain and Anne Hodgkinson, my mother's brother and his wife. He'd served in the War of 1812 and was tough as nails. But he was good to me and he let me have coffee. I'll never forget it."

The fire crackled. He drank his coffee and set the cup down gently. And then he started on honor and kin.

"Your bad manners have been an embarrassment to me and your mother. As guests in this house we have the obligation to contribute to the tranquility and pleasure of our hosts and uphold our honor and that of our kin."

He was very angry, but he hid his anger well.

"Now, you will kindly tell me, why your petulance and bad manners got out of hand last night."

"You won't like it."

"I don't expect to."

There was nothing for it but to tell him. So I did. He listened solemnly. "Did you inform your mother about this?"

"Yes, sir."

He got up to stand in front of the hearth. "I dearly wish you had come to me first. Well," he turned to face me. "As head of the family, what do you intend to do about it?"

I stared at him, open-mouthed. "What?"

"You consider yourself head of the family. Do you want to ask me about Annabelle Hurst and why I pursued her?"

This was a trick, certainly. The man was full of tricks. But for the life of me, all I could do was blush. "No, sir."

"Then perhaps you'd like to ask if I'm marrying your mama for her money. Ask away."

I rallied. "Are you?" I asked.

"What do you think, Oscie?"

I studied him as he stood there. He'd been out riding already. I'd seen him from my window, bounding across the frozen fields on his horse, Pathfinder. Probably got up at six after card playing all night. Yet his face didn't have the look of late hours, hard whiskey, and women, as my daddy would call it. He was as elegant in his riding clothes as he'd been last night in his dove-gray swallowtail and silk pastel waistcoat.

Frantically, I searched my mind for what I knew about him. I minded hearing something about his mercantile business in Centreville not doing well. I stared up at him. He was awaiting my answer. Did I think he was marrying my mama for her money? Oh, I was so confused. *His business in Centreville was not doing well.* The words went round in my head.

Then a name came to me. *Willow Spring Farm.* Yes. I'd heard Mama mention it as a place he'd owned near Centreville. So he was not landless. And Mama had said he owned a house in Centreville, too. And just before I'd come into the room, I'd heard him arguing with Julia's stepdaddy. Mr. Wilcher had asked him to join his group of men who wanted to ask Franklin Pierce, who was to be our next president, to make a raid on Cuba.

McLean had said no, that the antislavery papers up North were calling the Southerners highwaymen for raiding Cuba. And that all he wanted was to settle down and be a family man, that wheat would go from thirty cents to a dollar seventy a bushel this year and he aimed to take advantage of it.

He would take care of Mama and little Sarah and Maria, I thought. I knew my own daddy would want that.

"No sir," I allowed. "I don't think you're marrying Mama for her money."

"Because you consider me honorable and trust-worthy?"

"No sir. Because my daddy said you were honest. And you're not jittery as a grasshopper all the time like Julia's stepdaddy, who's not used to nice things."

He smiled. "You are very forthright, Oscie."

"But Mama's still upset because of the gossip. So does that mean you won't get married?"

"Would that bother you, Oscie?"

"I wouldn't want to see Mama unhappy."

"I assure you, we'll marry. The gossips won't stop us. And now we must speak of other matters."

He smiled again and I felt a knell in my bones. "I never saw such a household as yours. You girls are absolutely undisciplined and in real danger of growing up uneducated. Maria has a startling talent for the piano, but no one to teach her properly. Your penmanship is terrible. Little Sarah doesn't even know her alphabet yet. Do you think your daddy would want that?"

"No sir. Mama had an Episcopal theology student here for a while to tutor Sarah. He read to us from scriptures on the Sabbath."

"Don't you all go to church anymore?"

"Mama let the pew rent lapse. She couldn't bear sitting there without Daddy. We have prayers at home."

"And I suppose you and Maria are truant from Van Sickle's Institute for Young Ladies so often because you can't bear it there, either."

I stared at him. "How do you know such things?"

"It is my business to know them."

"Then you should know that Maria and I think the girls at Van Sickle's are all featherheaded gooses."

"You decided that, not Maria." His face darkened. "You are filling Maria's head with your notions. She is strongly under your influence and she must learn to think for herself. That wild nature of yours needs tempering, or you will ruin your life and break your mama's heart."

For a moment we glared at each other. Then his voice got milder. "Education is a tradition in my family. At your age, in the Alexandria Academy, I studied Greek and Latin."

My knees, under my calico skirt, were shaking. "Are you going to send me away to school?"

"Send you away?" He laughed. "Of course not. I'm going to get you girls a tutor."

"A tutor?" What was he saying? Why did I feel a deepening shadow come over me?

"Yes. I have someone in mind who will not only nurture your good mind and bring out your beautiful qualities, but help you learn to master the womanly arts. Someone who will help you recognize the fine line between appropriate and inappropriate anger, for instance."

I was too stunned to answer. But from what I could grasp of the situation, it was not good.

"Does Mama know about this?"

He gave a little half bow. "Your mama has put the education of you girls in my hands."

I felt abandoned, betrayed.

"Running to your mother about it will do no good. Now I will offer you some advice. Don't draw battle lines with me. Once they are drawn, there is no going back. We're stuck with each other. We might as well make the best of it."

He looked down and scowled. "Will you please tell me why you are wearing riding boots with a calico dress?"

I blushed. "I can't explain it."

"Try."

"All right." I took a deep breath and tried. "I pondered that if I had to meet with you first thing this morning, before breakfast, like you were God on Judgment Day, and answer for my sins, and tell you everybody in the county thinks you're marrying my mama for her money, and not shame my mama or daddy while I did it, well then, I pondered I'd feel a sight better doing it in my riding boots than in some silly satin slippers."

He laughed, throwing back his head. "Oscie Mason, I could think of a dozen ways to break your spirit and enjoy every one of them. But you're worth winning over with persistence and firmness and charm."

I did not answer.

"Another thing. Didn't that daddy of yours ever tell you that men like to hold sway over women?"

"No, sir, but Mama did."

He scowled. "Your mama?"

"Yessir. She told me about the iron fist in the velvet glove. She said that Southern men take care of their women. But that they love to be masters. And they think a woman has only one right. Only I don't know as I should go on here, sir."

"I insist." He gestured politely.

"She said that right is to protection. But Southern men think that makes us beholden to them. That we must always obey. She said thank heavens my daddy wasn't like that."

His brows arched. "And did she put me in that class?"

"No, sir. She never said anything about you."

He nodded. "I'm nobody's fool, Oscie Mason."

"I never thought you were, sir."

"Part of me is a Southern gentleman, and part of me isn't. The part that is, insists you offer an apology to Julia and her parents before we leave here today."

"Yessir."

He put his arm on my shoulder and walked me to the door. "War with me all you wish in private. I am a worthy opponent and I fight fair. But don't play this struggle against your mother or belittle me in front of the servants. Or you will see the part of me that isn't a Southern gentleman, the part I have fought all my life to hide. Even from myself."

His soft words fell on me like cold rain. I curtsied and left the room. I ran for dear life. For I had just felt on my shoulder the iron fist in the velvet glove.

Julia and I stood on the portico of Lang Syne while my family waited in the carriage. We were leaving, after another sitting with the artist and a noontime meal.

"I'm supposed to apologize for hitting you," I said.

"Then, heavens, do as you're supposed to do and get it over with."

"I'm sorry for hitting you, Julia."

"Are we still friends?"

"We never were. You like Maria better."

"But it's you I tell things to. What is your mama going to do about everybody gossiping?"

"I don't know, but she'll do something."

"I told you about the gossip because I wanted to help you. My stepdaddy gambles away all my mama's money, and I'm miserable. I can't wait to grow up and get away from here. Now I'm going to tell you something else to help you. Only don't even hint of it to anyone."

I promised I wouldn't.

"Your new stepdaddy bought Mary Ann from us. Be careful around Mary Ann. She conjures."

"What?"

"She has doings with the supernatural. Lots of nigras do. Mama says it comes from their traditions. Mary Ann makes hair wreathes. Don't ever let her take a piece of your hair. So far, two nigra servants here died after she took their hair."

"Has she taken your hair?"

"She wants to. I won't give it. She says she'll take it while I sleep."

I thanked her. She smiled. Why did I feel I should pay heed to what she said? I waved and ran, leaving her there on the portico, a fragile figure, the cold December wind whipping around her as she waved.

Chapter 4

Two days after Christmas, Mama summoned us into the parlor where she stood with Will McLean to tell us that their wedding was postponed.

"Instead of being married here New Year's Day, we'll wed in Alexandria in January," she told us. "You'll still wear your new dresses and capes. It will be a smaller wedding, with only family."

Before we could absorb that, and while Maria was still carrying on, Mama told us she was putting her property in trust.

"What does that mean?" Maria asked.

"It means," McLean said, in a soft and solemn voice, "that I have no right, whatsoever, to hold, possess, and enjoy your mother's real estate and personal money."

"Oh, Daddy Will, how horrible!" Maria said.

He smiled. "I had no intention of holding, possessing, and enjoying anything but my wife and family," he smiled. Then he sobered. "Now I have an announcement of my own."

We waited. What more could there be?

"I've written for a tutor for you girls. Her name is Elvira Buttonworth. She's from Cambridge, Massachusetts."

No one spoke for a moment, but for once Maria understood before I. "A Yankee?" she asked.

"That's right," McLean said, "a Yankee. She's a clever and virtuous woman."

"But you said Yankess are taking all our money," Maria wailed.

"They are, because they're smart. They invented the steel plow, the clipper ship, the typewriter, the telegraph, the friction match, and the safety pin, among other things. I've ordered you a new Yankee piano, Maria. There are a hundred piano makers in New York and none in the South."

"Yankees are ill-bred and I don't want a new piano if a Yankee tutor comes with it," Maria shot back.

"Good for you, Maria," I said. I was glad to see her speak up to McLean for once. Of course, everybody just *knew* you didn't have truck with Yankees. They were coarse and vulgar.

Will McLean glared at us. "Then you can all stay at Van Sickle's and turn into featherheaded gooses!"

"Will!" Mama turned to us. "See how you all have upset him. And he only wants what's best for you!"

"I'm sorry, Daddy Will." Maria ran to put her arms around his middle. How could she? I'd die first!

Four-year-old Sarah ran to hang onto his arm. "I thought you were buying *Mary Ann* to teach me, Daddy Will! She knows how to play hide 'n seek. And stealin' bases."

"Mary Ann can't teach you," I scolded Sarah. "She can't read."

"Don't have to," she retorted. "Mary Ann knows

how to put a poker in the fire when an owl comes 'round screechin'."

"That's stupid."

"Ain't," she argued. "Screechin' owl means some-body gonna die. Hot poker burns out his tongue so he can't screech no more."

"Any more, darling," McLean said.

"You see? Daddy Will knows about screechin' owls. And Mary Ann can tell stories! And she's gonna marry Allie and have babies and make candy outa sorghum molasses and I can watch!"

Will McLean roared with laughter. "Well, that's a sight better than learning two plus two, isn't it, sweetheart?" He took her on his lap and smoothed back her unruly curls and explained how our tutor would teach her to write her name.

"But Mary Ann tells stories to make your skin crawl. She told me some when we were at the Wilchers'."

"You hush about Mary Ann," I scolded. "I've told you stories, haven't I?"

"Enough!" McLean ordered. "I'm giving you girls a chance for the best. Up in Cambridge, where Miss Buttonworth comes from, they encourage women to be educated. The world is changing. And I want you girls to be ready for it."

"How is it changing?" Maria asked.

"In many ways. New railroads are being built, new political parties are being formed, new territories are being settled. And there are bitter fights about slavery in every one of them. People bought 300,000 copies of *Uncle Tom's Cabin* up North last year. Think on that! A book! Now I want you all to be good to your tutor. There's a bad feeling growing between us and the Yankees and we're lucky to get her."

Maria and Sarah promised to be good to the tutor, I didn't. And when the others left the room, I stayed.

McLean leaned back on the settee and lighted a cheroot. "Speak your piece," he said.

"You bought Mary Ann," I accused.

"Yes, and that's my business." His eyes narrowed.

"Then you'd best make it your business to keep Sarah away from her. The woman's crazy. Julia told me."

"All of a sudden you and Julia are friends? You were ready to kill her, as I recollect."

"That has nothing to do with it. I care about Sarah."

"So do I, in case you haven't noticed. I think I'm capable of taking care of this family. Now is there anything else?"

"You went and got the Yankee tutor to punish me."

He scowled. "If you choose to see it as punishment, you're the loser."

I raised my chin. "Is there anything in Mama's agreement about changing our name? Julia said you were going to make us give up our daddy's name."

"Oh, I see. Don't like the sound of Oscie McLean, eh? Didn't I ever tell you I'm descended from one of the historic clans of Scotland?"

I stared at him, stone hard. "I want to keep my daddy's name."

"I'm joking, Oscie. I'd never make you change your name, if you don't want to. Even I am not that despicable."

I turned to go. "I'm going to learn from that smart Yankee tutor how to best you, Will McLean."

He roared with laughter. "When that happens, I'll

know I haven't wasted my money on your education, Oscie Mason."

I left the room with his laughter ringing in my ears. He was a proud man. Take away a man's pride, my daddy had said and you might as well take away the bread he eats. I was to blame if McLean's pride had been taken away by that agreement of Mama's. And he would blame me for it, no matter what he said.

"Girl, you'll be down with the quinsy throat, the way you're dressed in this weather," Maum Hanna said.

We were making cookie dough at the table in the log cabin kitchen which was detached from the house. Maria and Sarah and I looked up to see Mary Ann in the doorway, wearing only a thin woolen shawl. Her meager possessions were wrapped in an old blanket. She was rail-thin and looked dumbstruck, like a bone was caught in her throat.

"Mary Ann!" Sarah started to run to her. I reached out to try to stop her. "Don't!" Sarah pulled free.

Mary Ann hugged my little sister and I felt a stab of jealousy. Then Maum Hanna told her to set and eat. We stared as Maum Hanna put hot coffee, ham slices, and fresh buttermilk biscuits before her.

"Girl, what you good for?" Maum Hanna asked. "We ain't had need for a new servant round here in years."

Yes, that was what I wanted to know.

Mary Ann took her time about answering.

"Doan be scared," Maum Hanna insisted. "Nobody here gonna hurt you."

She didn't look scared to me. She looked wise as a fox. Her eyes went round the table and studied us, every one.

"I be trained up as a baby minder since I wuz seven. I minded all the darkie chillens when their mamas wuz in the fields over to Lang Syne. I knows 'bout growin' herbs, how to wash and iron Massa's shirts real proper like. I clean my irons."

She swallowed and continued while we sat entranced. "I knows how to make a chemise outa flannelette an' underpants outa homespun. How to make lye soap in a hopper an' candles from tallow and beeswax. I kin make ash cakes outa meal and water an' a little pinch of lard. I kin talk low and act real good servin' company. I been raised up proper and religious. I kin be a maid for fancy ladies, make candy outa sorghum molasses, keep away screechin' owls, and tell stories to chilluns."

"That's a lotta knowin'," Maum Hanna said.

"I ain't finished. I doan work in the fields. Never have. Even Massa Wilcher, mean as he wuz, never put me in the fields." Her eyes once again swept around the kitchen. "Allie tol' me Massa Will and Miz Virginia got married. Talk over to Lang Syne wuz that they wouldn't. Counta all that gossip 'bout Massa Will."

"They wuz married on the 19th of January," Maum Hanna said proudly. "In St. Paul's Episcopal in Alexandria. They be back from their weddin' trip soon."

Mary Ann nodded. "Massa Will, he wuz hurt by all that gossip. Tol' me so. Tol' me they wuz gettin' married, no matter. An' that when they had a baby, I wuz to care for it."

Maria and I stared at each other. We'd never considered that our mama and Will McLean would have a baby. I felt outraged at McLean. Didn't he know any better than to confide in a darkie? And if

he and Mama did have a baby, what right did he have
to turn it over to this woman?

"Are you and Allie going to have babies?" Sarah
asked.

"Sure aims to, honey. Can't wait to have chillens."

"I heard that there was trouble with you over to
Lang Syne," Maum Hanna said.

"Miz Julia, she done everythin' mean to me she
could. Made me hand her water, fan her in summer,
acted like mistress. Pinched me every chance she
got."

"Our girls ain't like that," Maum Hanna said.
"They's quality."   .

"Miz Julia made me sleep on the floor by her bed."

Liar! Julia had told me she'd slept on the floor next
to Julia's bed, so she could get a piece of her hair! Oh,
I was furious! She was a no-count liar and she was
trouble.

"You kin sleep in the room off the pantry," Maum
Hanna said. "I gots the keys to the pantry."

Mary Ann's eyes widened. Everybody knew that if
a servant had the keys to the pantry, they were held
in high esteem.

"I doan know nuthin' 'bout no new babies,"
Maum Hanna said. "Mister Will doan tell me such
things. But you kin help me wif the cookin' and carin'
for the girls. I'se gettin' old."

"Massa Will hired me to do his shirts," Mary Ann
said. "He say I do shirts fittin' for the Prince o'
Wales."

"Mister Will doan have enough shirts to keep you
busy. So I 'spect you'll be helpin' me in the kitchen.
Mister Will doan come inta the kitchen. But Paula
and Fanny does. And you gotta get along wif 'em.
Miz Virginia doan tolerate no fightin'. Any com-

plaints you got, see Hiram. He's in charge of the servants."

"Or me," I interrupted. "The servants always come to me with their problems."

Maum Hanna laughed. "Thas right, child."

But Mary Ann stood up. "Much obliged for the food," she said. "If you show me where Massa Will's shirts be, I'll get to launderin' em." And she sneered at me. "You're just a child. Had enough of a child givin' me orders with Miz Julia. I got any complaints, I goes to Massa Will hisself."

Maum Hanna got up, too, pointed her in the direction of the laundry, then came back into the kitchen. "We got trouble wif that one," she mumbled.

I was still smarting from Mary Ann's sass. I nodded. "Wait until the first time she goes up against Massa Will," I said.

In the two weeks that Mama and Will McLean were on their wedding trip to Washington, Yorkshire was in *my* charge. Probably for the last time. And I loved every moment of it. McLean had taken Maria and me out of Van Sickle's right before the wedding and assigned us some reading to prepare us for our tutor's arrival. They would bring her home with them from Washington, where she'd been teaching in a young ladies' seminary.

I read some, but mostly I rode around the plantation, inspecting the damage winter was doing to the outbuildings, plantings, and fences. I did my best to keep Sarah away from Mary Ann. I wrote out the menu plans every morning for Maum Hanna, as Mama had done. And I insisted we eat in the dining room evenings and not in the kitchen with the servants. Maria read from Scriptures, as Mama did, before we went to bed.

I stayed up late, reading, was down at the barn early, and prepared myself for the changes McLean said were coming. I was nobody's fool. I knew things were going to change.

I may have been still a child whose formal schooling had been dismal, as McLean suspected, but my daddy had filled in the gaps. So I knew about old Henry Clay's Missouri Compromise and how it drew lines in the country where a person could and couldn't own slaves.

I knew about the Fugitive Slave Act and how darkies were running away by the Underground Railroad.

My daddy had told us how up North Quakers were hiding runaway nigras. And I recollected the admiration in his voice for both the Quakers and the nigras.

My daddy had had feelings for people. Didn't matter a lick if that person was nigra or white. We owned slaves, yes, but our nigras were family.

I had my daddy on my mind a lot that last week of my freedom. Mama's marriage, the way she'd put her property in trust, the birth of a foal by his Mirabella all conspired to make me miss him something powerful.

The last afternoon before Mama and Will McLean returned, I took myself upstairs to my daddy's dressing room, off Mama's bedroom, where I often went to be close to his things.

I found Hiram there. And Paula and Fanny.

The house girls were packing away all my daddy's clothes, his robe, night clothes, trousers, shirts, cravats, boots, the long duster he wore in bad weather when he made his doctor's calls. His cherry highboy was empty, his shaving things gone from the washbasin.

The place was stripped bare. I watched Paula and Fanny close one of the last trunks and carry it out.

"What are you doing?" I asked Hiram.

He folded some clean towels and put them over the back of a bench. "Making this room spotless. It'll be Mister Will's now. He should know this is a quality house."

I never felt so forlorn in my life. It was as if they were sweeping every trace of my daddy from the earth.

"Mister Will is the master of the house now, Miz Oscie. You gotta get used to it. We all do." He patted my shoulder.

Tears came to my eyes. I felt like my innards were being pulled out of me. "I can't abide it, Hiram. As long as my daddy's things were still here it was like part of him was still around. I used to come in here when nobody was around and just sit. And pick up his shaving mug and razor. And touch his duster."

"I know, I know. But you doan need no shavin' mug or razor to remember him, Miz Oscie. You got him in your heart."

I watched him wipe an imaginary spot off the mirror. "Are you going to be Will McLean's personal man, Hiram?"

"I reckon I am. He said he knew I had my loyalties, but he'd be honored if I served him like I served Doctor John. I said if'n he took care of Miz Virginia and my girls like Doctor John did, I'd serve him well. An' see to it that all the servants do likewise. We got this arrangement, him an' me."

I nodded. I respected Hiram. He'd been second in

command to my daddy. And if he said the servants should serve Will McLean, I'd give him no grief over it.

"Mary Ann aims to marry your Allie," I told him. "She's trouble, Hiram. She's no-count and she's crazy as a hooty owl. Even Maum Hanna says so. She told Maum Hanna she takes orders only from Massa Will. You better watch out for her."

He smiled. "We'll leave her to Mister Will then, won't we? We'll worry 'bout ourselves. Here, Miz Oscie." He brought some keys out of his pocket. "They be to your daddy's trunks. I give 'em to you. Those things be yours now."

I clutched the keys to my bosom and let the hot tears roll down my face. He hugged me. No words were necessary.

In spite of all my efforts to keep them apart, Sarah had been following Mary Ann around for the week Mary Ann had been with us, close as a burr to a dog's tail. When Mama comes home I'll put an end to it, I'd promised myself. I'll warn her about Mary Ann. What I would say, I didn't know. For I had nothing solid to tell Mama. Only whisperings from Julia. That was the problem. Such whisperings had already caused enough trouble in our household.

That last night before they came home, I lay propped against pillows on my bed catching up with my reading.

Suddenly I stopped. "Did you hear that, Maria?"

"All I hear is Mary Ann's voice from across the hall, telling Sarah a story." Maria was already half asleep.

"Exactly! *I* told Sarah a bedtime story. It isn't as if she hasn't had one! And that sly wench sneaks in there to tell one of her voodoo stories."

"Don't be silly," Maria said. "Sarah misses Mama something awful. She needs all the stories she can get."

"Didn't you just hear the word *gris gris?* It means voodoo!"

"Sarah loves ghost stories. All little children do."

"I'm going in there to stop it!" I started to get up.

"You're making a fool of yourself," Maria warned. "The more you tell Sarah to stay away from Mary Ann, the more she wants her. There now, she's finished. Sarah's probably asleep. Turn your lamp down now. I'm tired and I want to get up early to make a chocolate cake for when they come home."

I watched from the second story front window the next day as the carriage, driven by Hiram, pulled into the front roundabout.

Sarah and Maria ran down the porch steps. McLean's dogs appeared from several directions. Hiram jumped down from the carriage and helped Mama get out. She was dressed in a cloak the color of old rose petals and a darling velvet hat with feathers.

Will McLean embraced Maria, then swooped Sarah up in his arms. As he did so his greatcoat opened and I saw a brass-handled pistol stuck in the waistband of his gray trousers.

My daddy had carried a pistol only once in his rounds of the county, when local people said they'd seen a wild boar in the area.

McLean glanced up, caught sight of me, took off his black hat and gave a sweeping bow. I started to turn from the window to go downstairs when another figure caught my eye.

She was dressed in dark blue from head to toe. Her hair was piled high on her head. My heart sank. There was our Yankee tutor. She stood out like a crow among birds of Southern plumage. I felt a shiver of fear, then caught myself.

This was the woman who was going to teach me to best Will McLean. With the exception of wanting to learn that, I thought I knew everything as I went down those stairs. But I didn't realize how little I knew until I met Miss Elvira Buttonworth and until Mary Ann came to live with us. Both these women came into my life the same week. And both were brought by Will McLean.

Chapter 5

I leaned against the doorjam of the room assigned to Miss Buttonworth. She was unpacking. Her portmanteaus were open all over the place and Sarah was inspecting the contents. Maria sat primly in a chair across the room. Miss Buttonworth had sent Paula downstairs. She was not accustomed to a maid, she said.

"Don't Yankees have servants?" Maria asked.

My sister was intent on being Miss Prissypants, acting important.

"Yes," Miss Buttonworth answered, "sometimes. But we pay for them. And I'd much rather save my money to see Jenny Lind perform at the National Theater in Washington."

Now she had Maria's interest. "Oh! Did you attend one of her performances?"

"I did. Cost me seven dollars for a ticket. For a New England Yankee, that's dear, but it was worth it."

"Does she sing like a bird?"

"No, like an angel. Washington has many attractions, you know. In the new Smithsonian Museum they have a stuffed orangutan. At a party with your mama and stepdaddy we met women writers."

"Harriet Beecher Stowe, I suppose," Maria said disdainfully. "She got rich writing *Uncle Tom's Cabin*. I think it's vulgar for a woman to earn money writing."

"No, we met Emma Dorothy Eliza Nevitte Southworth. She writes of women who make it on their own, with no male protectors. I have her novels, right here."

Maria got off her chair to look at the books. "Mama said she's a feminist."

Maria was ahead of me sometimes. I didn't even know what a feminist was.

"Are you a feminist?" Maria goaded.

Miss Buttonworth was unflappable. "Well, I support myself, but I like to think I'll marry someday."

"Will you have babies?" Sarah asked.

"Feminists don't have babies, silly," Maria chided.

"Oh, yes, they do," Miss Buttonworth said.

"Are you against owning nigras?" Maria asked.

"Yes. And then I consider how mill towns in New England employ child laborers who work longer and harder than your servants and aren't cared for half as well."

Maria preened. "Our servants are family," she said.

"Don't know what to think half the time," Miss Buttonworth told her, "do you?"

Maria yawned. "About what?"

"The questions of the day." She folded some

homespun nightdresses and put them in a drawer. "There's enough questions out there. Why doesn't the South have more shipping lines? Should secret societies be allowed in public high schools? Why does a city like Washington have only thirty-seven teachers for two thousand children in their public schools? Should Nebraska territory be slave or free soil?"

Maria looked stunned. "Do all Yankee women talk like you?"

"Not all. But where I come from, we believe in being educated. Thanks to fast trains that carry Mister Greeley's newspaper thousands of miles, everybody can be. I notice your Daddy Will gets the *New York Tribune,* as well as the *Lexington Observer and Reporter.* Do you ever read them?"

"My Daddy John used to read us the Lexington paper and the *New York Sun,*" I volunteered.

"Good. We'll read the papers you now get every day." She started lifting her frocks out of one of the trunks.

"Why are your dresses all so dull?" Maria asked. "Are you in mourning?"

I had to agree with Maria there. If the woman's gowns weren't dark blue or gray, they were the color of the dung heap. Only a white collar and a cameo at her throat relieved the drabness and I wondered if she tried to look that way on purpose.

She had no figure to drape gowns on in the first place. She was too tall and rail-thin. All sharp edges. You would no more think of putting your head on her bosom than on a possum's. Fact was, she had no bosom. And her complexion looked as if it'd just been scrubbed with Mathilda's lye soap.

But there was something regal about her. She

carried herself like she was wearing pink moire. And that powderless complexion glowed. Watching her, it came to me that she must have some Yankee strength that didn't need frippery. I must learn what it is, I decided.

"I always admired the Quakers," she told us. "Ever wonder why they're so sure of themselves? I figured it must have something to do with dressing so plain. Must help them to think plain."

"In Virginia, ladies have a love of fashion," Maria said. "Lace and ribbons are important to us as the air we breathe. Mama says a proper lady is well-schooled in the quality of fabrics and the fine points of dress."

"A proper lady is well-schooled in everything," Miss Buttonworth replied. "Above all, I've always tried to teach my students that each individual has the right to think for his or herself. About everything, from the questions of the day to how they want to dress."

"What's this?" Sarah was pulling something out of a trunk.

"My bathing costume."

"Your *what?*" Maria gaped.

"My bathing costume. It has a cloth cap, drawers, stockings, a tunic, and shoes. Made it myself. I have a pattern. I'll teach you all to make your own."

"For what?" Maria asked.

"That's a nice creek you've got down the end of the knoll. Tell you the truth, when Mister Will told me about that creek, I just couldn't say no to him about coming here."

"You *swim?*" The idea took Maria's breath away.

"Every morning, soon as the weather breaks.

Nothing like it to give a body stamina."

"I'd die before I put that thing on!" Maria said.

"Mister Will said he wants me to teach all of you to swim." Miss Buttonworth informed us. "For your own protection."

"There's *dragons* in the creek!" Sarah's brown eyes were wide with fear.

"Nonsense, there's no such thing as dragons," Miss Buttonworth said briskly.

"Yes, they *is!*" Sarah informed her. "Mary Ann says if I play near the creek they'll reach right up out of the water and pull me in!"

"Mary Ann tells stories," I explained. "About voodoo and dragons and I don't know what else. I don't approve of any of it. But nobody else around here seems to care about it but me."

"Mary Ann is only trying to keep Sarah from going near the creek, Oscie, and you know it!" Maria snapped.

"I see," Miss Buttonworth said. "Well, learning is better than fear. And that's why you'll all learn to swim."

"I won't," Maria announced. "And I'll never wear your old swimming costume, either!"

"We'd best defer that question to the future," Miss Buttonworth said, "and go down to supper. It's very special tonight. It's the first time your Daddy Will presides at the table as head of the family."

It was different, Miss Buttonworth was right. In the dining room, where the table was laid with Mama's best crystal and china, Hiram served wine from a silver decanter. He was dressed in a fine new white jacket and he took his cues from McLean's glances. I could see by his demeanor that this did not diminish Hiram in any way. He seemed prouder than ever. Like he used to be when he served my daddy.

McLean filled the room with his presence. His shoulders seemed powerful beneath his dove-gray frock coat, his moves were both confident and graceful. He made a toast, saying something about his new family. Mama looked up to him adoringly as he did so.

When he said grace, he included a prayer for Franklin Pierce and his wife who had just been in a train wreck. Their eleven-year-old son, Bennie, had been crushed to death.

"What did your friend, Miss Kent, in Washington, tell you about the tone of the inauguration plans?" he asked Miss Buttonworth. "The talk we heard is that Mrs. Pierce has taken to her bed after losing a third son. Will we have a first lady?"

I could not believe it! McLean was talking politics with a woman! My daddy, the only other man I'd known to do such a thing, had told me that Southern men didn't want their women bothering with such talk. Maria and I both stared, waiting for our tutor's reply.

"When I saw Abby in Washington, she said she would act as official hostess if her niece, Mrs. Pierce, could not. Don't worry, Mister Will, we'll have a first lady."

McLean beamed. "Now, girls, you see? Your tutor knows the woman who will be hostess at the White House. Perhaps she'll get us invited there sometime."

"You didn't vote for Pierce," I blurted out. "You voted for Winfield Scott because you said he's a Virginian and not a slave holder."

McLean fastened a cool gaze on me. "Do you *know* how I voted?"

"No, sir."

"Exactly as it should be. I would hope that privacy in such a matter is still one's privilege."

I was put in my place. Sarah attracted attention then, slumping in her chair and refusing to eat despite Mama's coaxing. "Wanna eat with Mary Ann like I does alla time."

"You ate in the dining room with me and Maria these past two weeks," I reminded her.

"And you'll be eating in the dining room with us all the time now, darling," McLean said.

"Ate bweakfast with Mary Ann," she insisted. "I want Mary Ann!"

Good, I thought, let Will McLean see what the wench has done to her.

"My love," McLean said softly, "sit up and stop acting like a spoiled brat. We're doing our darndest to make Miss Buttonworth think she won't be equal to her task, aren't we?"

Sarah sat up. "Mary Ann says there's bad voodoo on the new pres-a-dent and that's why Bennie was killed."

"What?" McLean asked.

I gloated. This was better yet.

"Mary Ann just tells her ghost stories sometimes, Daddy Will," Maria put in.

"They're more than ghost stories, Maria," I said.

"What are they?" McLean asked.

But I met his eyes and I couldn't answer. Because I had nothing *solid* to tell him. And he'd had enough whisperings and rumors. Oh, I would get something I could sink my teeth into about Mary Ann. As soon as I could.

"Do I have to learn to swim, Daddy Will?" Maria

was saying. "I think I'll die if I have to wear that horrible costume."

He smiled indulgently at her. "It's a long time until spring," he said. Maria always used her feminine wiles on him.

"And must we read Miss Buttonworth's feminist novels?"

I saw right off what Maria was doing. Such novels were not read by proper Southern girls. And she sensed that McLean did not know Miss Buttonworth had brought them.

McLean was the suave gentleman. "We'll discuss your lessons another time, Maria." But I saw the eyebrows go up. And they said so much.

Miss Buttonworth was flustered. "Those books are for my own edification," she said. "Perhaps I was premature in speaking of them to the girls."

"You're a little sneak," I told Maria.

"Oscie!" Mama was shocked.

"I can't abide it, Mama. She is trying to get Miss Buttonworth in trouble."

"Oh dear, it's quite all right, child," old Buttonworth assured me.

"Quiet, all of you. In heaven's name, this sounds like a ladies' social." But McLean's voice was rich with amusement. "Miss Buttonworth is not in trouble with me, Oscie, but you are. I trust your tutor to expose you to all schools of thought, without influencing the values your mother and I hope you will hold onto."

Everyone settled down. His voice was velvet soft.

"And one of those values is courtesy, Oscie. Now apologize to your sister. She is not a sneak."

"I'll never apologize to Maria," I said.

"Then you are excused," McLean said quietly.

"Miss Buttonworth, I apologize for Osceola. No doubt you see here what an impossible task you have taken on."

I ran from the room. When the soft tapping came on my door about an hour later, I figured it was Mama. But it was old Buttonworth, standing there with a covered tray.

"You never got beyond the soup at supper," she said. "You missed the chicken, fried squash, carrots in cream, and chocolate layer cake."

I could have eaten the side of a hog. From downstairs I heard Maria hit a discordant note on the piano.

"She doesn't play very well," Miss Buttonworth said. "I'll have to work with her."

"She did her darndest to get you in trouble tonight. I know my sister. She figures if she makes you fall from grace she won't have to take swimming lessons."

"I know that. So does Mister Will."

"Then why did he take up for her? And give me the rough side of his tongue?"

"Because he knows she needs taking up for. That you're the stronger one. He expects more from you."

"That isn't fair."

"It never is. Now are you going to invite me in or do I stand here in the hall all night?"

She set the tray down on a small table and pulled up two chairs. "When we first met in Washington, before he was married, Mister Will told me he had three girls who needed schooling. One sweet as honey who was one of God's own little angels."

"Sarah," I said.

"The other a dreamy and romantic sort who was always running a foot race with herself to try to please. And who had to learn she didn't need to do that."

"Maria."

"And the third wild as a colt in spring, who occasionally had the wisdom of Methuselah, but ran off at the mouth so much she got in her own way and acted like she didn't have the sense God gave a goose."

I knew that was me. "Who's Methuselah?" I asked.

"A patriarch who lived about eight hundred years ago. I thought you Southerners knew your Bible."

"He's Old Testament. Don't like Old Testament much."

"You're wrong about him, you know."

"Methuselah?"

"No. Mister Will. He likes you."

"He hates me. My life's been like hog-killing time since he got here."

"He admires your spirit, Oscie. Says you've got a good brain and your daddy encouraged you to have opinions."

"Then why won't he let me *have* opinions?"

"Because he wants you to learn, first, when to talk and when not to. It'll save you grief in later life. From what I can see, he's afraid to let up on you, too proud to let you know he likes you and wants you to admit he's to be reckoned with as head of the family. And I agree with him on one thing."

"What?"

"Anybody who'd sit and talk and let this food get cold hasn't got the brains God gave a goose."

I commenced to eat. She poured two cups of tea and sipped her own appreciatively. "Your stepdaddy asked me to bring this food up to you. Your mama found a good daddy for you girls. He's smart and very handsome. In Washington he attracted women like flies. He loves your mama and holds her in high esteem. She needs him, Oscie. The lot of a widow isn't a good one in our society."

"I know that."

"He doesn't drink, gamble, or take up with loose women."

"Julia Stratton-Wilcher says she heard that he has a past with women. He was courting someone else before Mama."

"Past is past. He's no saint. No man is. What counts is now. But most important, he wants you girls to get a good education and not grow up to be simpering, empty-headed Southern belles."

"I don't simper. Maria does."

"I think you like him, but you won't admit it. And I hope when you are ready to admit it, it isn't too late."

"Too late for what?"

But she wouldn't say. "He'd be proud to have you love him, but he won't ask it of you. Neither will I."

Our eyes met. I looked at my plate.

"I know you don't like me." She set her cup down carefully. "But you're stuck with me. I'm here to teach you languages, grammar, mathematics, history, and geography. I'll also teach you to sew, swim, and recognize a fool when you see one. Even if that fool is sometimes yourself. We can have fun doing this or it can be a chore. It's up to you."

"Will you teach me to best Will McLean?" I asked.

"I will teach you to hold your own with everyone," she said sadly. "He wants that more than anybody. But I hope that when I'm done you no longer will have the need to best anybody."

"How long are you going to be with us?"

"Some days it will seem like forever," she told me. "And then one day you'll wake up and our time together will be finished. And we'll both cry. So, I don't know about you, but I'd like to make the best of this arrangement. What do you say?"

She had freckles across her nose. Didn't anybody ever tell her she should stay out of the sun? For a moment I thought I saw something shining in her eyes. But it came and went so fast, whatever it was.

It would be years before I knew that it was an inner light. And when I knew that, like she said, our time together would be finished.

Chapter 6

May 1853

It was a fair morning in May when I found out my mama was in a delicate condition. It was the kind of morning in which, if you told a person the world was filled with danger and mystery and betrayal, they'd say it was folderol and you needed a dose of Maum Hanna's crushed peachtree leaves for a bad stomach. But I'd known the world for what it was ever since my daddy died.

I slept too long and missed breakfast and was late getting to classes. Will McLean had converted a third floor room that had lots of windows into a schoolroom. In a quick detour through the dining room to grab a warm biscuit and ham, I ran into him. He was lingering over his coffee, reading his newspaper.

"You might pay your mama a visit. She didn't come to breakfast," he said.

That was the second morning in a week. "Is she sick?"

He smiled. "I'm sure she'd want to be the one to tell you."

Tell me what? I felt fear flooding me as I raced upstairs. Julia Stratton-Wilcher had been sick for weeks now. A few days after Will McLean had allowed Mary Ann to go home to Lang Syne to visit her mama, Julia had taken to her bed.

I knew Mary Ann was making a hair wreath. I'd seen her working on it. Had she gotten a piece of Julia's hair on that visit, finally? Had she now taken some of my mama's hair?

And then, as I raced down the hall to my mama's room, I saw Mary Ann standing over little Sarah who was on the floor in the nursery.

Mary Ann had a scissor in her hands!

"Stop!" I bounded into the room just as I heard the snip of the scissor. Out of breath, I glared at Mary Ann. "Give me the hair! Give it to me!"

"Mary Ann's gonna put it in her hair wreaf," Sarah said.

I started to tremble. Mary Ann smiled at me. She had slanty, amber-colored eyes and high cheekbones. And I recollected then something I'd heard Allie say, that Mary Ann was part Indian. Nobody knew who her daddy was, he'd said once.

"You're not going to use my sister's hair for your old wreath," I told her. "Don't you think I know you cut off some of Julia's hair when you went home to visit? She's been sick ever since."

"Julia caught the quinsy throat from her mama," she told me. "What's hair got to do with it?"

"You take people's hair and make them sick. I heard about that. Now give me Sarah's."

She shrugged indifferently and handed the small piece of curl to me.

"Come along, Sarah. You're late for school. What do you have in that box there?"

"We's gonna bury it this morning, me and Mary Ann."

I peered down. Inside the box on some straw was a dead bird. "Let Mary Ann bury it. You come with me."

"We got to take the feathers off it first."

"What?" I took the box from her. "Never heard such a thing, taking feathers off a dead bird. Our daddy would whup you good if he was here."

"We needs them for our collection." Sarah ran over to the large window seat. There, indeed, was a collection. Trash is what it was. Looked like an old dung heap. There was an earthenware jar filled with old garden bulbs, another with a dark, evil-smelling dried-out mixture and still another with some syrupy stuff in it.

Then I caught sight of the piece of green-and-white striped material. It was from the dress Julia had worn at the party. "What's this?" I asked Mary Ann.

"Miz Julia give it to me. I collects pieces of cloth. Gonna make a quilt for when me and Allie is married."

I stood there in the warm sunlight that streamed in the window and felt dizzy. My daddy had told me the West African's world was full of spiritual forces and that we had to allow them their ties to their old villages. We were Episcopal, and sometimes it seemed that the African beliefs held a person in just as good stead. All white folk knew that certain nigra practices had deeper and darker meanings, of course. We just chose not to pay mind to them.

But I could not ignore this. "Come along and leave the bird, Sarah." I pulled her from the room, told her to go to class, and stood facing Mary Ann.

"I think you're evil," I said. "And I aim to tell Daddy Will."

"Thought you wouldn't call him that."

"It's my business if I do or not."

"Tell him all you wants. Massa Will, he understands me."

"I know you're his pet. But even he won't allow this." I couldn't see, I was so mad. Massa Will *understands* her! That was the trouble, exactly! Will McLean didn't know how to handle nigras. Most white folk didn't mind a nigra messing with the supernatural down in the cabins. But right in their own home? It just wasn't seemly! Then I pondered that Will McLean probably didn't know what Mary Ann was about.

Not only that, but she was part Indian. And Indians had powers. Everybody knew that. Mary Ann probably went out at night and breathed on Mama's azaleas, which was why they hadn't bloomed this spring.

And why did she always wear that shawl of hers? I'd never seen her without it. Probably hiding a witch's mark, I told myself. It made sense, her being a witch. Maum Hanna had told me that witches took pieces of people's personal things, if they wanted to bring harm to a person.

I went to see Mama. The world tilted when she told me her news. She was going to have a baby! Now I knew I had to get Mary Ann out of the house.

"Sarah is too young to understand," Mama said. "But you are old enough. Women sometimes feel a bit peaked mornings in the beginning."

I was frightened. I remembered Mirabella giving

birth and I hugged Mama. "I wish Daddy was here."

"Good heavens, if he were, I wouldn't be having this child. This is Daddy Will's baby."

"Mama, you mustn't let Mary Ann care for the baby when it comes," I implored.

She scowled. "Nonsense, she has experience with babies. Look how Sarah loves her."

"She's teaching Sarah bad things, Mama. Please don't let her near the baby. I'm afraid she's a witch."

Mama laughed. "I thought Button was the witch, making you sew hems all the time. I see you've ruined another white pinafore with ink. How many new pinafores has she had you hem now, since January?"

"Mama, be serious. I caught Mary Ann taking a piece of Sarah's hair for her hair wreath. Two nigra servants at Lang Syne died after she took their hair. She took Julia's hair on a visit there and now *Julia's sick!*"

Mama patted my hair and tucked it behind my ears.

"You haven't allowed her to take a piece of *your* hair, have you, Mama?"

"Sshh."

"Have you?"

She held me close. "She mentioned it, but, no, I haven't."

"Don't, Mama, please. Please, don't."

"Oscie, I know how you miss your daddy. And since he died, you've had terrible fears. And you're trying to take care of all of us. It's been such a burden on you. But you must stop worrying now. Daddy Will is taking care of us. Why, he's working sunup to sundown on this farm. He's joined the school board, though you girls don't attend the local school. He's paid up the pew rent so we can be proper church members again and he's been made captain of the local fire brigade."

I didn't see what being captain of the local fire brigade had to do with Mary Ann being a witch. Not unless she started a fire at Yorkshire. But I said no more. It wouldn't do to upset Mama. Anyway, she thought Daddy Will was the answer to all our problems. But this wasn't about him. This was about evil in our house. And Mama was so trusting, she wouldn't know evil if the Devil himself came dressed in good broadcloth and asked her to do a quadrille.

"Well, I see you have decided to come to class, Miss."

Ever since her first day here, Button and I had become friends. But in the schoolroom she was harder on me than on Maria or Sarah. Yet, I was learning. From *Greenlief's National Arithmetic* and *Mitchell's Geography* and *Webster's Spelling Book.* She read to us from Washington Irving's *Life of Washington* and Charles Dickens' *Nicholas Nickleby.* She made us memorize Shakespeare's sonnets. She spent hours teaching Maria on the new piano.

Sometimes in class she told us about New England, especially Cambridge where, she said, "Longfellow and Lowell were writing their poems, and John Bartlett was writing his quotations."

I sat down to commence penmanship. For the next fifteen minutes I struggled while she walked up and down chanting, "One, pick up the pen, two, elbow on the desk, three, dip pen in ink, four, lift the pen, five, position pen to paper."

I wrote the day's assigned words, by Frederick Douglass. "Are the great principles of political freedom and of natural justice embodied in the

Declaration of Independence, extended to us?" Yesterday we'd done Henry David Thoreau. Tomorrow it could be Senator Henry Clay from Kentucky. Button didn't hold much with politics. She did hold with greatness.

I spilled some ink on the paper and when she said start again, I begged off. "Please, I can't write today. My head is so full of worries."

She pounced on me like a cat on a butterfly. "Are you worried about the price of wheat?"

I was obliged to answer. "No, Ma'am."

"About the Kansas-Nebraska Act Congress just passed?"

"No, Ma'am."

"About the crime rate in Cincinnati which has tripled between 1846 and last year?"

I was sinking fast. "No, Ma'am."

"Then what are you worried about, Osceola Mason?"

"I'm worried 'cause my mama's going to have a baby. And Daddy Will's going to let Mary Ann be the nurse."

"A baby? A baby? When?" Sarah asked.

"Now, look what you started," Maria groaned. "I hope you're ready to explain things to her."

"Never mind," Button said, "any explaining that needs to be done, I will do. After class. It's part of my job."

She had the *Married Woman's Private Medical Companion* ready after Sarah left the room. Maria gaped.

"How can you have such a book when you aren't married?"

She smiled. "Does a woman have to be married to be intelligent? Now any questions you have, I'll answer another time. Let me talk to Oscie first."

Maria sniffed. "Don't need any old book," she said. "I'll ask Mary Ann." And she walked out.

"You see?" I said. "That's just what worries me." And I told her my fears about Mary Ann being a witch.

"Nothing about witchcraft in this book," she said. "It's all scientific. But we have a fine tradition of witchcraft in New England. We started the whole business in this country." Then she told me about the Salem witch trials.

"So you don't believe in witches then?" I said.

"It's what you believe in that counts, Oscie. There's so much evil in the world, I can't be bothered with witches. My own father is fighting slavery up North. He's running a way station on the Underground Railroad. One night last year he was shot in the leg while helping two slaves get aboard a tugboat to Canada. I fear he'll be killed, but I won't give in to my fear. I won't live that way."

"I'd be obliged if you told me what to do about Mary Ann," I said.

"Can't do that. Wouldn't if I could. But I've had conversations with the woman and I've found some real substance in her. Before you go condemning Mary Ann on the evidence of a dead bird or a piece of hair, like they did up in Salem, don't you think you should talk with her first?"

That's all she would say. The subject was closed. We'd talk more about Mary Ann when I heard the woman out and gave her a chance.

That night I went to Will McLean with the problem.

I waited until I heard Mama come up to bed, then I crept downstairs in my robe. McLean was burning the oil lamp late in the library again. Mama had been right, he was busy these days. I'd seen him get off Pathfinder and work side by side with the nigras in the field, just like Benjamin Chinn. He came in so late that we children were often in bed already and he and Mama took supper alone.

Wheat was climbing in price, I'd heard him say. It was already a dollar fifty a bushel.

These nights he'd pore over his plans for the new barn. Or go over his ledgers. Or figure out how much slave labor his new McCormick reaper had saved him. That's all he cared about anymore. That and Stephen Douglas in the Senate. Or that new upstart Whig party man, Abraham Lincoln, who was talking about running against Douglas next year. Or whether Kansas should be a free or slave state.

It made no difference to me if Kansas was free or slave. Oh, Will McLean went around saying that slavery was an evil that had to be contained. Like he didn't have fifteen nigras running the place for him. How else did he think he was going to run it?

The oil lamp on his desk threw his shadow, larger than life, against the wall. The floor creaked beneath me. He looked up.

"Well," he said, "speak your piece."

"You told me to come to you with problems."

He nodded, encouraging me.

"I want to ask you to take Mary Ann out of the house and put her in the fields to work."

"Why?"

"I think she's a witch."

To his credit he did not mock me. He listened politely while I told him about the dead bird, Julia, and the hair wreath. Then he leaned back to ponder on it. His face was very sun-browned and his white shirt stood out sharply against it.

"Do you think you're giving Mary Ann a fair chance?"

"Julia's sick, isn't she? And what about Mary Ann taking a piece of Sarah's hair for a hair wreath?"

"Hair wreathes are a custom. I don't care for the practice, but many white women make them."

"And what about the way she wanted Sarah to take feathers off a dead bird?"

He lit a cheroot with one of those new-fangled Yankee matches. "You'll have to do better than that, Oscie."

"She's asked Mama for some of her hair. You want something to happen to Mama? Or the new baby?"

"Your mama can take care of herself."

He was so calm. Didn't he care about Mama? Why didn't anyone listen to me about this? "Mary Ann is part Indian."

"Good Lord! Then ask her to do some incantations so the weather holds until we harvest the wheat."

"If you're going to joke about it."

"Well, good heavens, Oscie. Witches? In 1853? In Prince William County?" He shook his head. "Look, I agree that part about the bird isn't so good. But Mary Ann's been invaluable to your mother. She brings her breakfast every morning, she knows remedies for morning sickness. And she loves Sarah."

"She tells her stories about voodoo. You want us to learn to swim when the weather gets warm. Well, Sarah won't. Because Mary Ann told her there's dragons in the creek. And Sarah won't go near it anymore."

He saw how upset I was. "Sarah will learn to swim. I have some influence over her myself, you know. Look here, Oscie, your mother has told me all the fears you have had since your father died. I can understand that. I lost my parents when I was your age, too. I know how terrible the world can look to you. But taking it out on Mary Ann this way will not do you any good."

"Get her out of the house and put her in the fields. Or sell her."

"Haven't you heard *anything* I've said?"

"I heard."

"I told you once, I don't buy nigras. But I bought her with good reason. Now I'm telling you that I don't sell 'em, either. I'm not in that business."

"You don't know nigras, Will McLean. Wasn't ever a darkie I couldn't get along with on this place. This one's different. Bad."

He leaned forward. "Could that be because she's the only one on the place who won't do your bidding? Or because you're jealous that she has your little sister's affections?"

Tears came to my eyes. "No," I said. "It's because she's your pet. You don't know any better than to pamper her. You can't pamper darkies. My daddy never did, but he was good to them just the same."

"Your daddy was a good man, Oscie. One of the few customers I had who paid his bills. He just had different methods for running this place than I have. I had enough conversations with him to know he was Old South. I'm New South."

"What does *that* mean?"

"I'm hard put to know." He sounded sad. "But I'm doing my darndest to find out."

"I think you're an abolitionist, Will McLean, is what I think."

He shrugged his broad shoulders. "Could be I am,

Oscie. New winds are blowing. Don't know what's coming with them."

"That's why you won't put Mary Ann in the fields."

He turned sharp. "She's never worked in the fields. It'd kill her. You don't have to be an abolitionist to know that."

"Did you know that Button's father is in the Underground Railroad?"

"Yes."

"What do you think of the Fugitive Slave Act?"

"I think if a nigra has the gumption to run like all hell and make it North, he should be left in peace and not brought back into slavery."

I nodded. "My daddy thought so, too."

"Well then, maybe your daddy and I aren't so different, after all."

I shook my head. "You are."

He smiled. "How?"

"My daddy knew he was a slaver. Didn't make a fuss over it, like you do. Just treated them good. Didn't pamper them, though. He knew what he was about."

His stare was dark and grave. "Thank you for the advice."

"You talk out of both sides of your mouth about slavery. Nigras pick up on that, you got trouble."

"I shall keep your words in front of my mind." His voice had dropped to a deadly whisper.

I had an idea I'd come too close to some truth in him he didn't like. "Don't know what you mean by Old South," I said. "There's only one South I know. Right here, like it's always been. Place hasn't changed since my daddy ran it. And he would put Mary Ann in the fields to protect his family."

"You may go," he snapped.

I went. New South! Never heard such folderol. Man was crazy, is what he was, full of fancy notions. And if he was New South, whatever that was, then we had a heap of trouble.

Chapter 7

June 1853 to January 1854

When June came, lessons did not stop for us. Button moved them outside, to the peach grove, mornings, before the sun was hot. There she would read to us. Perhaps Edgar Allan Poe's *The Raven,* or she might tell us a story. Like how Elizabeth Barrett wrote to Robert Browning in 1846, saying, "If it will satisfy you that I should know you, love you, why then indeed, you should have my soul to stand on if it could make you stand higher."

Maria loved that story, but I didn't think anybody should stand on anybody else's soul. I wouldn't want anybody standing on mine.

After morning lessons, we'd have a picnic lunch. Then we were ready for swimming.

Just like I told Will McLean, Sarah didn't learn to swim in the creek that summer. She was terrified of it. Maria and I both ventured into the water and, as the heat strengthened in June, looked forward to our daily lessons. Sarah would sit on the bank with Mary Ann, watching for those dragons in the water. Nothing we said could persuade her there weren't any dragons. And if Button took hold of her and held her, even for a second in the water, she would scream like a stuck pig.

Of course, Will McLean couldn't abide her screams. So he relented and said she didn't have to learn to swim that year. I didn't know how I felt about that. I was beholden to McLean because he was so tender and gentle with Sarah. But in the next minute I knew it was wrong that she shouldn't learn to swim.

"I should think you'd *tell* Sarah there aren't any dragons in the creek," I said to Mary Ann one day.

She just gave me that slow, Miss Sly Boots smile of hers. "Better she thinks there be dragons in the creek if'n she doan swim," she said.

I couldn't comprehend such fool logic. But I knew that Mary Ann was certain she had Will McLean behind her. I would just have to do something to make her look the fool in front of him, that was all.

By fall I had carried out three elaborate plots to get Mary Ann into trouble. None worked. On the fourth try, I sneaked into Will McLean's dressing room after Mary Ann had delivered his freshly laundered shirts and cut the buttons off them. Mama caught me and made me sit down right there and sew all the buttons back on again.

Will McLean came in while I was sewing and sat down and told me, with most proper seriousness, that I was wearing his patience thin with my obsession about Mary Ann.

"What's the profit in it for you, Oscie?" he asked.

I kept right on sewing. No sense dragging it out again like an old chicken bone. He wouldn't understand. Mary Ann had wormed herself into everybody's favor. She sweet-talked Mama, so that

Mama was planning a celebration for her when she married Allie right before Christmas. She was absolutely possessive about Mama and her "condition." She rubbed Mama's back and had remedies for her swollen ankles. And all she talked about was the "hunnert" of babies she'd minded back at Lang Syne.

But I was determined about one thing. When the new baby came, she wasn't going to be nurse for it. And I told Will McLean so, right out.

"Do you think that's your decision to make?" he asked me.

"I don't want her near my new brother or sister," was all I would say.

He sighed wearily and got up. "You stop tormenting that poor darkie," was all he would say. "Or I'm going to have to teach you a hard lesson."

Then he took my horse Cottonwood away from me for two weeks. And that only made me madder than a wet porcupine. So when Mary Ann and Allie got married, two weeks before Christmas, I took to my bed with a convenient stomach upset. Let everybody else celebrate. I wanted nothing to do with the woman.

Christmas, Will McLean's older sister Hannah came to visit with her husband and ten children. The house was filled to overflowing and when I found out that their oldest son, John, was studying to be a doctor at the University of Maryland, where my daddy had gotten his medical degree, I attached myself to John right off. I took him to the barn and showed him my daddy's old doctor's gig. I unlocked a trunk in the attic and brought down my daddy's doctoring things and talked Mama into allowing me to give them to John. I liked John the best of all Aunt

Hannah's brood. And he treated me kindly, like a grown-up, not a child. I think he was glad to have somebody in the family interested in his doctoring.

Daddy Will gave us all ice skates for Christmas. Button had said she'd teach us to skate. The creek froze before Christmas. It was so cold a person's bones got petrified just going out the door.

Mama's time was coming fast. The new baby was due in the middle of January. Right after Christmas I found out that Mama had given Mary Ann a piece of her hair for the hair wreath. And I set my mind to it. I had to get Mary Ann out of the house for good.

I don't know what made me think of the idea to take Mary Ann's shawl. But the plan was so simple it was downright brilliant. Why hadn't I thought of it before? I minded how, the one time the woman had misplaced her shawl, she'd gone plum crazy. All I wanted was for everyone to see how contentious she was and what an evil heart beat under her ribs.

So I sneaked into Mama's room one morning when she'd set the shawl aside to rub Mama's ankles. And I ran off with it.

Well, you never heard such caterwaulling in your life. Mary Ann ran right to Will McLean who was in the library, bent over his ledgers. He sent for me. And there in the library was Mary Ann, weeping like a peacock whose feathers had been stolen.

McLean stood up when I came in. "Did you take her shawl?"

I said yessir, I did.

"I'm going to put an end to this benighted nonsense for once and for all," he said. And he closed the door.

My bones turned to mush then. But all he did was

take Mary Ann by the wrist and ask her, real gentle like, to show me.

"Uh, uh no, Massa Will," she said, "please."

I stood puzzled. What was she supposed to show me? McLean talked the kindest to her then that I'd ever heard him talk. So she turned away from him and undid her dress in front and slipped it down over her shoulders.

And then I saw why she wore that shawl like it was a second skin.

Somebody had whupped Mary Ann so bad once that her shoulders and back were full of scars.

I recoiled, seeing those scars. I backed away.

McLean wouldn't have that, though. He came and pulled me over to stand right by Mary Ann. Just held me by my wrist and made sure I got a good look at those scars. "You see?" he said. His voice was raspy. I nodded yessir.

"You going to stop tormenting this poor woman now?"

I said yessir and Mary Ann buttoned her dress back up. McLean looked at me with eyes so fierce, my soul shriveled. "Go get the shawl," he said.

I ran to fetch it. When Mary Ann left the room, he sat back down at his desk and picked up his pen.

"Why didn't you tell me?" I demanded. "Who did that to her? Who could do such a thing to a person?" I'd heard of nigras being beaten. But I never believed it and nobody ever talked about such things in my presence.

"Does a person have to show you their scars before you decide not to inflict your own?" he asked. "What kind of a person are you, anyway?"

"Who *did* that to her?"

"Mr. Wilcher."

"Julia's stepdaddy?"

"That's the only Mr. Wilcher I know. The man never did treat his darkies right. Emily Stratton-Wilcher begged me to buy Mary Ann to get her away from him. Now is there anything else you need to know?"

"I thought she wore that shawl to cover some old witch's marks," I said.

"Those scars are witch's marks, all right," he said bitterly.

I stood pondering. There were a lot of things I still needed to know. My mind was whirling, fast. Had Mary Ann become evil because of what Mr. Wilcher had done to her? *Was* she evil, or was I imagining things? What about the two nigras who died at Lang Syne after she'd taken their hair? What about the scrap of material she had from Julia's dress and Julia's sickess? What about her voodoo stories?

My daddy had always insisted that the nigras never be mistreated. The only time he'd ever whupped *me* was when I was about four and had thrown hot soup at Maum Hanna and scalded her hands in a temper tantrum. I knew that what had been done to Mary Ann was horrible and wrong.

But I was still convinced of one thing. *Something* was wrong with Mary Ann.

I minded it was not the time to ask Will McLean what he thought it was. I still had to study on the question myself. So I said nosir, there's nothing more I need to know and left the room.

Chapter 8

January 1854

Nobody could ever figure out why Sarah would ice skate on the creek when she wouldn't swim in it. But she took to ice skating like Moses to the Promised Land. I figured that Sarah conjectured that the dragons were petrified under ice. So she hounded Mary Ann all day long to take her down to that creek and ice skate. And since Sarah didn't have lessons in the afternoon, she had more time to hound.

The end of the second week of January my brother Willie was born. It was a day of white mist that hung over the plantation so a person couldn't see the log cabin kitchen from the house. The whole place seemed sealed off from the rest of the world. And the temperature had risen so that the snow outside was turning to mush.

Will McLean had sent Hiram that morning to the junction to telegraph Doctor Moore in Alexandria. After a noon meal, he went to the station himself to meet the doctor's train. Maum Hanna was with Mama in her room. Button insisted that everything was normal and that lessons should continue as usual.

Everything was normal, I suppose. Except that nobody thought to question where Sarah was. Maria and I and Button thought she was with Mary Ann. Nobody thought to question Mary Ann's whereabouts until, halfway through afternoon classes we heard a ruckus downstairs and Will McLean's voice, yelling.

We ran downstairs and there was McLean, in the front hall, coat off, hair soaked and plastered against him, clothing wet, holding a limp, dripping Sarah in his arms.

Doctor Moore was with him, calling for warm blankets and rum. It was Button who galvanized the servants into action. The whole house went suddenly crazy, with everybody running and bumping into each other and Button and Doctor Moore giving orders. I couldn't hear or think or breathe. It was worse than hog-killing time.

We found out what had happened in scraps of information. Daddy Will's carriage had been approaching the house when he and Doctor Moore saw Sarah, through the mists, skating alone on the creek. They also saw her go under the water, heard her shrieks turn into thin wails. Will McLean leaped out of the carriage and ran as fast as he could across the meadow to the creek, dove in, and pulled her out.

Doctor Moore stayed for three days. But it was Mary Ann who delivered Mama's baby, because the doctor was attending to Sarah and Maum Hanna was making sure the servants kept a steady stream of heated blankets ready, and giving Sarah salt rubdowns. The doctor tried everything he could for Sarah's frostbite, brandy, terrible medicines. Sarah lay limp and shivering with cold. Until she started shivering with fever.

We walked around the house on tiptoe. Candles threw threatening shadows. Outside the mist became thicker, but inside I felt like I was walking through it.

Within three days, Sarah died. All I recollect from that time was that I was under a spell. My head pounded. The sound of my new brother's wail in the night got all mixed up in my head with the cries of Sarah. Once, in the middle of the second night, the day before Sarah died, I got up as if in a bad dream, to see Will McLean standing in the hall outside the nursery. He turned to me. His eyes seemed sunken, his face covered with a stubble of beard, his shirt collar was open. He seemed not to recognize me. From inside the nursery I could hear Sarah's pitiful cries and see the huge shadow of Doctor Moore on the wall. He went from the nursery to Mama's room.

Every once in a while I heard Mama calling, "Will, Will, how is my baby? How is my Sarah?"

Will McLean would go in there and lie to her and tell her Sarah was coming round. Then the doctor would give Mama something to make her sleep.

I recollect the way they laid Sarah out in the parlor, evergreens and holly berries in place of flowers. And I recollect how Will McLean collected our ice skates and had Hiram put them away.

And how finally Button convinced him to tell Mama that Sarah had died. And Mama, in her blue robe de chambre, came downstairs, held up by Will McLean, to view her baby for the last time. I thought she would faint, standing there. But she didn't. Then Will McLean whispered something to her and picked her up in his arms and carried her back upstairs.

After he came down he went directly outside.

Maum Hanna went up to Mama, then came down to say that Mama wanted to see me. I went upstairs. She was against pillows in bed, her face almost as white as the lace. The baby slept in a cradle nearby.

I stood there, trembling. She gestured that I should come closer to the bed and sit.

"Dear Oscie," she said, "you must do something for me."

All I could do was nod.

"My Will is talking of selling Mary Ann."

It took me a moment to comprehend.

"Maum Hanna just told me a moment ago. Said Mary Ann's down in her cabin, wailing. My Will's gone out for a ride on Pathfinder and Maum Hanna's given me a potion to sleep."

How could she care about Mary Ann *now?* "Let him sell her," I said. "It's her fault. She was so fixed on showing you what a good baby nurse she could be that she forgot Sarah!"

"No, dear, it's nobody's fault. We all forgot Sarah."

"No!" I began to cry. I couldn't bear it.

She hushed me and went on. "Mary Ann is married to Allie. And she's with child. Your daddy never sold any darkies off from here. And he'd never split up a family."

Through my blurred eyes I stared at her. "Do you think Daddy would *care?* After what's happened?"

"Yes, your daddy would never do a wrong to make a right. He always minded Yorkshire's long and venerable history. It's times like this we have to hold on to what we are."

It was the potion speaking, I decided. It'd made her mind daft. "Mama," I began.

"My Will is so distraught. If he sells Mary Ann

he'll be going against everything he believes in. I don't want him ever to do that. I don't want this tragedy to destroy us any more than it's done." She closed her eyes and for a moment I thought she was asleep. Then she opened them and smiled weakly at me.

"In his heart, Will is an abolitionist, Oscie. Only he doesn't know it yet. Why do you think he hired Button? Because he so admires the way they do things up North. And he believes our way is doomed. But at the same time he wants, more than anything, to run this place as good as your daddy did for us."

I nodded.

"Now will you do this for me? Go to him and tell him he mustn't sell Mary Ann? But don't say anything about going against his principles. Say that I ask him not to do it because I want to uphold what we've always been about here at Yorkshire. Do it for your daddy, darling, please."

I just looked at her. Do it for my daddy? For him, Sarah, and all of us, I was for selling Mary Ann. The one time I agreed with Will McLean, I had to go to him and tell him he was doing the wrong thing?

It made no sense at all. But what did *that* matter? Nothing under God's sun made sense anymore. So I got up and said yes, I would do it. Then I kissed her and left the room.

The funeral was the next day at St. Paul's in Alexandria and so neighbors who couldn't make the trip started coming to pay their respects that afternoon.

When I got downstairs, Lucinda Dogan was in the parlor with her brother John. Benjamin Chinn was there, too, and he said the Carters were on their way.

I saw two more carriages pulling up in the front drive. All the people brought food and stood around saying how lifelike Sarah looked and kissing me and Maria.

I still couldn't believe Sarah was gone. And as far as I was concerned, the waxy figure in that coffin in the center of the room had nothing to do with my little sister with the unruly curls who ran through the house and kept everything so lively. So I didn't look at it. I had enough to attend to with the tearing feelings inside me. How could such a little person fix herself so deep in everybody's heart?

So as I sat there next to Maria I minded Sarah's little ways. I thought about the things she'd say; I hated myself for every mean thing I'd ever done to her.

How were we going to live without Sarah?

How could we take her to St. Paul's tomorrow and stand there and watch her be put into the ground? And come home without her? I got to trembling again, pondering that.

Button had taken charge of things. Will McLean would be along shortly, she told everyone. And Hiram had gone to the junction to fetch the minister. There would be services this evening. Mama would be down then. No, Mama wouldn't be going to the funeral tomorrow.

Then Button told me to go and get some milk and cookies for myself. Like that would stop the awful miseries inside me. "And if you see Will McLean, tell him his neighbors have come to call," she whispered.

Just as I left the parlor, McLean walked in the back entrance of the center hall and went quickly into the library and locked the door. I knocked softly.

"Go away."

"I can't. I have a message from Mama."

Footsteps inside, the door opened. He waved me in, then crossed the room to his desk and refilled a glass from a silver decanter. He'd been riding. His boots were muddy, his cravat askew, his hair mussed.

"Fine mess, isn't it?" he said. His back was to me. He drank down whatever was in the glass in one gulp, and gestured that I should sit. Then he looked at me and I never saw a face so taken with grief. The man appeared haunted. And I minded that it had to do with more than the stubble of beard on his face or his bleary eyes.

"How is your mother?"

"Sleeping. Maum Hanna gave her a potion."

"Good. Has the minister arrived yet?"

"No, sir. But lots of people have. Button says she'd be obliged if you came soon into the parlor."

He nodded and ran his hand over his face. "I've got to shave and change my shirt. How are you and Maria holding up?"

"Fair to middling," I said. "But I can't stand being in there and hearing all those people saying how alive Sarah looks. She's dead and she looks dead."

He nodded and took a seat. He rested his forearms on his knees and leaned forward to look at me. "What message from your mother?"

"She heard you're selling Mary Ann."

He nodded, waiting.

"She doesn't want you to."

He stared at me long and hard. "Your mother is bearing up well under the strain, Oscie, but . . . "

"She says I should tell you that no darkie ever got sold away from Yorkshire. And my daddy would never split up families."

He sighed wearily. "You were right about Mary Ann, Oscie."

"Yessir," I said. But I didn't gloat. Who could? There was a stab of sorrow in me so bad it was like a knife.

I'd bested Will McLean finally. But it didn't feel like I thought it would. Fact was, if I had it in my power to bring Sarah back again, I'd settle for never besting him at all.

". . . suppose I just don't understand how to handle darkies," he was saying. He got up to look out the window. "With the thaw, the ice was melting, but I never dreamed . . ." He stopped speaking and commenced again. Like he was trying to get it right.

"All that business about the dragons being trapped under the ice, and not being able to get her. She was spellbound by that. All Mary Ann's nonsense. I should have listened to you, Oscie. I thought you were being a pesky, mean-spirited little girl."

He turned to look at me. "You were. But I should have paid heed anyway. When you said your daddy would have put Mary Ann in the fields to protect his family, I thought you were sassing me. Well, you were doing that, too. But you were also telling me there was something wrong with Mary Ann, even though you didn't know what it was."

I could scarcely breathe. My chest hurt.

"I know now," he said softly. "She's obsessed with babies. Has a regular fixation on them. All her life, at Lang Syne, she minded the children until Mr. Wilcher came and took that job away from her. All she wanted here was to get it back again. Which is why she was with Mama that morning instead of watching Sarah. Maum Hanna couldn't get her out of the room."

A clock ticked on the mantel. Otherwise the room was silent as a tomb.

"I don't want you thinking I hold with any of that witch business you were throwing at me. And I don't want you blaming Button because of the ice skating."

"I don't blame Button," I said. "Or you."

He looked at me quickly. And before he turned away, there was a moment of something unspoken in his eyes. Like a question, drawing an answer from mine. And I felt the warmth that sometimes comes between kindred spirits. But only for a moment. Surely not enough to make up for anything. Yet it was enough for now.

"Thank you for that, Oscie, but I should have seen this for what it was, and I didn't. When I'm wrong I admit it."

"Then don't sell her," I said.

He smiled sadly. "Your mama's on some sleeping potion. She doesn't know what she's saying."

"Yes, she does! This means a lot to her! She said it's times like this that we have to hold onto what we are. It means a powerful lot to her, sir."

"What are we, Oscie?" he whispered hoarsely. "Dear God." He slumped back down in the chair. "What kettle of fish have we gotten ourselves into, keeping these people as slaves?"

My face flamed. And I felt like I was defending my daddy, then. "We take care of them," I told him. "Even when they get old and sick and can't work anymore. Even Mary Ann, after what she did. That's the kind of people we are."

He nodded and stood up. "I've got to get cleaned up and go into the parlor. Your mama's a good woman," he mumbled.

"What will you do, then?"

He faced me. "Honor her wishes. But I can't have Mary Ann in the house anymore. I'll put her in the

In My Father's House   79

fields as you once suggested. It'll be best for every-one."

Yes, I thought. Best all around that she be out of the way.

It wasn't until that evening at the services for Sarah that I recollected that Mary Ann was going to have a baby. I suppose I should have told Will McLean about it. Could still tell him, I pondered, looking across the room to where he sat with Mama.

But I didn't. Not that night, not the next day, and not any time after. Part of me wanted to, but every time I felt the urge, I thought of Sarah. I felt the gaping wound inside me, saw Mama's stricken face, heard Maria crying in her bed at night, and saw Sarah at every turn in the house.

So I decided to let the matter be buried with Sarah. Mary Ann was out of sight now. Mama was too deep in mourning to even ask for her. Will McLean stayed clear of Mary Ann whenever he could. And whenever I sighted the woman in the distance, I noticed she was wearing that shawl of hers draped over her front now instead of her back. Like she didn't want anybody to know she was having a baby.

Probably thinks Will McLean will sell her off, I pondered, that if she can't work in the fields, she'll have to go. So I'm not the one to give away her secret.

I told myself that when I wasn't reminding myself that nigra women worked in the fields all the time when they were having babies. Why should Mary Ann be any different?

Chapter 9

January 1854 to May 1857

Willie was one cunning baby and I was devoted to him from the start. He was less than five pounds when he was born, but he grew and changed fast. His real name was John Wilmer. Was his first name in memory of my own daddy? Had McLean been kind enough to allow Mama that? I don't know. I never asked. But in my mind it was. Although the baby was never called anything but Willie.

Thanks to Button, I was apprised of the fact that the January Willie was born, the Republican party came into being and wheat jumped to $1.70 a bushel. The world was changing fast.

Right after Willie was born, Will McLean's younger sister Ann died. He had more brothers and sisters than you could find in the Old Testament.

When Willie was four months old, I read *Jane Eyre,* and I could pen the whole Bill of Rights in beautiful script without spilling a drop of ink. Will McLean had promised me that if I learned to do this, he'd allow me to ride with him once a week around the plantation and survey the progress of the spring planting.

We didn't fuss at each other so much anymore since Sarah died. It was as if her death had made us all step back and look at each other with new eyes. Will McLean and I didn't exactly love each other, no. But I no longer bristled like a porcupine when he came near. And though he still teased me a lot, he allowed me my say. But I hadn't figured him out yet and I suppose I was still wary of him. And he knew it.

I started calling him Daddy Will that spring. Riding around Yorkshire while he showed me the repaired fences, the carefully pruned peach orchard, the lush corn fields and pasture lands, the newly started barn, with him seeking my approval for all the improvements, I couldn't very well avoid it.

Besides, Mama wanted me to call him Daddy Will. And I would have done anything to bring a smile to Mama's face again.

By the time Willie was a year old and starting to toddle, Button was teaching us how Stephen Douglas and Abraham Lincoln had debated in Illinois in October of 1854. Later, in late fall of 1855 she told us how five thousand proslavery people from Missouri had crossed over the line into Kansas and seized the polling places and made speaking out against slavery a crime.

By the time Willie clapped his baby hands together and learned to say words, Button was telling us about Senator Charles Sumner of Massachusetts who was beaten on the floor of the United States Senate by Congressman Preston S. Brooks of South Carolina in 1856.

It was in an argument over slavery.

A few days after that, Button told us about a man

named John Brown. With six of his sons and a son-in-law, Brown abducted five proslavery settlers from their cabins in Kansas and split open their skulls with broadswords. Then Brown evaded capture.

This upset Button very much.

But I'm getting ahead of myself. Back to the year Willie was born. I grew two inches. Daddy Will had a new smokehouse built. Christmas was a mixed blessing holiday. Our spirits were all still afflicted from Sarah's death, so, while we had a tree and presents and a great feast and Aunt Hannah came with her family again, there was no music and no holiday ball.

The new store barn was finished at Christmas. It was very solid and handsome. The nigras had a party in it. Daddy Will and Mama went and gave out presents.

Later I heard Mama saying something to Maum Hanna about it being a shame that Mary Ann had lost the baby. And how she should have known better than to let Will put Mary Ann in the fields.

"It wuz that or sell her," Maum Hanna answered. "You couldn't of stopped that man no how. He wudda sold her, Miz Virginia, if'n he'd a known. Which is why she kept it so quiet. An' why she still doan want him to know."

I was in the hallway, listening, and I stood stock-still. *Mary Ann had lost her baby!*

I felt flooded with guilt as I stood listening. I minded how Mary Ann loved babies so.

"You doan blame yourself," Maum Hanna was saying, "you wuz too upset by the death of your own to know what wuz goin' on. That girl just too skinny an' ornery to have a chile anyhow."

"I should tell Will," Mama said.

"You doan put that man on the spot," Maum Hanna advised. "He cain't keep her in the fields, what's he gonna do wif' her? He sell her off, you be guilty. He bring her back inna house, he be. You know Mister Will still blames himself for bringin' her here and what happened. Doan raise it all up agin, Miz Virginia, please. This house needs some peace."

I tried to push the guilt aside. Maum Hanna had known of Mary Ann's condition. *She* could have said something, but she held back, too. Because her first loyalty was to Mama and Daddy Will.

And so it was that I attempted to cleanse my conscience. If Mary Ann had wanted Will McLean to know, she could have told him. Like Maum Hanna said, we needed some peace.

Christmas of 1855 things were almost back to normal again. Mama almost seemed her old self and any shadow that lingered around Daddy Will from Sarah's death seemed almost gone.

We were becoming a family. Little Willie helped that happen. You couldn't have bad feelings when he was around. And by the following summer he was riding up front of Daddy Will in the saddle when his father was out in the fields.

Fall of 1855 Button read us a letter she'd received from Harriet Beecher Stowe.

"I am a little bit of a woman. Somewhat more than forty, about as thin and dry as a pinch of snuff, never very much to look at in my best of days, and looking like a used-up article by now."

In 1856 we got a new president. James Buchanan. Daddy Will said he had charmed Queen Victoria when he was minister to Great Britain, but he would need more than charm to keep the Union from falling apart.

People were talking a lot about the Union falling apart. Summer of 1856 Button read to us from the newspapers about how men were killing each other in Kansas over slavery.

Mama got a hoop skirt that summer. Button read us *The Charge of the Light Brigade*. Maria played "Listen to the Mockingbird" on the piano without missing a note.

By the time Willie was baptized in St. Paul's Church in Alexandria that October, Mama told us she was in a delicate condition again.

In March of 1857 Button read from the paper about Chief Justice Roger B. Taney, who had liberated all his own nigras. Yet he declared that a slave would always be a slave and neither he nor his descendants could ever have standing in court or be American citizens.

Button then told us that it had to do with a slave named Dred Scott who had lived on free soil in Missouri for several years already and now wanted his freedom.

Daddy Will said Taney was a jackass. And we'd all see the punishment for such a decision. I decided that our family had already been sufficiently afflicted with Sarah dying. Now we were happy for the first time since my daddy had died. So I wouldn't concern myself with Dred Scott's descendants.

In May 1857, little Lula, named Lucretia after Daddy Will's mama, was born. I was twelve years old. In June Button took Maria and me on a trip to Washington. We stayed at Aunt Hannah's and saw the new B & O Railroad Depot which had a seventy-foot tower, a sky-lighted hall, and was elegantly furnished.

Mary Ann still laundered Daddy Will's shirts. But

she never ventured up to the house. Not even to deliver them. And as far as I could see, she wasn't having any more babies.

Chapter 10

Christmas 1859

"I'm worried about Button," I told Daddy Will. "Ever since crazy old John Brown tried to start a slave uprising at Harper's Ferry this fall, she's been sad."

It was a Saturday in late December and we were riding out to get a Christmas tree, he on Pathfinder, and I on Cottonwood. Those Saturday rides were the best times to discuss things with him, I'd found, when everyone else was out of earshot.

"She has been kind of under the weather lately," he agreed.

"She's got a fixation with Brown," I said. "Every day, from October until he was hanged on the second of this month, she read to us about him from the newspaper. Maria says Button is worried about a slave uprising."

"I don't think it's that," he said.

"Maria says Julia's stepdaddy isn't allowing his nigras their usual ration of rum this Christmas. And he's forbidden the nigra preacher who rides circuit to come onto the grounds of Lang Syne. Do you think there's going to be a slave uprising?"

"No."

"Julia told Maria that her stepdaddy instructed his overseer to shoot the first darkie who acts suspicious."

"He never gave his darkies any quarter, remember."

"But what do you think is wrong with Button? She's been so sad lately."

"She told me she's disappointed in Henry David Thoreau and Longfellow and William Cullen Bryant for saying Brown is a noble, crucified hero. Button knows Brown was just a madman who became a martyr after he was executed. Don't forget, her father is in the antislavery movement in New England. And they gave Brown moral and financial support. She may now be questioning her beliefs."

"She told us once that it's good to do that."

"It may be good but it's never easy," he sighed. "And don't be surprised if she wants to leave us soon."

"Leave?" I drew up the reins. "She can't!"

He smiled wryly. "Whenever she wants to go, she can. She's a Northerner and we must consider her feelings. The whole country is in an uproar since Brown's execution. People right here in Prince William County are forming military companies."

"For what?"

"To defend hearth and home against the Northern fanatics who would interfere with our Constitutional rights."

"Is there going to be a war?"

He'd reined Pathfinder in and we sat our horses on a hillock overlooking a field of evergreens. "We have to pick a tree today," he reminded me.

"Is war coming?" I asked again.

"It's been coming for a while now, Oscie."

I felt a sense of dread, not so much from those

words, but from the calm with which he uttered them. As if he'd known it all along.

"Don't go frightening your mother or the children," he said. He urged Pathfinder on. "A lot depends on what happens at the Democratic Convention in Charleston in April. We have time yet. War isn't going to ruin our Christmas. Come on, let's get our tree. We're going to have the best Christmas ever. I've bought a lot of presents in Alexandria, a new tin fire engine for Willie, a rag doll for Lula, and lots of frippery for the three grown women in my life."

Willie was six and Lula two-and-a-half and crazy about rag dolls. Maria was fifteen and I was fourteen. We had new ball gowns. I followed Will McLean down the slope, my mind dizzy with what he'd said about war coming.

"I've hired musicians," he was saying, "and everyone's coming. I want to see what you and your sister learned from that fancy dancing master I've been paying."

Daddy Will was right about military companies being formed in our county. Most of our male neighbors showed up at our Christmas ball wearing some version of a military uniform. Josiah Tidball Carter even wore his granddaddy's Revolutionary War sword. Two of Mrs. Judith Henry's sons pushed her into the house in her special chair looking prouder than peacocks in right fine broadcloth versions of the Southern soldier.

But Cousin John shocked me most. He had graduated from medical school and was a practicing physician in Washington. But all he talked about was raising his own company if war came.

"Isn't it exciting?" Maria asked. She looked like a

freshly iced cake in her blue velvet. Maria had grown a bosom and the dress was low cut with a skirt draped and pinned with pink satin rosebuds.

"What's the matter, Oscie?" Cousin John came up to stand behind me. "Why the long face?"

I watched Maria swirling around on the floor with one after another of Cousin John's handsome brothers.

"My bosom isn't as respectable as Maria's. It never will be," I said dismally.

He laughed. I could talk to Cousin John like he was an older brother. Always had. "Maria will tend to fat when she's thirty," he said. "And you'll still have your figure."

"I'd just as lief take the bosom now and the fat later, if I had my druthers."

He put his hands on my shoulders and turned me to face him. "You look like a French porcelain doll I saw in a shop in Washington," he said. "Your green taffeta brings out the color of your eyes. I know six girls who would hate you into next week for your dark curls and tiny waist."

My face flamed and I looked down at his boots.

"Now what's wrong?" he asked.

"I'm not good at flirting, like Maria. I couldn't make eyes behind a fan if our wheat crop depended on it."

"I'm not flirting, Oscie Mason. I'm telling you the truth. Now come on and let's not waste this good fiddle music. Let's dance."

"Would you really go to war, John?" I asked him, while dancing.

Something in his smile tore at my heart. "I'm not raising my own company for a turkey shoot."

"But you're a doctor."

"So I'll be needed. Most of the good doctors will go with the North. The South lacks the materials and facilities to produce medicine. And I'll wager the first thing the North does is impose an embargo on medical supplies."

"My Daddy John said medicine hasn't any race or color."

"It's a good thing he isn't still around then, Oscie. We get everything from the North. I'm forcing a committee now to try to get as many medical books as I can shipped South."

The music stopped. It had been lively, but now the fiddle players started in on something downright soulful and stirring, the kind of music that seemed to rise right out of the land around us. I became sad again. He steered me to a sideboard and handed me a cup of punch.

"We'll probably have to smuggle medical supplies in from the North or Mexico," he said. "Run any blockades the North sets up or capture medicine in battles. We'll need chloroform, morphine, quinine, paregoric, laudanum, and calomel."

"Doctor talk." I smiled at him. "I miss it. It reminds me of Daddy."

"I'll be using his instruments when war comes. And I'm drawing up a list of four hundred plants that can be grown by Southern citizens as substitutes for medicines. Jimson weed for fever, balsam or cucumbers for burns, watercress or wild yam for scurvy."

"Oh, John, I'll grow them! I'll grow a whole garden full!"

"I'll mail you a list of plants." He smiled at me. "I'll write to you," he said.

Chapter 11

April 1860

"I need Button."

I was all ready for a set-to with Daddy Will at breakfast. "If she can't come with us, I'm not going."

He smiled at me across the table. "I thought you were your father's daughter. How can you be afraid?"

We were to take the ten o'clock train to Alexandria because I'd come up with the Devil's own toothache late last evening. I was petrified of Doctor Chaffin and his horrible instruments, ever since I'd made a visit to his office last summer. But I saw no reason to admit that to Will McLean.

He was just back from a week at the Democratic Convention in Charleston and he was bright-eyed and bushy-tailed and spoiling for a fight. And although we may have arrived at a "plateau of understanding" with each other, as Mama liked to put it, we still enjoyed a good feather-raising argument now and then.

"When Cousin John gave you that gum last Christmas, he told you it might take the filling out of your tooth," Will McLean reminded me.

Chewing gum was all the rage in Washington and Cousin John had given me some, along with a leather-bound copy of *A Christmas Carol,* for presents.

"She's refused to share the gum with me," Maria said. "Yesterday when we were writing in our journals, she said I was a ninny because I wrote about the barbecue at the Carters' yesterday. And she took her last piece of gum and put it in her mouth right in front of me. And do you know what *she* wrote about? That you said anti-Douglas Southerners are fools for walking out of the convention and nominating John Breckenridge of Kentucky for president. She doesn't even know what an anti-Douglas Southerner *is,* Daddy Will. And she laughed at *me!*"

"I do so," I countered.

"Leave your sister be," McLean told Maria. "She's suffering enough for her sins. Although I am flattered to be quoted in your journal, Oscie."

I was about to lash out at Maria, bad tooth or no, when Button came into the room.

"Quiet you girls. Your mama's been up half the night with Lula and is trying to catch up on her sleep."

"Why can't you come with us, Button?" I asked.

"I didn't know that I couldn't." Button reached for a cup of coffee.

"I'd rather you didn't," Will McLean said. "There's a lot of bad sentiment in all our cities about Northerners. In Boggy Swamp, South Carolina, they ran two Northern tutors out of the district recently."

"This isn't South Carolina," I argued.

"The president of a college in Alabama had to flee

for his life last week. Simply because he's Northern born."

"You mean people in Alexandria would attack Button because she's from the North?" Maria asked. "You *come* from Alexandria, Daddy Will!"

Button spoke then. "If it's all the same to you, Mister Will, I think it's a lovely spring day for a trip to Alexandria. And Oscie does need me."

"You don't have to," he said.

"Of course I don't. But I want to. Maria, you stay home and help your mama with Lula today. She's feverish. I'll ask Maum Hanna to pack us a lunch for the train."

All I could remember about being under the nitrous oxide in the dentist's chair was Will McLean's voice from across the room telling Dr. Chaffin that Abraham Lincoln was a force to be reckoned with.

Button held my hand. The nitrous oxide put me into a lovely dreamy place, so that I wondered why our neighbors would all rather use opium from the garden poppy and corn whiskey for a toothache.

After I was rested a bit, Daddy Will went outside to get a carriage. I was in the waiting room with Button when he came inside, pushed us back into the surgery and asked the doctor if there was a back way out. Outside I heard angry voices.

"If they damage my place . . ." the doctor was saying.

I must have missed something because of the nitrous oxide, because the next thing I knew the doctor was showing us through a back hall that led to an alley. Outside the April sunshine was bright. Button gripped my arm. Will McLean put two fingers in his mouth and emitted a shrill whistle. A young boy at the end of the alley came running. I saw money exchange hands and the boy ran off.

"How did they know?" Button was asking.

"You spoke to that man in the waiting room," he told her. "You don't have a Southern accent."

So, the angry crowd, now in the doctor's office, was after Button! I felt the bright blue sky swirling over my head. Then the boy came running back. "I got your hack, Mister."

The back door of the dentist's office burst open and six or seven women and men came running out. "Take your abolitionist whore out of town, Mister," one man was saying.

I saw the hack at the end of the alley. Before I realized what a bad turn matters had taken, Daddy Will had drawn his gleaming, brass-handled Colt pistol.

"Step back, all of you," he said. He sounded the way he did when he told Maria or me to go to our rooms for misbehaving. But the angry people stood their ground. And in the next moment nobody knew what to do as Daddy Will stood there with that pistol drawn and they stood there glaring at us.

"You're a Southerner." One man stepped forward. His face looked like a cornshuck. "You'd shoot your own for a Yankee whore?"

"Call her that one more time and you'll be sorry you drew breath this day," Daddy Will said. His voice had dropped to a rasping whisper and I thought, if they know what's good for them, they'd go back to where they came from. You didn't trifle with Will McLean when he spoke like that.

"We don't need any Yankees in Alexandria!" A woman yelled it. Her mouth looked like she ate raw rabbits.

Then I heard a click as Daddy Will pulled back the hammer of his pistol. And they heard it too.

"Seems to me, you all need someone in Alexandria to teach you manners," he said. "You all make me ashamed of my hometown."

"Why, it's Will McLean." Another man stepped forward. "We'd best get back, folks. Will here belonged to the Alexandria Militia. I know him to shoot the core out of an apple at two hundred yards."

"Get 'em back, Ambrose," Daddy Will said quietly.

The man named Ambrose did as he was told. And I found myself wanting to both laugh and cry. I made a gurgling sound in my throat. Will McLean looked down at me quizzically, and the next thing I knew he was lifting me off my feet.

I held on, with my eyes squeezed tight. He smelled of tobacco, harsh soap, and horses, like my daddy always did. I heard Button's quick steps behind us. Then we were inside the carriage and the door slammed. The carriage jolted to a quick start and Daddy Will gave orders for the train station.

Behind us we heard the sound of voices yelling and running feet. *They were trying to follow us!*

Then something hit the carriage with a thud. I whimpered.

"That's it," Daddy Will said, "no more chewing gum for you, young lady."

I looked up at him. "What's a whore?" I asked.

"Someone who disgraces her town by trying to attack innocent visitors," he said dourly.

I knew there was something wrong with that explanation. But I just closed my eyes, secure between the two of them, knowing something horrible had just happened to us which meant that things couldn't be the same anymore. We'd always gone to Alexandria. And Button had often gone with us. But it wasn't until we got to the train station that I conjectured about a larger truth.

Although I was sitting between them in the carriage, it was Will McLean I was clinging to.

Chapter 12

May 1860 to April 1861

I sat on the back portico pretending to read. From upstairs came the laughter of the children as Mama oversaw their bathing. The evening air was like silk, and the spring lawns and pastures, lush with green and iced with pink and white blossoms, were a sight for the eyes. From inside the house came the sound of Maria's piano playing. She played for Daddy Will every evening after supper while he sat on the portico—as he was doing at the moment—and read his paper.

On the surface we'd never had such a sense of well-being in our house. But underneath it all I perceived a deepening shadow. Will McLean had been somber since the incident in Alexandria. He'd bade both me and Button not to say a word about it to anyone.

I looked across at him. Something was wrong, I just felt it in my bones. At supper he'd told us he wasn't going to Baltimore where the Democrats were to have a second convention this year because the first one had ended up like a hog killing.

Whatever was wrong, he wasn't talking about it.

"You don't have to worry about the farm if you want to go to Baltimore. The planting's all finished and I can see to everything else for you," I said.

He looked up from his paper. "Thank you, Oscie, but that isn't it."

"What is it, then?" I asked. "You can tell me. I'm almost fifteen. I can keep a quiet tongue."

He smiled at me. "You are growing up very nicely, do you know that?"

I blushed. "Isn't anything I wouldn't have said to my daddy."

"Exactly. So I'm gratified that you'd say it to me."

Silence for a moment. I waited. Mama had told me that if you didn't push a man into a corner, soon enough he'd come around.

"The Democrats have splintered themselves into pieces over slavery," he said quietly, gazing out over the peaceful landscape. "They're laying the groundwork for chaos. I'll not go to Baltimore, because I'll not be a part of it."

I waited again.

"Lincoln has emerged as the dark horse and a hard rival for Seward at the Republican convention in Chicago."

Lincoln again. That name was all you heard anymore, whenever people gathered. A visitor didn't step across our threshold but they were mouthing off things about Lincoln. Now here was Daddy Will brooding about the man.

I must ask Button how dangerous this Lincoln person is, I minded. Daddy Will expects me to know such things. I didn't want to seem ignorant in front of him.

"Is Lincoln dangerous?"

Button was in her room, writing a letter to her father. "As dangerous as a person can be who has a reputation for integrity," she answered.

"Then why doesn't Daddy Will like him?"

"He doesn't dislike him. He just knows that the South will secede if Lincoln is elected."

"Do you want Lincoln to be elected?"

She smiled sadly. "I adore Abraham Lincoln. He comes to us out of the frontier, where things are still new and clean. He represents all that is honest and good in us. But part of me doesn't want him to be elected."

"Why?"

"Because then we will become two countries," she said.

It became plain to me all too soon that I had to pay mind to politics. Because what went on out there in the world that seemed so removed from our peaceful life at Yorkshire, would soon affect us.

The Republicans had nominated Abraham Lincoln for President at their convention in Chicago. And in November he was elected President of the United States. Now the fox was in the henhouse, all right.

On December twentieth, South Carolina seceded from the Union. I was fifteen, finally. Mama's dressmaker came from Alexandria to make Maria and me four good dresses each, two for winter and two for spring.

But there were to be no ball gowns this year.

Maria came crying to me after our first session with the dressmaker. "Mama says no Christmas ball this year. Aunt Hannah writes of a frenzy of parties in Washington. Oh, I do hate that old Lincoln for getting elected and ruining everything! Oscie, you've got to convince Mama and Daddy Will to have our Christmas ball!"

"Don't you care about anything but a Christmas ball, Maria?" I asked? "War could be coming."

I wasn't breaking any promises I'd made to Daddy Will, telling her such. If Maria kept her eyes and ears open, she'd be sensible of what was going on. As for frightening her with war talk, well, it seemed to me she could do with some frightening.

"I think you're mean, Oscie. What do I care about an old war coming? I'm going to ask Daddy Will to let me visit Washington. Aunt Hannah has invited us. And if *you* don't want to go to all the parties, you can just stay here and mope!"

So she asked. And of course, Daddy Will said it was just the thing. "You never know when you'll get to see Washington again," he said. "Oscie, you'll go, too. We'll send Button with you. She knows Washington and can be chaperone. Aunt Hannah's boys will squire you around."

So we got the ball gowns anyway. But Washington was terrible. The streets were muddy and mobbed with people Button called "crude office seekers." The grounds around the unfinished Capitol dome were cluttered with workmen's equipment.

We went with Aunt Hannah's girls, Eliza, Mary Jane, and Catherine to party after party, to luncheons and teas. Button took us to see *Othello* at the National Theater.

Daniel, Douglas, and Bethannah squired us about. But I missed Cousin John who was at the University of Maryland, begging his old professors for medical textbooks for the South.

One evening we were invited to a hop at Willard's Hotel. The mood was that of controlled chaos. Most of Washington's citizens were for the Union, but there were many Southern sympathizers. And when Maria danced with a young man in the Washington Volunteers, and Daniel went to fetch her, words broke out between him and the young Union man and they almost came to blows.

We left early and I told Maria that she'd caused more trouble than if she was wearing a secessionist cockade.

I was glad to find myself in the center hall of Yorkshire again, enveloped by the grand old house's familiar and solid graciousness. I looked around the rich carpeting and draperies. At supper I minded the orderly elegance as a white-haired Hiram poured wine and Paula and Fanny served.

"Washington was so exciting!" Maria said.

"It was vulgar and loud," I countered.

"If you think that now, wait until March fourth when Lincoln is inaugurated," Will McLean said.

I looked at him, in his white ruffled shirt and gray broadcloth, presiding over the table, Lula next to him in her high chair, Button next to her, Willie on Will McLean's other side. He insisted on having the children at the supper table always. He was tender and indulgent with them. I looked at Mama, serene and glowing in lavender silk. This is home, I told myself. It doesn't matter what happens out there. I'll always have this to come to.

On January ninth, Mississippi left the Union. Florida left on the tenth and Alabama on the eleventh, to be followed by Georgia on the nineteenth and Louisiana on the twenty-sixth.

Button doubled our studies. She lengthened the school day. On clear February nights she kept us up late to observe special constellations in the sky with the new telescope Daddy Will had given us for Christmas.

Cousin John wrote from Washington with a list of plants for medical substitutes, and Daddy Will helped me draw up a diagram of my garden. One morning in February we were in the schoolroom. A cold, drizzling rain was falling. Outside we heard a horse galloping up to the house. It was a nigra messenger from the telegraph operator at the junction. Daddy Will called us all down and read us the message.

"Two days ago, former Senator Jefferson Davis was inaugurated as president of the Provisional Government of the Confederate States of America," he read.

Mama cried. Will McLean looked up at Button, who was standing with us on the stairway. "Any time you want to leave, you can," he said. "You are now tutoring in a different country."

"I always wanted to travel to a foreign country," Button told him. "I'll stay until the shooting starts."

She did. And I will never forget that day in April when Daddy Will stood in the doorway of our schoolroom, fresh from the fields in his planter's straw hat. "I wanted to bring the news myself," he said.

We all turned to stare at him. Along with everyone else in the country we'd held our breaths since the day after Christmas, when sixty-eight Union men huddled inside Fort Sumter in Charleston Harbor, besieged by six thousand South Carolina militiamen.

"Our new government gave Major Anderson until four this morning to surrender," Daddy Will said quietly. "Anderson refused. At four-thirty this morning, South Carolina batteries opened up on him."

Button gasped. "I was hoping Lincoln could keep the peace," she said.

"So was I," Daddy Will answered. "But a rider just brought the news from the depot. God help us all."

The tracks at Manassas Station stretched, deceptively silent, in the warm spring sun of the next day. Button's baggage was all around her on the platform. I and Daddy Will and Maria stood around her, locked in misery and waiting for the train to take her to Washington where she would stay with Aunt Hannah until her plans were worked out. Maria, who could normally talk the ears off a donkey, looked about to cry. "What will you *do* in Washington?" she asked.

"Find a way to make myself useful in the war."

"That means we'll be on different sides," Maria said. "Oh, why did the South have to go and fire on Sumter?"

Maria was starting to learn that what happened out in the world would sooner or later be felt by us.

"Because Southerners impatient for action, wanted to bring Virginia into the Confederacy," Button explained.

Daddy Will stared silently at the shining tracks.

"Do you want to know the most interesting part about the Sumter story?" Button asked.

We both said yes. Anything to break the dreaded silence.

"General Beauregard, the Confederate commander, was well taught in artillery at West Point. Do you know who taught him?"

We both said no.

"Anderson! The man he fired on at Sumter!"

"Do you think it was right to fire on his teacher?" I asked.

"Absolutely," she said. "If Beauregard thought that what he was doing was the right thing. And I'm sure Anderson was most proud of his former student."

"Would you want us to fire on you, Button?" Maria asked.

"If I taught you artillery, yes. For with the lessons I would have taught you when to go into action and when to hold your fire. As I am sure Anderson taught Beauregard."

We hugged her. In the distance we heard the chug-chug-chugging of the train, its shrieking whistle coming closer. Maria started to cry.

"I've left lesson plans in the schoolroom," Button said. "You are to continue your studies. Maria, keep up your piano." She hugged me again. "Oscie, keep up your French and finish your Virgil." And, holding me close, she whispered in my ear. "Be good to Will McLean. He's going to need you now. Know when to go into action and when to hold your fire."

The train pulled into the station with a hissing of steam and an iron-clanking of wheels. The baggage master loaded Button's belongings. Daddy Will held her elbow as she went up the step. Then she leaned down and pecked him on the cheek. "Bless you, Will McLean. It's been an honor working for you."

I saw the fractured look on Daddy Will's face as the train moved slowly, laboriously, in a vaporized dream, away from us. Maria was bawling like a stuck pig. I wouldn't cry, leastways not out loud.

We stood there, the three of us, like jackasses in the rain, watching that train pull away. I knew it was the end of my school days. Button took my childhood with her. She'd taught us to sew, appreciate learning, write without spilling ink, understand current events, swim, ice skate, and behave. She taught us to question, to keep going no matter what happened, and she pushed us when we stopped.

"Come along girls," Daddy Will said. "We've lost a good friend. I hope you remember all she taught you."

There was a hurt inside me worse than a toothache on that ride home, almost as bad as when Sarah died. But I kept the conversation up, like Button would have done.

"I didn't think I cared a frog's feather about Alabama and all those states leaving the Union," I told Will McLean.

"And? Do you care now?"

"No. But I wonder if Mr. Lincoln is hurting because those states left, like we're hurting for losing Button."

"I'm sure he is," he said. But he looked straight ahead, driving the carriage.

"I don't think I'll study anymore. My school days are over."

"You'll keep studying, I'll see to it." His voice brooked no argument.

"I could read to you and Mama of an evening, if you want. Like Button did sometimes."

"That would be nice."

"Tell you what I would like." I looked at his somber face, outlined harshly against the blue April sky. "I'd like to commence teaching Willie. Button started him on his letters and sums. I could study mornings and teach him afternoons. If it's all right with you."

He said that would be fine with him. But still he didn't look at me.

"Lula will be four next month. 'Bout time she learned her letters."

He said yes. About time. And it was most gracious of me.

I was worn out by then, trying to bring that man around. He just wouldn't be brought. What I wanted was to soften him up. Ask him if he thought Virginia was going to leave the Union. But I saw that he was set-back then. And I minded what Button said and held my fire.

It was April thirteenth, a bright spring day. Three days later Virginia seceded. It was raining.

A week later we had a letter from Button.

> Have arrived safely and am being coddled by Hannah and her brood. She has a sewing machine and the girls asked me to show them how to make shirts, trousers, and jackets for their soldiers. I gladly did so, though it seems strange, with me a Yankee, yet none of that came into it. We feel like family, or as they put it, kin.
>
> Hope you are doing your studying. Hannah and her husband are speaking of moving but I shall stay here and seek a position as a teacher. Oscie, you and Maria should know that on April 19, a Baltimore mob opened fire on Yankee soldiers as they passed through the streets on their way to Washington. What is significant about this is that Massachusetts men were the first to be wounded in this war on the same day the Revolution started in Lexington and Concord. Will write soon again, Button.

Chapter 13

June 1861

"And what did you do with the buffalo you shot, Captain Alexander?" Mama asked.

Candles reflected off our best crystal and china, and flickered in the mild June breeze that came in the dining room windows. Paula and Fanny moved about like dusty shadows, serving. Mama was entertaining our guests, Captain Edward Porter Alexander and General Pierre Gustave Toutant Beauregard, as if Confederate troops had not been gathering at the junction for almost a month now. As if the fields around the junction where cattle once grazed, were not now filled with trenches and tents and cannon.

As if war were not coming.

But it was, though the only time we heard Daddy Will and Mama refer to it was when they discussed what to send in the wagon to the camps of the 1st, 11th, and 17th regiments of Virginia volunteers. Pails of fresh buttermilk, baskets of bread, dozens of eggs, and a smoked hog went. And Maria and I, Willie and Lula had been allowed to go along.

But after Daddy Will saw the way the soldiers had

looked at me and Maria, he not only refused to take us again, but he forbade us to ride away from the house unless given permission.

I fastened my attention on Captain Alexander again.

"Why, Ma'am," he answered pleasantly, "the Indians butchered the bull for us and we brought it back to camp."

"So there are friendly Indians on the plains out West then," Daddy Will said.

Alexander smiled, showing a flash of white teeth beneath a neat blond mustache. His face was so very brown, his eyes so blue. "I've had proud moments in my life, suh. But when that Indian named Wolf told the others that I made a good hunter, I can say it was the proudest I've ever known."

Everyone laughed politely. I just stared. Never in my life had I met anyone like Captain Alexander. I could not eat. How could anyone be concerned with such ordinary pursuits as eating when someone who filled all the requirements of a god sat so nearby?

Ever since I'd ridden out on Cottonwood to meet him and General Beauregard earlier that afternoon, I'd been in a feverish state, though I knew he was a married man.

Coming into the house, he'd drawn off his doveskin gloves, tucked them in his mustard-colored officer's sash, swept off his plumed hat, bowed, kissed Mama's hand, and given her regards from his wife who was my Daddy John's niece.

But his being married had nothing whatsoever to do with the way I regarded him. I had decided that the very moment I saw him lean low in the saddle, one with that great bay horse of his named Dixie, to clear the fence at the foot of our property.

The graceful and disciplined energy of the vision they made burned into me. On his feet he moved like a soldier, erect and with a dignity that came from generations of good breeding.

He was from Georgia. He'd graduated from West Point. He'd hunted on the Great Plains, spent six months in Washington Territory, and resigned the United States Army to join the Confederacy. He was now General Beauregard's chief signal officer.

A forelock of sandy hair fell across his forehead. He was confident and there was an air of contained excitement about him. I had learned all that in the few hours since he'd been in our house.

His uniform was meticulously hand-tailored to accent his wiry tallness; his shoulders, under the good broadcloth of the tunic, were sufficient in their breadth to draw a line across my heart.

Watching him, I ached with a longing I could not name. It had to do with sadness. And loss. And the moment we met I recognized something in him that my spirit rose up to greet. And that I knew I would soon be asked to give up.

"And how are your accomodations at Liberia?" Mama turned her attention to General Beauregard.

"Most commodious, Mrs. McLean. Our hosts, the Weirs, have taken their leave, you know."

Mama's hand flew to her heart. "It is so sad to see so many of our neighbors leaving."

"I understand, Ma'am. But it's what we're advising everyone hereabouts to do. It won't be for long, however. The enemy is little more than an armed rabble, gathered hastily on false pretenses. We are certain to triumph, and soon."

I did not like Beauregard, the hero of Sumter. Maria did. She saw him as dapper. I thought him showy, and secretive. I did not like the look of him. He was Creole with high cheekbones and deep-set crafty eyes, a pointed chin, and a mustache that curled down over his mouth. Just the kind of mouth and chin I'd expect to find on someone who fired on his own teacher.

And I knew he was wrong in his opinion of the North. Button had written just the other day in a letter that came to us by private hands, because there was no longer any mail between the North and the South:

> Every Southerner has fled Washington. Your Aunt Hannah and Uncle Will took the girls to Charlottesville. The boys all joined your Cousin John's company. I am renting the house. It seems so strange that you have your capitol in Richmond now and we have ours here. I went for a drive last week and stopped at the 7th New York's encampment. They have a wonderful military band and they look to be a most fine group of young men. Whole towns have signed up for President Lincoln's call that went out right after Sumter. The volunteer Union Army is now 37,000 strong.

"You're not eating, Oscie," Mama chided.

I blushed, feeling Captain Alexander's eyes upon me. Thankfully, Maria demanded attention then. "Is it true that you gave Major Anderson the American flag that flew above Fort Sumter, General?"

Maria was a shameless coquette. But Beauregard preened under the question. "Yes, I presented it to him when he and his men sailed North. It was shot-torn, but he said he intended someday to be buried in it. Mrs. McLean," he turned again to Mama. "Tell me about your neighbor, Mrs. Henry. She's an invalid, is she not?"

"She is eighty-five and bedridden," Mama said.

"As you know, we've been studying the topography of the land since we've been here. We believe, with the coming, ah, events, she's in real danger on that hill. Can she be convinced to leave?"

"People have been begging her to," Mama said, "but I don't know what her decision will be."

"She won't leave." My face burned as the two officers fastened their gazes on me, Beauregard's dark and intense and Alexander's blue and most kind. "I went yesterday to see her. She said she wasn't leaving."

Will McLean scowled at me. "You rode out without an escort?"

My face burned. "Billie was supposed to ride over with me, but was detained. I thought I could convince her to leave."

"Is she fond of you then, Miss Oscie?" Alexander asked.

"I've known her since I was a little girl," I said. "Daddy John used to take me there when he paid her doctor visits."

He turned to Daddy Will. "I wonder, suh, if you'd allow your daughter to accompany me there tomorrow. We must convince this elderly woman to abandon that hill."

Daddy Will scowled. Alex saw the hesitation and smiled. "You outrank me, suh, as a major in the Alexandria Militia. And I hope you don't consider me facetious when I say that my wife's kinship with Mrs. McLean is near enough relationship, in Virginia, to make me regard you-all as family."

Everyone laughed politely.

"Your daughter would have not only the escort of a Confederate officer," Alexander said solemnly, "but that of a protective older cousin as well."

I saw Maria raise her eyes to the ceiling.

"Very well." Daddy Will smiled agreeably. "But I'm no longer a military man, Captain. Only a father. And believe me, with two pretty daughters on my hands and an army camped on my doorstep, it's easier being a major in the militia."

"He's married," Maria said.

We lay on our beds. Our guests were gone. It was late. Sweet June air drifted in the open windows, making me restless. I could not sleep. Every time I closed my eyes, I saw Captain Alexander taking our fence on Dixie.

"That has nothing to do with anything, Maria," I said. "My feelings toward him are beautiful and noble."

"You're smitten with him. Don't give me that noble nonsense."

"Well, you weren't above flirting with General Beauregard at supper. And *he* dyes his *hair!*"

She sat up in her bed. "How dare you say that? Can't you see how cultured he is? A true gentleman!"

"Alex told me."

"Oh, it's Alex already, is it?"

"When I showed him my herb garden after supper, he said that's what his fellow officers call him. I told him I was growing my herb garden in case the North blockades us. And he said that Beauregard is worried that if that happens he won't be able to get his hair dye from France anymore."

"No true gentleman would say that about a fellow officer."

I stared at the patterns cast on the ceiling by moonlight coming through the lace curtains. "He is a gentleman of the highest order, Maria. But he thinks Beauregard is a jackass for saying the war will soon be over. Alex says it won't be any ninety-day affair."

"And I suppose *he* knows better then President Jeff Davis."

"He knows, Maria. He told me how we have only nine million people. And three million of them are slaves. And the North has twenty million. And we have no treasury, no organization, no manufacturing. He fears for our cause."

"Then why didn't he stay with the Yankees?"

"He could have. He could have been the only engineering officer on the Pacific coast and in charge of all the government reservations. And made good investments and become a rich man if he stayed. But he said his people were at war and he had to come home."

"You're smitten with him," she said again. "I suppose you made an absolute fool of yourself when you went bounding out to meet them this afternoon."

"Do you think I'm completely brainless, Maria? I took a side path in the broomsedge when I saw them coming. Then I rode out into their path and pretended surprise."

"Well, I see you haven't read about Elizabeth Barrett and Robert Browning for nothing," she said.

"Oh, Maria, Alex is so beautiful. Do you think there are many more out there like him?"

"The South is full of them, Oscie," she sighed. "I heard Daddy Will tell Mama that we've got more brave young warriors than common sense."

"He is brave, don't you think?"

"I think you're on the road to perdition, Oscie Mason," she said. "And I think he'd better be brave if he's to face Mrs. Henry tomorrow."

"That woman isn't leaving, Maria. She said let the Yankees come."

We lay quietly, for a moment, each wrapped in our own thoughts. Then Maria spoke, her voice dreamy and sad. "I wish we weren't moving," she said.

I sat up in bed like a shot then. "*Who* said we were?"

"Julia."

"Julia! When?"

"If you'd come with me and Mama yesterday when we called on Emily Stratton to welcome Julia home from school, instead of riding that horse of yours around like a heathen all the time . . . "

"I wouldn't believe a word Julia says. Too bad the Yankees didn't carry her off from that fancy school when they took Alexandria."

"The Yankees didn't take Alexandria, they only occupied it."

"Lincoln sent troops in. If that isn't taking it, I don't know what is. Tell me what Julia said about our moving."

"She said Daddy Will asked Mr. Wilcher if he'd make accomodations for some of our animals."

I felt as if the world was tilting under me. It had a habit of doing that lately. "Daddy Will would never give our animals to Mr. Wilcher. He's liable to sell them off next time he loses at cards. Anyways, Daddy Will hasn't said a word about it to me."

Maria turned over, her back to me. "Believe as you wish."

"Has he said anything to you?" I asked. "Have

you heard him talk about it to Mama?"

"He's trying not to *upset* anybody, Oscie. He and Mama never talk about the war. Not in front of us, anyway."

I was sick for believing her. Move? Away from Yorkshire? From everything I held dear? Move where? I'd never leave here. Daddy Will would have to get past my dead body to make me move. I felt fear rising up inside me. I'd take to my bed like Mrs. Henry and refuse. I knew how she felt. I didn't hate the Yankees like everybody else I knew. I didn't care if they took tea on the roof of the Hotel Alexandria. But they weren't going to make me leave Yorkshire, I knew that. "It's ridiculous, moving," I said. "Why should we?"

Maria turned in her bed to face me. "What do you think General Beauregard and your precious Alex are *doing* here, Oscie? Paying a social call? They've come to fight a *battle!* Honestly, and everybody calls *me* the romantic one! Ask Alex tomorrow, why don't you? According to you, he knows everything."

Chapter 14

June 1861

On our ride over to Mrs. Henry's, Alex complimented me on the lush wheat and oat and corn fields we rode through as if I personally had something to do with them. But it was a compliment, I came to realize, from someone from Georgia to someone from Virginia. His parents owned two plantations, he told me, rice and cotton, with fifty or sixty nigras on each place.

He also told me that his father had imported a Northern tutor for his four sisters and I told him about Button then. But we didn't talk the whole three miles. We rode much of it in companionable silence, broken only by the creaking of saddles, the cries of crows overhead, and the summer wind whispering through the cornfields.

Mrs. Henry's door was always open. Visitors tied horses out front, drank water from her well, and left food in the springhouse. I called up to tell her who we were and Alex followed me up the winding stairway. The room was sparse and spotless, bright with sunlight and colorful curtains and quilts and fresh flowers in vases. The Robinsons, her closest neighbors, always looked in on her, as did her children.

"Child," Mrs. Henry held out a thin, bony hand. "How good of you to come. And who is this magnificent creature you have brought with you?"

Ah, I thought, to be old and say such things out loud. Alex bowed and kissed her hand. We pulled up chairs and sat.

"So you've come to ask me to leave again, have you? And this time you've brought reinforcements," she teased and smiled. Her face was a roadmap of Prince William County. "Since she was a little tyke of four, she'd come see me with her daddy," she told Alex. "He was my doctor. Had me up and around and moving, arthritis or not. I gave up, after Doctor John died. Just took to my bed. If he was alive, I'd be on my feet today."

Alex nodded politely, hat resting on his knee, his tunic open at the top button. Then he leaned forward. "Mrs. Henry, I've been all over this area for a week now, studying the lay of the land and . . . "

"Studying the land, eh? Have you ever seen such beautiful country, Captain?"

"No, Ma'am, I haven't," Alex allowed.

"This is peaceful country, Captain. Rolling fields, sudden patches of woods, clear streams. We call them runs, you know."

"Yes, Ma'am."

"People raise cattle, wheat, oats, tall corn, and tall sons. And beautiful daughters. The land is part of us. My family's been here for over a century. I know the history of every plantation around here, the name, weight, and hair color of every child born in these parts for sixty years. People have been looking after me since I took to my bed. My Isaac died in 1829. I birthed and raised my children on this hill. Now why should I want to leave, young man?"

"There's going to be a battle, Ma'am," Alex said quietly.

"Is there now?"

"I'm afraid so, yes."

"Heard tell about the soldiers down to the junction. Know you-all have been fussing with the Yankees. Been going on so long now even the horses and cattle know it. My boy Arthur said the Yanks have come spoilin' for a fight. My John says it's over slavery. Arthur says it's over states' rights. You know what it's about?"

Alex spoke plain and quiet. "We're fighting for our liberty, Ma'am."

"Thought we did that already."

"Well, we have to again. It's not about slavery, Mrs. Henry, it's about the sovereignty of the states and their right to secede and have self-government."

"My, such pretty words. Look at the view I have from this window." She pointed. "If everybody in the country had such a view, seems there'd be no need for war. Most of the small farmers around here don't even have nigras. Those who do, treat them right. Do we go up North and demand that they take the children out of their factories?"

Alex suppressed a smile. "We don't mean for the fight to be on your land, Ma'am. But we know the Federals are organizing and will soon take to the field. War is a science, Ma'am, like a game of chess. We know where our cavalry and brigades are, where we want them to repulse the enemy. We know our strengths and weaknesses. We can only guess at theirs. But we do know one thing for certain."

"And what is that, Captain?"

"You're on a hill, Ma'am. Armies like hills."

"Do they, now?"

"Yes, Ma'am. Generals are downright fond of them. Always want to take the high ground. Why, an artillery shell could hit this house."

She closed her eyes for a moment and her lips moved silently, as if in prayer. All the while she was patting my hand. "Captain," she said.

"Yes, Ma'am?"

"You're a good boy, Captain. Your mama should be proud of you. You've done your job. But I'm downright fond of my hill, too. I was here first. And I'm not moving from this house. So let your armies fuss at each other. Let them come."

We stayed a while longer and, true gentleman that he was, Alex did not push her. When it was time to leave, Alex said good-bye and left the room. I bent to kiss her, knowing in my bones that I would never see her again.

She beamed at me mischieviously. "Is he your beau?"

"No. He's kin. Sort of. His wife is my daddy's niece."

"Nothing worse than sort-of kin," she said, "especially when they look at each other like you two do."

"We're friends," I told her.

"Sometimes that's better. Husbands and wives often grow tired of each other. Friends are forever."

I hadn't thought of it that way.

"Don't mourn me, child. I have the high ground and it's taken me years to get here. There is peace in my heart."

Tears came into my eyes.

"Remember what your daddy always said. Don't

give in. I forgot his advice and here's what happened to me. Well, I have another chance now, to hold on. I'm an old lady, the country I love is going to pieces around me. All I can do is not give in. So here I stay."

Tears rolled down my face. "My deah," she said. "Don't cry. There's always a snake in the garden. The trick is to know it's there. If you do, its bite doesn't hurt as much."

I left crying, and went outside where Alex was waiting. Before we mounted our horses he stared around at the peaceful countryside dotted with cedars and pines. I minded how far-reaching his gaze was, then remembered that he'd spent months on the plains.

"She'll die here, won't she?" I asked.

We mounted our horses and went down the hill. "Most likely," he said.

"Do you really think this is a fight for our liberty, Alex?"

"I have to, or I wouldn't be wearing this uniform."

"Daddy Will is all torn up over secession," I said. "And he isn't even Old South."

"He appears to be the perfect Southern gentleman."

"In some ways, yes. His family is old. And Southern. But he's a merchant. Took him a while to get to learn how to handle the nigras. I still don't think his heart is in it. Mama says he's an abolitionist at heart."

"Is he?"

"I don't know what he is. Don't think he does yet, either. But he saw the war coming a long time ago. Says all he wants to do is get his family through it."

"And you? What do you think of the war, Oscie?"

"I never bothered my head with all that talk of

slavery and states' rights. It's been going on for years. We treat our nigras well, is all I know. So do all our neighbors. Except Mr. Wilcher. I don't think the war's about that. But it's come, anyway. And now we may have to move!"

We drew up the reins of our horses on a hillock, overlooking a clear stream. "But you're confused," he said.

I nodded. "I wish I knew what to think. Like you. And Mrs. Henry."

"I was thirteen when I first heard that the Southern states might secede, Oscie. I recollect the awful sense of dread I felt."

I waited. He went on.

"A few years later, feelings in our neighborhood were heightened because one of our neighbors was a Union delegate to a state convention. I got into an argument with two town boys who were for the secession candidate. I borrowed an old pepper-box revolver from our overseer and met them in a field. There was a fight and I aimed at one boy's heart and pulled the trigger."

I gasped. He smiled ruefully at me and patted Dixie's neck. "The gun misfired. I tried again. Again, nothing. Then, just as his friend was about to fire at me, some other boys took our pistols away. One of them fired my gun into the air and it went off."

"Oh, Alex!"

"Yes. If it hadn't misfired twice, I'd have killed Jim Hester and destroyed myself and my parents. I was that much against secession. I've avoided politics ever since, Oscie. I become too passionate arguing such issues."

"What made you change your mind about secession then?"

He urged Dixie on down the hill. "I haven't," he said. "Come on, our horses need water."

At the stream we dismounted while the horses drank. I decided then and there that I loved him. A sadness ran in him, as unswerving as the current in the stream. But a sense of purpose, also. Does love happen that way, I asked myself? Is it a configuration of events, glances, concerns and feelings shared, hearts unburdened, and words left unsaid?

"Any more questions?" he asked me.

"Are you sorry you left the Federal army?"

He sighed. "Oh, I sometimes miss the old camaraderie, the good life I had in the Engineer Corps. But I've never regretted my decision. I'm not altogether daft, Oscie. I know the risks. But I'm young and willing to take them. Not only for myself, but for those who depend upon me. If we can't do that, what good are we, hey?"

He squatted down and cupped some water into his hands and drank it and I did too. Kneeling on the soft sweet grass I looked over at him.

"We're going to have to move, aren't we?"

He stood up, his tall figure straight as an arrow against the blue sky. "Hasn't Will McLean said anything to you?"

"No."

"Then I shouldn't."

"I won't tell him you told me."

He sighed. "Very well, Oscie. Surgeon Thomas Williams, the medical director of the Army of Northern Virginia, has authorized me to rent your fine stone barn and out-buildings for a hospital. I've asked your step-daddy and await his answer."

I drew in my breath.

"There's no reason to think he'll refuse. Will

McLean is a patriot. He's welcomed us into his house and been most helpful in showing us the lay of the land."

I nodded. Tears came to my eyes.

"I'm sorry, Oscie," he said.

Suddenly it seemed like the midday summer sky was bearing down on me. I tried to mount Cottonwood and my boot slipped from the stirrup. He helped me. "Are you all right?" he asked.

He was so proper! Such a gentleman! I was not all right. I pondered that there was probably some deficiency in my soul, but I cared about my home more than the Confederacy. Was that selfish?

"Perhaps the army surgeons who come to Yorkshire can use the herbs in my garden, after all," I said brightly.

We rode home in companionable silence. Several times he smiled at me and each time he did I felt a stab in my heart.

The war had brought Alex to me. I was in love with him. But I hated the war. Because it meant we had to move. Because it was what Alex, in his fine uniform, stood for. Even though he knew that Beauregard was a jackass, that it would be no ninety-day affair, that we didn't have enough people or money or manufacturing.

Yet, with some sense of honor that I could not yet understand, he would take the risks. Because, as he had said, if he couldn't do that, what good was he?

Oh, I was so confused! If this was what Maria had meant by being on the road to perdition, she was right. For I knew no good would come from any of it. I was trapped, like a fox by a bunch of hounds. But I knew one thing. I wouldn't have given up knowing Alex. Not for anything.

Chapter 15

June 1861

Alex must have said something to Daddy Will, because the very next morning we were all summoned into the library after breakfast.

"Tomorrow more Confederate officers will be here to inspect our barn and buildings," he said. "I'm renting them for a hospital."

I watched Mama. She could make better use of her face than any woman. By her placid expression I calculated that Will McLean had already told her. And she'd accepted the telling.

"This means we have to move away from here," Daddy Will said quietly.

"Where will we go?" Maria asked.

"For now, I've written to Aunt Hannah. She and her husband and girls are in Charlottesville. We can rent a house there."

"Where's that?" Maria's voice cracked.

"Don't you know your geography, Maria? What did I pay Button for?"

"It's Albemarle County," I said. "It's where Thomas Jefferson lived. The University of Virginia is there. Mister Jefferson built it."

"Very good, Oscie," Will McLean said. "Now there's no fear that the war will come there. The town isn't yet a prime rail center. But it has a weekly newspaper and five churches. Many of its young men are in the Nineteenth Virginia, camped at the junction. They tell me their town has much to recommend it."

"Are there *bears* in Charlottesville?" Lula had developed as much a fear of bears as she had a fondness for rag dolls.

"No, sweetie," her father said. "It's quite civilized."

"I don't wanna go," Willie said. "Captain Alex promised me a wood musket. And he's gonna teach me the manual of arms. And he's gonna take me to Wilcoxin's Hill to his signal station. And I wanna see the war happen."

"You can do all those things with Captain Alex while we're here, son," Daddy Will said gently, "but you don't want to see the war happen. It's not a nice thing to see. People get hurt."

"Will Captain Alex get hurt?" Willie adored Alex, who inspired adoration in seven-year-old boys. To say nothing of how he affected fifteen-year-old girls.

"Captain Alex is a soldier, trained in war at West Point, son. He knows how to keep from getting hurt. We're civilians. We don't know how to protect ourselves. And we'll only be in the army's way here."

"Can I take my Maggie?" Willie was scared and bargaining.

"Yes, son, you can take your pony."

"Can I take all my rag dolls?" Lula asked.

"You all can take everything that means much to you," their father promised.

I tried to recollect what it was like to be seven and

have the world fall out from under you. Then it came to me. I was that age when Daddy Will married Mama. I looked at Maria. She was crying, shamelessly.

"Now, Maria," Will McLean admonished gently, "you're not giving the little ones a good example."

"I don't care. I don't want to leave here. It's my home. What will happen to it when the Yankees come?"

"Our home will be fine," Will McLean promised. "This is just for a little while. I'm taking you all to Charlottesville, staying to set things up, and then coming back after the battle to see to the harvest."

Pandemonium broke out then. Maria became racked with sobs, Lula ran to wrap herself around her father's legs and entreated him not to leave us in Charlottesville alone, where she was certain there were bears. Willie begged to be allowed to come back to Yorkshire with his father.

Will McLean looked besieged. Like the Yankees were already in our peach orchard. We need Button, I told myself. And then I spoke up.

"I think you're all behaving shamelessly," I scolded. "Willie, do you think Captain Alex would like to see you carrying on like some sniveling Yankee? Now you hush, or I'll tell him and you won't get that wooden musket!"

Willie hushed. Everybody looked at me. I drew myself up, strength coursing in my veins. "Lula, I promised you could come along with me and Willie when Captain Alex takes us to see his signal station, but unless you behave, you won't go!"

I could feel Will McLean's eyes on me. "Maria, for heaven's sakes, stop being the helpless Southern belle. You yourself told me that war was coming! Now take the children to the kitchen for some cookies and milk."

To my surprise, Maria dried her eyes and obeyed. Mama got up and kissed me. "You always were my mainstay, Oscie. I must go and tell Paula and Fanny to start packing the silver, china, and crystal." She left the room.

"Thank you," Will McLean said, "for being so strong."

"I didn't think I could be. I hate the idea of leaving here. I was going to fight you about it."

"What changed your mind?"

"Alex. He's against secession. And he says we don't have enough people, money, or manufacturing to win the war. But he'll fight it anyway. I pondered if he can do that, I ought to mind what I have to do."

"Alex is a fine person," he agreed.

I nodded. "How long before we have to move?"

"I'd like to have my family out of here by the tenth of July. Beauregard has thirty-five thousand troops. And the Yankees have thirty-seven thousand. This won't be a turkey shoot."

"We aren't ever coming back here, are we?"

"I told you, I'm coming back for harvest."

"But what will the armies do to our house?"

"Oscie," he said, "I promise you, if we can't come back, I'll find us another home. Haven't I always taken care of this family?"

"Yessir. I'm beholden to you for that."

"It's my job, you don't have to be beholden. But in the days ahead you can help me by keeping the children from being frightened. I can't depend on Maria for that."

"Captain Alex is taking us to see his signal station this week. Willie and Lula are daft over him. And he's offered, when he has time, to take us trout fishing, too."

"Fine, yes." He was poring over some maps on his desk.

I stood in the doorway. "I know it costs money to get letters hand-delivered North. But could I write and tell Button?"

"Of course. She should know we're leaving. Have her address any mail to Aunt Hannah for now. Just don't allow Willie to play the hooligan with Alex and hang all over him. That man has enough on his mind these days."

"Captain Alex, did you bring it? Did you?" Willie ran down the stairs in front of me the next day when Alex came in the front door.

"Is that any way to approach a senior officer?" he scowled at Willie.

Willie saluted.

"That's better. Yes, I did bring it. It's tied to my saddle. Go outside and wait. I'll be right there."

Willie ran shrieking from the house. Alex smiled at me. "He takes me back to my childhood. In the middle of preparations for war, I can't think of anything sweeter. Are you ready, Oscie?"

"I've got my best boots on under my calico." I smiled at him. "Is it all right if Lula comes? I promised her."

"The more the merrier," he said. "She can ride on the front of my saddle, if you wish."

On Wilcoxin's Hill he gave us presents: the wooden musket for Willie, carved by one of his men; a signal flag for Lula. Then, when two of his men were showing the children the rude log hut that was their station, and his flags and torches, he gave me a package. I untied the string and there in the brown paper was a buffalo robe. "Oh, Alex!" I gasped.

"The Indians gave it to me on the plains," he said. "I'd be honored for you to have it, Oscie. I don't know where you all will end up, but you might need it some cold night, away from home."

Tears came to my eyes. "I'll always think of you when I use it, Alex," I said. He had given me a present! Surely that meant he felt toward me as I did toward him! Oh, he had given me a present! I would treasure it always!

For the rest of June he came around almost every day. He'd spend a great deal of time with Daddy Will in the library, going over maps of the land. He was at our table often, taking meals with us. He sometimes stayed evenings and played chess. He took Willie and me and Lula fishing for trout in Bull Run on a hot June afternoon. And when I told him how Sarah had died from a fall in our creek, he told me about his wife saving an orderly from drowning.

"In 1860 we were stationed in Washington Territory," he said. "There was a little pond and my colonel thought he wanted to cut some ice. The orderly walked out to where the water was deep and the ice was thin and fell through. My wife took an oar and gave it to him to hold onto until others came to help."

I listened, gravely. A shadow fell over me, though I did not know if it was from remembering Sarah or from hearing him speak, so calmly and fondly, of his wife.

Washington, June 22nd, 1861

My Dear Oscie: Your letter finally arrived and I shall not write again until you are in Charlottesville in July. I know how you feel about moving. I have such fond memories of Yorkshire and like to think of all of you there. But war always means an uprooting of what we hold dear, as well as a change of social order and an absence of reason. I know you will like Charlottesville. Did you know that Doctor McGuffey, who authored the *McGuffey Spellers and Readers* you used, lives there? Perhaps you will meet him.

Washington has become an insane asylum. Rhode Island boys are camped in the Patent Office, New York regiments in the House of Representatives, and Massachusetts troops are in the rotunda of the Capitol, baking bread in the basement.

What is love, you ask. Dear child, love is like light and there are two kinds, the bursting fireworks of the moment and the solid, fixed stars that sometimes become obscured in the heavens, but are always there, year after year, for a lifetime.

You must experience the first in order to appreciate the second. But be careful with the fireworks. They burn out quickly. And if you get too close, they can hurt. Your Alex probably needs a friend right now. He sounds like a true Southern gentleman. I wish I could meet him. I wish I could be there for you. Be careful. Your very dear friend and teacher, Button.

I could not keep track of those June days. Mama and the house servants were packing all our belongings. Daddy Will was busy in his library and out in the fields. Everyone was in a whirlwind of activity, except me. I seem to have stopped.

I went to sleep thinking of Alex, of every word he'd spoken to me that day, every look exchanged. I kept the folded-up buffalo robe next to my pillow at night.

"You'll die with that thing next to you in this heat," Maria warned.

I didn't care. I dreamed about him and I woke thinking of him. I stayed close to the house so as to be near when he arrived. When our eyes met my face burned and my hands went cold. I was in the depths of misery and supremely happy at the same time.

I lived for our moments alone. Often we took rides out together, without the children. Nobody seemed to care or notice. I rode circuit with him as he checked his signal stations, from the one on our farm to Wilcoxin's Hill and another on Van Pelt's place near Bull Run.

He confided in me that he was worried about Beauregard. "He's never commanded more than a company of men on the field," he said.

I stored his confidences in my heart, honored that he should trust me so. His voice became part of me. I knew his every expression, felt proud riding beside him in the lush green fields. The days passed, stretching time like a quilt on a frame, as summer days tend to do, with the colors heightened when Alex was around. I never felt so shamelessly alive.

When he was not around, everything seemed flat and lifeless and it was as if the summer air would suffocate me. I waited for him to take my hand, went hot at his touch as he helped me down from my horse. I waited for him to take me in his arms and kiss me.

He did not. But that was all right, too. I put that down to his honor and loved him more for it.

And then it happened. One day, in the hustle and bustle of all our preparations for moving, my world fell apart.

Chapter 16

June 1861

"Oscie, Mary Ann's in your herb garden again. Me an' Willie saw her."

I went bounding out of my room and downstairs when Lula said that. It marked the fourth time in two weeks that Mary Ann had wandered up to the house and into my garden. I hadn't caught her the other times, but I would now. She is up to something, I minded. And I'll find out what it is.

Heat lay in waves over the plantation this last week in June. The sky was white with it. We prayed for rain, for the smallest breeze. But my garden was growing dutifully. I was so proud of my neat rows of jimson weed, wild mustard, my knob grass, cucumbers, and other herbs.

Mary Ann stood there in the garden. I almost ran into her as I came around the corner of the house. I stood stock-still for a moment, staring at her. She was as thin as ever. Her hair was cropped short and sprinkled with gray. And there were lines on the side of her mouth that were never there before.

"What do you want?" I demanded. Willie stood on

one side of me and Lula on the other, clutching one of her favorite rag dolls.

She smiled at me knowingly. She was barefoot and in one hand she held a small stem of one of my lovage plants. "Lovage no good for any infirmities I know about," she said.

"I'm growing it for Maria. It removes freckles. It's called Levisticum Officinale." I used the Latin Alex had taught me. "I don't allow anyone in my garden."

"You 'lows that fancy captain. He's here alla time."

I felt anger rising in me. "What do you want?"

"Plants kinda puny," she said. She sighed and looked around, hands low on her hips, sassy-like. "You gotta know 'bout the earth to grow herbs. But I reckon it's your business if'n they be puny."

She was after something. "That's right, it is."

"Girl like you makes everythin' her business. Made it her business to get Mary Ann put inna fields, didn't you?"

"That was Will McLean's decision, not mine."

She raised her chin defiantly. "You pushed for it. Even before . . . what happened with Sarah. Then after, you knowed Mary Ann wuz gonna have a chile. Your mama tol' me you wuz the only other one 'side Maum Hanna who knew."

Something was coming now. I held my breath, waiting for it.

"Your mama, she wuz crazy wif' grief. Maum Hanna," she shook her head, "*she* wuz just as glad to be ridda me. You cud of told him I wuz havin' a baby. But you didn't."

"Why didn't *you* tell him? Because you were afraid he'd sell you, that's why. You were down there in your cabin, wailing because he was going to sell you."

She shrugged, as if the whole matter was of

complete indifference now. But I recognized the look in her almond-shaped eyes. "Maybe Mary Ann shudda tol'. Would of had my baby now. All that hot sun in the fields. Killed my babies. That one an' the one that followed. Jus' like the hot sun here killin' your plants."

I felt the same hot sun bearing down on my head. In the distance, the insects chorused out their celebration of the heat. I felt dizzy. *Babies!* More than one! So, she'd lost two, working in the fields! Nobody had told me that! Had anyone known? Even Mama? Was it my fault? I couldn't think!

"Massa Will, he wuz so crazy after Sarah died, he wudda sold me, fer sure. Away from my Allie. But he wudda listened to you."

I could barely breathe. I had difficulty swallowing. "He doesn't listen to me," I said weakly.

"Does sometimes." Then she sighed again. "No end o' times, Mary Ann asks herself when she shudda tol' and shudda kept quiet. If'n you ask me, too much tellin' goes on 'round here 'bout some things. And not 'nuf 'bout others."

There was a threat in her voice. "You have something to say to me, say it plain," I advised.

She smiled sweetly at Lula. "You need a new rag doll, little girl? I kin make you a nice new rag doll."

Lula clutched her doll close. "No," she said.

"Child's puny," Mary Ann said.

Before I could retort, Willie stepped forward and planted himself firmly in front of me. "My sister's not puny," he said. "She's my sister. And you don't say things about her. And get out of Oscie's garden."

I loved Willie then more than I ever thought I could. He was so often willful, a plague to me. But just then I wanted to hug and kiss him.

"Go into the house, children," I suggested. "I'll be along directly. Go on now, and I'll make us all some nice lemonade. I'll be all right."

They went, slowly. Then I faced Mary Ann again. She was trying to make friends with Lula now, the way she'd once done with Sarah. Any guilt I felt, vanished, remembering Sarah. I felt rage boiling in me, but Mama had schooled me never to show anger or helplessness or fear to the nigras. "Now say what you have on your mind," I directed.

"Nuthin' I wants to tell *you*. The tellin' I gots to do is fer Massa Will."

"Tell me first," I demanded. "It has to do with me, or you wouldn't be here plaguing me like this."

She smiled secretively. "Seems to me that Massa Will, bein' the gentleman he is, wud wanna know certain things goin' on around here right under his nose. That's what it seems to me."

"What things?"

"Things like you ridin' around the countryside wif' that fancy captain. Ain't right. He bein' married an' all. My Allie, he says your Daddy John wouldn't like it nohow."

I felt faint, but I composed myself. "Tell Allie I can take care of myself, thank you."

"He ain't the only one noticin'. Everybody in the quarters seen you an' that fancy captain flyin' by on your horses, laughin' an' carryin' on."

"We don't carry on." So, she had found something to get back at me for losing her babies. How long had she been watching me, from down at the quarters, waiting for the chance?

"Oh, I reckon you do. Miss High an' Mighty." She laughed. "See how high and mighty you be, when Massa Will finds out."

"How *dare* you!" I stamped my feet in the garden dirt. "You so much as go near him with your lies about me and I'll see he sells you off."

But she had worked that out too. Hands still on her hips, she turned to go. "Doan matter no more. Cain't you even figure? War comin'. My Allie, he say, be no more workin' in the fields, once the Yankees come. Lucky we get in the harvest. Massa Will doan need us nomore after that. He probably sell us off together."

My spirit was so afflicted in the next twenty-four hours I didn't know which way to turn first. One minute I was so angry with her for her threats that I wondered how I could care what had happened to her. Ever since she'd come to us, she'd been a shadow hanging over the place. Trouble. That's what she'd always been. And the next minute I was overcome with guilt, pondering on Mary Ann's lost babies, knowing I was to blame and that I should have gone to Daddy Will in the beginning and told him.

The next evening I was to find out how much trouble she still intended to be. Daddy Will asked me to go out onto the back portico with him after supper. Maria was playing "Dixie" on the piano, in a slow, melancholy way. In the distance storm clouds hung flat over the fields.

Will McLean stood gazing off to the hills. "We won't be out of here until the fifteenth," he said. "That gives us two weeks yet."

I waited.

"Look here, Oscie, I think you ought to see less of Alex in the time we have left."

There it was. Thunder rumbled on the horizon. I looked up at him.

"All these rides you've been taking around the countryside with him. It isn't seemly. He's a married man."

Silence poured into the space between us, like molasses, thick and heavy. "Alex is my friend. And I won't have people saying things about him." My voice trembled.

"I can't have people gossiping."

"Nobody's gossiping but Mary Ann. And only because she hates me."

"She doesn't hate you, Oscie," he said wearily.

"Yes, she does! And I'll tell you why, though you're not supposed to know. They've all kept it from you. It's because she lost two babies after you put her in the fields. And she blames me for it."

He turned to stare at me. "She *what?*"

I held up under his glare. "She lost two babies, working in the fields. And she thinks I told you to put her there."

"Why wasn't I told of this?"

"Because you would have sold her. And Mama didn't want it. She was carrying one baby when Sarah died."

"Did you know this?"

"Yessir. But I figured that if Mary Ann didn't tell you herself, I wouldn't."

"You had a duty to tell me," he said angrily.

"Then what would you have done? Sold her? And made Mama unhappy?"

He leaned his elbows on the railing of the portico. "Good God," he said. "This is a terrible state of affairs!"

"And that's why she made up lies about me and Alex. To get back at me."

He shook his head. "You can't blame the woman,

Oscie. Losing two children . . ." He sighed. "But she isn't lying about you and Alex. You have been riding out together. And I can't have talk about it."

"It's just from the quarters."

"From *anywhere!* Don't you remember what gossip did to this family last time?"

Dear God, I pondered, he's never gotten over that.

"It is my duty," he recited carefully, "to safeguard the reputation of this family. As much as it's my duty to get you all to safety with war coming."

"But Alex and I haven't *done* anything! He's the most honorable person I know. If I tell him I can't ride with him anymore, it will put something on our friendship that isn't there."

"Don't be too sure it isn't there," he said.

I glared at him defiantly. He met my defiance with his own. And the old bad feeling was there between us again.

"I'm not going to end my friendship with Alex just because of gossip," I said.

"You will do as I say. I won't have the dark shadow of scandal on this family. Don't fight me on this, Oscie, I mean it."

He had the whip hand and he knew it. Tears came into my eyes. I turned to leave. "*Mary Ann's* the dark shadow over this place. Always was. You should never have brought her here, Will McLean. If this family's been torn apart at all, she's done it."

"I know that." He whirled around. "You think I don't know that? But you should know something too, Oscie Mason."

At the back door I turned to face him.

"She's what this slavery business is all about. Her fate being all tied in with ours. People owning people, buying them, selling them, *inheriting* them, like furniture. How old were you when Sarah died?"

"Nine."

"And you made the decision not to tell me about Mary Ann. Nine, and you had that power over her. You're going to have to live with that for the rest of your life, Missy. Just like I'll have to."

"And what about Mary Ann? Doesn't she have to live with what happened to Sarah?"

"We're supposed to know better. Which is, presumably, why *we* own *them*. What Mary Ann became isn't her fault, but the fault of others who had power over her." His voice dropped and he shook his head, sadly. "I tell you, Oscie, I'm almost glad this war's come. The South can't go on like this much longer."

The next morning, early, officers and men came from the Confederate army to start turning our barn into a hospital. There were dozens of them out there in gray uniforms, all looking like Alex. Their sleek horses were under our maple and hickory trees.

At breakfast Daddy Will told us he was off to the Wilchers' to make final arrangements for our animals. "Willie, you're to come with me. I don't want you underfoot."

"We must feed the men," Mama said.

"They have their own aides and supply wagons," he said. Apparently he didn't want them near the house. I stared at him across the table. I was bleary-eyed from lack of sleep. He scowled back.

"You're not going to give Mirabella or Cottonwood to the Wilchers," I told him. "You can do whatever you have a mind to with the other farm animals. But not them."

"Oscie!" Mama was shocked. "Daddy Will's been

working night and day to make this move easier for us. Apologize this minute!"

"She doesn't have to apologize." Will McLean stood up. "She knows what she does have to do, though. I hadn't planned on turning your horses over to the Wilchers, young lady. Don't plant any thoughts in my head. Come on, Willie."

"We'll have lemonade and cookies for the soldiers," Mama called after him. "Tell their officers to send them up to the house around three. You know how hot the sun gets about then." She turned to me. "Have you two been fussing again?"

I looked down at my plate, saying nothing.

"Honestly, Oscie, it's so hot. And we're all put out, what with moving. Do you think this is easy for him? Now, of all times, you should try to be helpful. He takes so much from you, that man. Your own daddy wouldn't take such sass. Sometimes you make me ashamed, Oscie."

"I'm sorry, Mama. I'll try to be nicer." I felt ashamed. I spent the morning in my room, packing. From my bedroom window I could see Alex's Dixie under the hickory tree. The enlisted men were cleaning out the barn. And then I saw Alex. I could pick him out of a crowd. And that was the problem, exactly, I told myself. I could sight him in the middle of a hundred officers if I had to.

The men came up to the house that afternoon at three. Mama called me to help serve the lemonade. And to make up for my behavior at breakfast I went down. Maria was making sheep's eyes at a young captain from Charlottesville.

"How many men from Albemarle County are up here?" Mama asked him.

"About eight hundred, ma'am," he said in a

marmalade voice. "All part of the Nineteenth Virginia. And proud to be here."

Somehow I got through the lemonade serving. Alex didn't show up. But he came the next day.

I was in my room in the middle of a muddle, still packing, when I heard a light rapping at the back door. I went down. All I saw was a tall shadow in the lemon yellow afternoon sunlight.

"Hello." Seeing it was Alex I struggled to act natural.

He took off his hat. "Hello, Oscie, is the major about?"

He insisted on calling Will McLean major. "He's been gone since early this morning with Maria and Willie and Lula to oversee the transfer of our animals to the Wilchers. Mama's lying down with a headache. Would you like some lemonade?"

He inspected his hat in his hands as if he'd never laid eyes on it before. "I wanted to ask the major what he wants done with that old gig in the barn."

He knew Daddy Will wasn't here, I told myself, so he's come to speak to me. "Why don't you come in out of the sun?"

He came to stand in the cool hallway.

"It was my daddy's old doctor's gig," I said.

"It's still in excellent condition."

His voice brushed the hurt places in my heart. "You can have it for the army, if you think it'll be of any use to them. My daddy would be proud for you to have it."

"I ought to ask the major," he said.

"It's mine to give." I said it almost defiantly. "He has his way about most things around here, but not about everything."

He nodded and studied the hat he was turning

around in his hands. "Not even Mr. Lincoln or Mr. Davis have their own way all the time, I hear."

We smiled at each other. The silence stretched out so long between us that I felt drawn and quartered on it. I thought of my Daddy John with a rush of tenderness. Talking of his gig made me conjure him up. And with the tenderness came a strength.

"Alex, did Will McLean tell you to stay away from me?"

He looked around the large center hall as if he'd never seen it before. "It wasn't my intention to hurt you, Oscie."

"You never hurt me, Alex. I told him you're the most honorable person I've ever known."

He nodded. "It's all my fault. I've been a guest at the major's table. He and your mother have extended every courtesy to me. I know better. I know how it looked, us riding out alone like that. I don't blame the major a bit. I have sisters. I'd have to feel the same way about them."

"You would say such a thing."

He smiled at me. "Why?"

"That Southern honor of yours."

He looked at me, not understanding.

"Don't you see, Alex? It's the same sense of honor that made you leave the Federal army, even though you haven't changed your mind about secession. Even though you know we're outnumbered and underequipped."

He looked at me in wonderment. "It isn't the same, Oscie."

Couldn't he see? Was he so dense? Oh, I loved him so! But at the same time I wanted to lash out at him. "It is the same," I said. "Why, I'll wager that if God appeared to us in a burning bush in our yard and told us our cause was lost from the start, you'd still persist in fighting."

He examined the plume on his hat. "I do what I have to do, Oscie," he said softly.

I stared up at him, filled with rage and love, all mixed together like a potion in me. "Will McLean doesn't care about Southern tradition, Alex. He was hurt by gossip that touched our family once a long time ago, is all."

"I find that hard to believe, Oscie, that he doesn't care about Southern tradition."

"It's twaddle. And he knows it. He just doesn't want our family touched with gossip again."

He nodded. "I can understand that, Oscie."

"You know who said something to him about us? Some uppity darkie from the quarters. Will McLean never did know how to handle the darkies. Would you let some nigra servant stop us from riding out?"

He searched my face. "No," he said.

"There's nobody around this afternoon. Ride out with me, now, Alex. One last time. Even if Will McLean comes back, he doesn't have to know it."

He shook his head sadly. "I can't do that, Miss Oscie. It wouldn't be honorable of me. I promised him. Even if he doesn't find out, it wouldn't be honorable."

Fool! Benighted fool, I thought. Honor! What good will all that honor do you on the battlefield. It can't take the place of the men and equipment the Yankees have. But I didn't say it. Instead, I cried.

"Don't cry, Oscie. And don't ask it of me. I am what I am. I don't want to hurt you."

"I'm crying because of what you are, Alex. I love you because of what you are. I'd die with you, standing here right now, if you asked me. And it's tearing me to pieces."

"You shouldn't say such things, Oscie," he said severely. "It isn't right."

"You saying our friendship wasn't right?"

"No. I shall treasure it always. You just mistook it for something more. I am ashamed of myself for allowing that to happen." He took a step closer to me.

He was so close I could smell the soap he used, the tobacco, the man smells of him. I looked up into those blue eyes under the long blond lashes. In a moment I could be in his arms, I told myself. How would his Southern honor hold up then?

But I could not do that to Alex. Because all the twaddle he stood for, which I could see so plainly now for what it was, had made me love him.

"I hold you in highest esteem, Oscie Mason," he said. "And I want you to meet some nice young man in Charlottesville and forget about me."

"I shall never forget you, Edward Porter Alexander."

He looked quite miserable.

"I have a right to remember my first love all my life."

"I should be shot."

"Don't say that. It's more my fault than yours. I knew the moment we met that you were married. And I never wanted you not to be honorable."

"Then what did you want of me, Oscie?"

"Just to *be* with you is all I wanted. To ride around Prince William County. Before the war started." I hesitated, thinking of what Will McLean had said about how the South couldn't go on being what it was any longer.

"Everything's changing, Alex. You mark what the South is all about. I wanted to spend time with you, before it all got different."

That *was* a great part of what I'd wanted from him, I realized suddenly. A great part of why I loved him. I'd seen our old way of life come riding in our front gate with Alex, etched sharply against the talk of war and change around me.

"Promise me that you'll find someone else, Oscie," he said. "You are a very sensible and brave young woman."

"If I do, he'll never wear a sword or take a fence on a horse like you, Alex."

"Good. Because that means he won't be a soldier. Don't give your heart to a soldier, Oscie."

But I already have, I told myself. I already have.

We spoke a few moments longer but it was finished then. And so he bade me farewell and left. I watched him walking down the path to the barn in the lemon yellow sunlight. And it was like the end of a dream. I felt a wrenching loss inside me. And I prayed we would leave Yorkshire soon. Our life was finished here. And I couldn't bear being out there on our land and not seeing Alex again.

While I stood there the chaise came up the lane. It stopped next to Alex and he spoke to Will McLean for a minute. I waited until it came into the backyard. The children and Maria scrambled out.

"You'll never guess," Maria said breathlessly. "Julia is betrothed. To a Yankee soldier! She met him in Alexandria, when she was in school and the Yankees occupied the place!"

"Well, I always knew the Yankees would get Julia," I said.

"I must tell Mama!" She ran into the house, the children with her.

Will McLean walked slowly toward me and paused with one foot on the bottom step of the portico. He looked up at my tear-stained face. "What's happened?"

"Alex wanted to know what to do with the doctor's gig. I told him he could have it for the army."

He walked up the steps. "Did you settle things with him?"

"Yessir."

"I'm sorry things have taken such a turn for you, Oscie."

"Do we have to wait until the fifteenth to leave here?"

"I'll have us out of here as soon as possible."

"Is Julia really betrothed to a Yankee?"

"She ran off on the train to Alexandria to marry him. Mr. Wilcher had to fetch her home. She swears she'll wait for him 'til the war's over."

"Lucky Julia. She has somebody to wait for."

He put his arm around my shoulder. "I am truly sorry, Oscie. I know you don't believe it, but I am."

"He's a fool," I said.

"Who?"

"Alex. He's a fool, pure and simple."

His hand gripped my shoulder. "Why is he a fool?"

"All that stupid honor. It's all he cares about. See what it gets him on the battlefield. Nothing matters but his honor. Nothing. Did you know that?" I stopped and looked up at him. "Are they all like that? He *knows* the South can't win the war, same's you do. He *knows* Beauregard's a jackass. Told me so. He *knows*," I broke off, unable to continue. I commenced sobbing.

Will McLean didn't say anything. Just put his arm around me and let me sob it out against his waistcoat.

"You won't want to hear this now, Oscie," he said,

"but you've turned into a lovely young woman. You have your whole life ahead of you." He gave me his handkerchief.

I dried my eyes. "I'm nobody to talk about anybody being a fool. I've made a brassbound jackass of myself in front of you."

"We're all entitled to make brassbound jackasses out of ourselves at least three times in our lives," he said. "It's written in that Constitution we've overthrown. Come, Oscie, we've too much to do with this move for recriminations."

I nodded. "Is Mary Ann coming with us to Charlottesville?"

"No. I need servants to keep the place running for a while. Only Maum Hanna and Hiram are going."

"Then I'm ripping up my herb garden."

"I beg your pardon?"

I pulled back from him. "I'll not leave it for Mary Ann. She can't wait to get her hands on it."

His eyes widened. "You'd rather destroy it than leave it to the army?"

"She'll get it first, for her herb concoctions. Anyway, the army's got our barn, our outbuildings, and probably our house. And now they've got my daddy's doctor's gig. What else do they want?"

He shook his head sadly. "I've got to get my family out of here, right quick," he said.

What more, indeed, I pondered. They've even got my heart.

There was a full moon that night. I put on my robe and slipped out of the house, after everyone was asleep. Moonlight flooded the fields and grounds with the light of day.

In that moonlight I tore up my herb garden.

I worked furiously until the roots were all exposed in the dirt. When it was done I stood gazing at the outline of the stone barn, the outbuildings, the quarters, the familiar trees and fences standing stark in the moonlight. The air was warm, a hooty owl called to its mate. I walked down to the barn.

Cottonwood and Mirabella, no longer young, came to the fence to be patted. But, with the exception of McLean's horse and enough livestock to keep the place going, the barn was empty.

I turned to look up to the house, solid and comforting on the knoll.

My daddy's house!

It was the only home I'd ever known, and now we were leaving. Probably forever. I thought of my Daddy John. I saw myself as a little girl, waving goodbye as he left in his doctor's gig. Then I saw myself as I was yesterday, saying goodbye to Alex.

Gone, all gone. Mirabella nuzzled me and I hugged her. My daddy's horse. He'd ridden her about on these fields, young and slim and tanned, many times with me on the saddle in front of him.

I stayed there a long time, hugging Mirabella and crying. For my father, for his house, for Alex, for Sarah, and for what we'd all lost. It was a bitter goodbye.

Chapter 17

July 22, 1861

I stood in the small hallway of the house we were renting in Charlottesville, summoned out of bed by Maum Hanna in the predawn gray. Outside it was pouring rain. Maum Hanna was fussing over Daddy Will.

"Doan you worry 'bout things here. Me an' Hiram'll see to the Missus and chillens." She handed him a package. "Food fer the train." Then her bulky form moved back into the kitchen.

Hiram helped him into his oilskins. Will McLean looked at me. "Sorry to get you up so early, but I stayed late at the telegraph office last night. Now I'm getting the six o'clock train to Manassas Junction and I wanted to speak with you before I leave."

I rubbed the sleep out of my eyes. "Yessir," I said.

"The battle is over at Manassas. General Johnston reinforced Beauregard. Our signalmen detected the Yankee movements and the Confederates rushed north to meet the Yanks head-on."

Alex at his signal station, I thought.

"Alex sent me the message. He said the first

Yankee cannon shot was aimed at our house. Beauregard set up headquarters there. The shot hit our kitchen. Another hit the cornfield, another the peach orchard, and still another went into the corncrib."

I could barely speak. "Was anybody hurt?"

"Lots of casualties on both sides, but none of our people. The Confederates were outnumbered, but the First Brigade of the Army of the Shenandoah was commanded by some general who was a college professor at the Virginia Military Institute—Jackson, I think his name is. He took a defensive position on Henry Hill."

"What of Mrs. Henry?"

"We don't know yet. The battle went on all yesterday. The Confederates kept bringing up reinforcements and the Yankees were disorganized and retreated back across Bull Run."

I nodded, trying to take it all in.

"I want you to keep an eye on things here."

"I hate it here," I said. "I miss my home."

"That doesn't matter. This is where I want my family. Out of harm's way. Keep an eye on Willie. He keeps running down to the telegraph office. He's made friends with Marco Paoli, the operator. I've spoken with the man. He doesn't mind Willie, but I don't want the boy neglecting chores and lessons. And I'd be beholden if you'd use your influence on Maria, too. She's still too flighty for my liking. I've enrolled Willie at Mr. Carrol's School. I'd also be beholden if you tutored Lula. Hiram will wire me if there's trouble."

"You won't be back?" I asked.

"I will, but I don't know when. I have to salvage what's left at Yorkshire, find a way to provide for my family, and eventually find us a new home. Are you going to say goodbye?"

Hiram was holding the door open, lantern in hand. Outside the carriage waited. Will McLean was head to toe in oilskins, revolver at his waist. I heard the train whistle in the distance.

I went to him and he kissed my forehead. "We haven't always gotten on, Oscie," he said.

This sounded serious, like a speech. Then he smiled. "We're both stubborn as Benjamin Chinn's mules. But I know you care about your mama and the children. Am I right?"

"Yessir."

"I know you lost any romantic notions you had about the South when we left Manassas. Am I right about that?"

When I said goodbye to Alex is what he meant. "Yessir."

"Well, the South will celebrate this victory at Manassas, but it doesn't mean a thing. Don't tell your mother that. But it's why I have to go now. To make a new life for us. I don't know how, but I'll find a way."

He went out into the rain with Hiram. I stood watching and I honestly hated to see him go.

The next evening, like everybody else in Charlottesville, Aunt Hannah had a party to celebrate the victory at Manassas. Her small parlor was crowded with people. Mama had just introduced me to Dr. McGuffey and run off to speak with someone else. McGuffey was thin and looked like a good wind would blow him away.

"You must bring your little brother to our place," he said.

I'm sure he'd profit from meeting you, Sir."

"He'd profit more from the sugar cookies my wife makes."

I smiled. "Willie can be a plague sometimes."

"My dear, it is the business of little boys to be plagues," he said. "They grow up to be big boys who will form an army for you if they have to. But more important, they grow into community leaders, and that's our purpose at the university. We don't overlook the women, of course. You and your mama and sister are invited to our evening lectures. I always thought it shameful we don't encourage our young women to go to college."

"My sister and I had a fine Yankee tutor," I told him. "She told me to look for you in Charlottesville."

"Ah, then you must write and give her my best. And now you must meet the Mosbys. They had an abolitionist tutor, down from Massachusetts, teaching their daughters. Come, I'll introduce you."

The woman called Virginia Mosby took my hand with such a firm grip I grimaced. "So you had a Yankee tutor, did you?"

"Yes, Ma'am."

"We're Virginia and Alfred. We don't hold with being formal. We have two sons and six daughters. All our girls can think and shoot as straight as the boys. And Abbey Southwick, the tutor our girls had, was a rock when we had the trouble with John."

I looked at Dr. McGuffey.

"Their oldest son was in his second year at the university when he shot a medical student in the jaw at the Brock Boarding House," he explained. "John went to prison and studied law. He was pardoned. The boy he shot started the fight and was a bully. John is married and a lawyer, now in the army."

"He's in the First Virginia Cavalry," Virginia Mosby said proudly. "He was under Jeb Stuart at Manassas."

"Was he hurt in battle?"

"My dear," she said, "Jeb Stuart's cavalry moves too fast. The Yankees can't catch 'em. Come see us. Tudor Grove, four miles outside town."

I said I would. Then I went to find Maria. She was falling quickly into the town rhythms, sensing the possibilities for the advancement of her personal aims, whatever they were. And Eliza, Aunt Hannah's twelve-year-old, followed her around like a lapdog, providing a constant audience for Maria's airs.

"Did you hear?" Maria said as I approached them at the punch bowl. "Eliza's brother John sent a telegraph message today. He's at Manassas! Doctoring! In our barn!"

"My other brothers were there, too," Eliza said. "Douglas telegraphed us that John is very busy with so many wounded."

I thought of my herb garden with a pang of guilt and remorse. I hoped John had enough medicines. I hoped Mary Ann didn't tell him I ripped it up. What would he think of me?

It was supper time and nobody knew where Maria was. We sat around the dining room table, waiting, while Maum Hanna kept the chicken warm. Mama insisted we all eat together, every meal. With prayers beforehand, this would keep us a family, she said.

"You don't suppose she's gone to the station in this rain to see the wounded when they arrive, do you?" she asked me.

It was only a week after the battle at Manassas, and the overflow of wounded was expected at the local depot this evening. The ladies of Charlottesville had been busy for two days, setting up the general hospital. Mama had worked with them and she looked drawn and tired.

"Not Maria," I said. "She and Eliza were going to the Female Institute to see a skit."

She unfolded a letter. "I'll read some of what Daddy Will writes. If Maria isn't here when I finish, we can eat."

"You know how I feel about this war, my dear, but seeing the wounded here, trying to assist our army in some way seems like the only decent thing to do. So I am using my merchant's talents to help the hospital surgeons get medical supplies. But I am sadly disillusioned to see large quantities of wine and whiskey being consumed by some surgeons and hospital attendants. And in our very barn! My nephew, John Cleary, works from sunup to sunset, under woeful conditions.

"He needs more blankets, mattresses, bandages, and foodstuffs. Billie and Allie have been drafted by county authorities to round up forage and blankets. Already in my travels in the Shenandoah Valley, I see that speculators are buying up all the flour hereabouts to drive up prices.

"I am giving a goodly supply of our crops to the army and have been asked to work for the Confederate Quartermaster. I shall donate my services free and ask only expenses.

"I am saddened to tell you that Mrs.

Henry died from wounds received when an artillery shell hit her house. I will attend her funeral for us all. Our house is intact. Give my love to the children. I miss you all."

"I'se hungwy," Lula said. "Wanna eat."

Mrs. Henry was dead. I pondered that while Maum Hanna served the chicken. Mrs. Henry had died on her hill then, on the high ground. I wanted to cry. I was tired too, for Willie and I had been out all afternoon collecting hand bells, fire fenders, candlesticks, and other household items as scrap for the war effort. The rain had chilled me, my head hurt, and in spite of all the lies I might tell myself about his being a fool, I missed Alex so much it was a dull ache inside me.

Then we heard the train whistle down at the depot. The front door opened at the same time. Maria came in, throwing off her wraps.

"Where have you been?" Mama asked.

"Why Mama, darling," Maria kissed her and sat down. "I went to the skit at the Female Institute with Eliza. She goes there. They had the most wonderful play. Can't I enroll this autumn?"

"Not now, Maria," I cautioned. "Mama's tired and Daddy Will wrote that Mrs. Henry died."

"Mrs. Henry should have moved," Maria said, loading her plate with food. "She was stupid. She knew the Yankees were coming."

"That's enough, Maria!" Mama spoke sharply. "The woman is dead. Have some respect."

"Stupid girls," Willie said, "having skits when we're at war."

"Hush, Willie," Mama admonished. "As for the Female Institute, Maria, Button taught you more than you'd ever learn there. And I *should* think you'd have more important things on your mind, what with wounded coming into town today."

"You want me to nurse the wounded?" Maria was aghast.

"I didn't say that," Mama answered. "But we could have used you rolling bandages this afternoon. Or helping to cook for them."

"I've never cooked in my life except to make sugar cookies or pull taffy," Maria said.

"Then perhaps it's time you learned," Mama said. "Oscie never collected scrap in her life but she did so today. Perhaps it's time we all learned a lot of things."

Even Maria knew better than to trifle with Mama now. "If you wish, Mama, I'll find something worthwhile to do tomorrow."

The door knocker sounded. Hiram ushered Dr. McGuffey into the room. He was wearing oilskins.

"I beg pardon for interrupting your dinner, Madam, but my visit is not social. I've come from the depot."

Mama waited. We all did.

"I was there with my colleagues from the university. They are taking wagonloads of wounded and putting them in the Rotunda. The hospital and private homes are filling up fast."

"How can we help you, Dr. McGuffey?" Mama asked.

"I have a special case. There is a young man I would vouch for personally, in a house full of women. He is from Ohio. And he is my nephew."

Mama's hand went to her throat. "But Ohio is Union," she said.

"Yes, Madam." Dr. McGuffey spoke softly. "So I

could not bring him to us at the university. The Southern sentiment there is too strong, as it is in most other households hereabouts."

"And so you come to us, Doctor?"

"Yes, Madam. I knew that people who hired a Northern tutor for their daughters would have open hearts. He is my sister's boy. From Marietta. Will you take him in please?"

We took the Yankee soldier into our house that night. They carried him in and put him on the settee in the parlor. And so it was that the next day Maria found something worthwhile to do.

She fell in love with a Yankee.

Chapter 18

July to December 1861

Ensconced on our settee in the parlor the next morning, with Lula sitting on a bench at his feet and Maria sitting on a nearby chair, Michah Stevens addressed Mama. "And so, Ma'am, while so many of our wounded fled back to Washington on foot, I was picked up by the Rebs." He stopped and blushed. "I mean by the Southern doctors. I was in a hospital at Manassas for a while. Big old barn it was. They treated me kindly."

"That was *our* barn. My Daddy Will built it," Maria said.

Maria had not been inside that barn more than three times since it was rebuilt. "I'm so glad our people saved your leg," she gushed. "And that Doctor Cleary said it would mend. He's our cousin, you know."

Maum Hanna came in with a tray of food. Immediately Maria commenced to try to feed Michah Stevens. He blushed. "I can do that myself, Miss Maria."

"But I *want* to do it. Mama wants me to do

something for our Cause. Now I've found something to do."

"Begging your pardon, Miss Maria, but I don't represent your Cause," Michah reminded her.

"Call me Maria," she said. "Of course, you're Union. But Mama wants me to be more considerate of people. And I just can't think of a better place to start. Isn't that right, Mama?"

"As long as you two behave with decorum," Mama said. "After all, Michah, you are Dr. McGuffey's nephew. And he has vouched for you."

Michah awarded Mama a flashing smile. "There's not much I can do right now, Ma'am, in the way of being improper."

This was not just an ordinary Yankee, I conjectured. Yankees were ill-mannered and coarse factory boys. Or backwoods people without any refinements. Surely they did not have blue eyes that laughed at you and grew soft when you spoke. Or such fine chestnut curls, or white teeth. God had not made Yankees with no-nonsense jaws and fine straight noses and dimples in their chins. Surely someone would have told us, if He had.

"Are you in pain?" Mama asked.

"Sometimes, Ma'am. But the doctors gave me remedies."

"Then perhaps the children shouldn't bother you."

"Glad to have them, Ma'am. Little Lula's an angel. And if the little boy wants, I could tell him about the battle."

Willie was hiding in the hall. "Don't wanna talk to any Yankee," he said.

"Oh, I'm so sorry," Mama apologized. "Willie's becoming a trial since his father left."

"That's all right, Willie," Michah called out. "I'll

tell Lula how the Confederate line was outnumbered when your generals sent reinforcements in. And how, about two in the afternoon, we surged up the slope that was covered with Confederates and mistook one of their regiments for our own. And they fired point-blank on us. Then, about four, they ripped into our right flank and we all skedaddled back across Bull Run."

Willie peeked around the door frame. "Tell me. Our soldiers are good, aren't they?"

"I'll tell you all the stories you want, Willie, soon's your big sister stops shoving soup into my mouth. Yes, your soldiers are good. We have a lot of respect for them." He sighed. "I think that by now," he said wearily, "we have a lot of respect for each other."

Michah became part of our household. Summer progressed, its hot days running into each other. I cooked delicacies for the wounded soldiers and, with Mrs. McGuffey, distributed them in the old Public Hall of the university, where men lay on pallets on the floor.

Michah, trained to be a teacher, tutored Willie to prepare him for school, with Maria and Lula in attendance. Mama worked almost daily at the Charlottesville General Hospital. In late August the *Richmond Examiner* praised the people of the town, saying it was now "a vast hospital for the sick and wounded." But it was not all work for us. Several times I went to lectures and recitals at the university with my cousins Catherine and Mary Jane. We even had a dance at the Town Hall to raise money to care for families of local soldiers.

But I went through all these doings like I was under a spell. For I still had a dull ache inside me because of Alex. The ache was so familiar to me now that it was part of my life. And, while there were times when I was so busy helping the wounded that I didn't even think of him, other times I'd stop in the middle of some chore and just stand there like one of Benjamin Chinn's mules. All because some soldier had the same color hair as Alex. Or some officer had the same sash. Or spoke with the same drawl. And it would come to me like a thunderclap, what loving Alex had done to me. I was not the same person as before. I never could be. What was I then?

I had no more romantic notions about the South, as Will McLean had noted. Impatient with Alex for the twaddle he stood for, sometimes angry at him, I still hadn't stopped loving him. Or missing him. Oh, I was so confused!

Button wrote from Washington in September.

> I am at Georgetown's Union Hospital learning to nurse. I met Louisa May Alcott from Massachusetts. She sprinkles herself with lavender water, to combat the smell. The biggest plague to us is the visiting families of the wounded. They overfeed their kin and overstay. We have to find places for them to sleep and cook their food. One wife came and had a baby here. The soldiers suffer so much from homesickness that many of them would profit from a furlough, but the officials won't allow that. It doesn't make sense to me, but then nothing about this war does . . .

In September everyone was wondering where the next fighting would happen. Robert E. Lee's son enrolled at the university and I danced with him at a party. Meanwhile his father had failed in a campaign in West Virginia and by mid-September the Yankees surrendered to our army in Lexington, Missouri.

Willie started school at Mr. Carrol's. Back on his feet, Michah helped Hiram with chores and was proficient at fetching Willie home. Without his influence I am quite sure that Willie would have become a complete ruffian in Daddy Will's absence. Nobody could make him mind anymore.

Michah fit right in. People in town accepted him, forgetting he was a Yankee, as he drove Mama about on some hospital mission, Maria beside him. And then one day some men came to our house to see Michah. One was the local recruitment officer. With them came Dr. McGuffey. They asked Michah if he would swear an oath to take up arms no more.

And, with Maria smiling up at him, Michah said yes.

"He'd have said yes if they asked him to run a Confederate gauntlet," Mama said, sighing. "I don't know what to do, Oscie. Maria's pure smitten with that boy."

There was nothing *to* do. Michah stayed. Neither the North nor the South knew yet what to do with prisoners, and so he was paroled.

Our President Davis met with generals Beauregard and Johnston in Centreville, up to home, in October, to plot grand strategy. Daddy Will wrote from Manassas saying their strategy wasn't so grand, that nobody knew what was supposed to happen in the war next.

The western part of our state broke away from us after many meetings, and went with the Union. Missouri came into the Confederacy in August. In late November, planters in Charleston and Savannah burned their cotton so the Yankees, who were in Port Royal, South Carolina, couldn't get their hands on it.

Up North they proclaimed a day of Thanksgiving. Button wrote to tell us that Prince Albert, consort of England's Queen Victoria, died in December. And to say that she and Louisa May Alcott were becoming soul mates and the hospital she worked in was becoming a perfect pestilence box.

I don't know how we endured Christmas. Everything seemed wrong. Daddy Will sent presents, but he disappointed Mama and didn't come home. Dr. McGuffey and his wife came to our home for Christmas dinner. That morning, on the walk home from church, Maria came up to me.

"You must help me, Oscie," she said.

"About what?"

"Michah and I want to become betrothed."

I wasn't surprised. "Have you told Mama?"

"Yes. Michah asked her last night."

"And what did she say?"

"That we must have permission from Daddy Will. And oh, Oscie, he won't be home until March! You know he's been traveling all up and down the Potomac, for the Quartermaster. I do think it's mean that he didn't come home Christmas. Mama is so sad."

"I'm sure he wanted to, Maria."

"I can't bear to wait until March. Oh, you don't know what it's like! I love Michah so, Oscie!"

I stared at her. Was it possible Maria didn't realize what I'd been through with Alex? It was. My sister always had thought only of herself. "What do you expect me to do, Maria?"

"Take up for me when he comes home," she

pleaded. "I know he won't like my being betrothed to a Yankee. He'll listen to you, Oscie, he always did."

"Me?" I laughed. "You're the one who could always wrap him around your finger."

"But you always stood up to him. He knows you're somebody to be reckoned with. And he respects that. Oh, please, Oscie, when he comes home tell him how wonderful Michah is. And that he comes from a good family back in Ohio and that he's had college and he wants to teach."

I promised I would. But it surprised me that Maria should see me in such a role. I pondered that we never see ourselves as others see us.

Something was worrying at Mama. And it was more than Daddy Will not coming home for Christmas. She seemed distracted all Christmas Day and when she retired to her room after the festivities, I went to find out what it was.

"It's my Will," she said.

"Is he sick?" Cousin John had written in November of typhoid, pneumonia, and even measles at Manassas.

"No. Oh, Oscie, I feel so disloyal, but I must tell someone." With that she produced a letter from him. "It arrived yesterday with a bank note for $825.00. Rent money for the buildings at Yorkshire from July to December. He advises me to buy clothing for us and stock up on provisions."

I waited. She went on.

"He writes that salt is worth $650 a ton in Nassau in the Bahamas, but it's bringing $1,700 a ton in the South. Coffee, selling for $249 a ton in Nassau, goes for $5,500 a ton on the Confederate market."

Still I waited. Clearly, I was missing something here.

"He's making money on the war, Oscie," she said.

Candles flickered in the room. Outside a chill rain fell against the windows. Mama balled her handkerchief in her fist. "My Will! He's making money on the sufferings of others!"

"Mama, are you sure?"

"He wrote in November that he sold a carton of candles for $156. In this letter he says he sold the same amount for $250. All part of the same shipment he got from Richmond at regular prices. He's now buying other scarce items in Richmond and selling them to the army for the highest price he can get!"

"There must be a reason, Mama." I couldn't think. But I had to say something. "He'll clear it up when he comes home." Here I was defending Will McLean. But I'd defend the Devil himself if it would make Mama stop crying.

"Oh, I know he wasn't for the war," she wailed. "And I know his heart wasn't in owning nigras. But he went back to Yorkshire to help the army. His family has always been so patriotic. It's tradition with them! What's happened to him?"

"Why don't we wait and see, Mama."

"I realize that merchants have always done this in time of war. But not even my great-grandfather, Bernard Hooe, made money from the Revolution. He was a skinflint of a merchant, but even *he* stopped selling to the British once the war started!" She was becoming agitated. I had to soothe her. "My Will is changing," she wailed. "He's losing faith in the Confederacy!"

He never had it, I wanted to say. But I didn't. I helped her take off her shoes and dress and got her into bed.

"And there's something else, Oscie. I put all my

holdings in trust. He can't touch my money. Does he need money now? Is that it? Did we lose everything when the battle came to Manassas? Have I driven him to this?"

"Mama, stop," I chided. "You know that Will McLean is no brassbound rascal, to want your money. And you haven't driven him to anything. Because you don't know that he's *done* anything yet."

That calmed her. I called down for some warm milk with rum in it, closed the draperies, and sat with her until she drank the milk and went to sleep.

Rain poured down outside. So, Will McLean, I thought, you've found a way to make a living for your family. Well, I don't care how many goods you sell to the Confederacy at inflated prices. Any fascination I had for the Confederacy ended the day I said goodbye to Alex. Like you said, neither of us has any romantic notions.

But I know one thing. If this is what you intend to do, Will McLean, you'd best start telling some fancy lies to my mama. Because she still has romantic notions. She still believes in you. I think I understand you, finally, much as we always disagreed. But Mama loves you. And I guess I'm just going to have to tell you the truth.

That night before I went to bed I penned a note to Will McLean in my best penmanship. The kind of penmanship he so prized. In the note I told him that it made no never mind to me if he was making money on the war, that I wasn't prying, but that if he was doing such, he shouldn't mention it anymore in his letters to my mama.

Chapter 19

March to April 1862

He came home, unannounced, on a cold blustery night the second week in March. An icy rain was falling. Seems like we had nothing else but rain that winter. I was in the kitchen fetching some warm milk and honey for Mama when Hiram answered the knock on the front door. I came through the hall to see Will McLean standing there in his oilskins, dripping wet.

"Hello, Oscie," he said, "where is everybody?"

"Mama's in bed with a chill. The children are sleeping. Maria's staying the night at the McGuffey's." I just stared at him. He seemed taller. And slimmer. His eyes were snappy and flinty. And he seemed more sure of himself, too, if that was possible.

Hiram brought claret on a tray. "We wasn't 'spectin' you, Mister Will. Why didn't you sent word so's I could fetch you at the depot?"

"You can't depend on the train schedules anymore." He sipped his claret. "I got a hack at the depot. I'll eat whatever's on hand, Maum Hanna. I've missed your cooking. You look as if you've seen a ghost, Oscie. What is it?"

"It was raining when you left," I said stupidly, for lack of anything better to say.

"That's right, isn't it? Nothing's changed."

But it has, I thought, as he took the tray from my hand and started up the stairs. "I want to see my wife. Then I'll be down to eat."

"Don't," I said.

He paused on the stairway. "Don't what?"

I put my hand on the newel post and peered up at him. "Did you get my note?"

"Yes. And I have honored your wishes. Do you think I now need further instruction on how to talk to my wife?"

"Nosir," I said. I stood looking up at him. He was home. In charge again. And he hadn't changed a bit. Only become more so of what he was.

Rain slashed at the dining room windows and the candlelight flickered on the polished table. I sat watching Will McLean eat. Maum Hanna had come up with cold ham and chicken, pickled preserves, that morning's biscuits made warm and light again, coffee, and chocolate cake. Hiram poured wine. A feast. McLean ate ravenously, inquiring after the children.

"Why is Maria staying at the McGuffey's? Does this happen often?"

"Michah moved in with his aunt and uncle after Christmas. They're very proper and didn't think Michah should stay here anymore since he wants to be betrothed. They've had a good influence on Maria. She helps Mrs. McGuffey roll bandages and reads to the wounded soldiers at the university. She's even learned to cook."

"What do you think of Michah?"

"Maria loves him," I said.

He sipped his wine and set the glass down. "You should know, better than anybody, that isn't sufficient to recommend him to me."

I blushed. He was referring to Alex. "He isn't married," I said. "Mama's made inquiries. His family is substantial, from pioneer stock. They have social standing back in Marietta, and of course his uncle is Dr. McGuffey. Michah was educated at the University of Pennsylvania before he joined the First Ohio. He can teach at college."

He was watching me with studied interest.

I went on. "He's wonderful with the children. I don't know how we would have managed Willie half of the time without him. And Lula adores him. He's helped Hiram and escorted Mama all over town. I think he has much to recommend him."

"Things *have* changed," he said. "You're taking up for Maria."

"I wouldn't, if I didn't think Michah was right for her. She asked me to. She's afraid you'll say no."

He nodded. "Thank you for your opinion."

"Are you going to say yes then?"

"Your mother and I must discuss it. And I'll speak with Michah. With the war and his being a Yankee, Maria stands to have her heart broken," he reminded me.

"She can take it."

"Are you sure of that? Maria isn't you. She never was."

Again I blushed. "Maria is stronger than any of us realize."

He nodded and sat back while Hiram took his plate and served coffee and cake. I took some coffee and waited, sensing more was coming. It was.

"In your note, you inquired if I was making profits on the war," he said quietly.

"I wasn't prying. I said that if you were, I didn't think you should tell Mama. It upsets her."

Silence. Rain poured against the windows.

"If you want to know if I'm making profits on the war, Oscie, why don't you just ask me," he said, quietly.

I didn't know which way to look then. So I looked at my coffee cup. "I figure that's your business, Will McLean," I answered.

"I suspect it wouldn't upset you if I were. Am I right?"

It came to me then that he wanted my opinion on that, too. "Nosir," I said.

"Why is that?"

"Can't rightly say."

"Try."

I knew a challenge when I heard one. He was pushing to see how much I'd grown up, to see if he could trust me enough with something he wanted to say. I knew I had to be honest. He'd sense in a minute if I wasn't. I'd never pandered to him, either, and he didn't want that now.

But if I spoke the truth and it didn't set right with him, I was in for the rough side of his tongue. I knew that my standing as somebody to be reckoned with depended on my answer.

It went without saying then, that my opinion about Maria and Michah hung in the balance.

"Well, sir," I commenced, "I've studied on the matter. And I see the future of the South when I look at you."

His face held no expression. "Go on," he said.

"It isn't the future Alex saw. All that sweet

tradition. You're brash, Will McLean. But you know about real things none of us have had to face before. I think you're all about what the South is going to have to be if we want to stay alive."

"And how do you feel about that?"

"It frightens me. Always did. Back when you first came to us at Yorkshire, I knew you were different. Where my daddy blended in, you stood out. Didn't know what it was about you, then. But I know now. And all those things you always said about my daddy being Old South and you New South, you were right about that. Only I don't think you knew what you were all about back then, either."

He nodded.

"But you do now," I said.

"Yes, I do now, don't I?" His voice was raspy. Silence for a minute, then he commenced telling me what he was doing.

"I'm trading in sugar. I'm not selling cheap shoes, or coats that will fall apart the first winter, to our government at exorbitant prices. I wouldn't do such. An army can fight without sugar. But it's a scarce and very expensive commodity."

He paused. I nodded.

"I'm buying up a large cargo of sugar now, to put in a warehouse someplace. It comes from Louisiana. It's costing me dearly to have it shipped, but I will make a profit. I'm doing it so I can take care of my family after the war is over."

"Are we going to lose the war?" I asked. "I know we took losses in Kentucky in June."

He lit a cheroot. "Stonewall Jackson took Romney, West Virginia. But wintering has weakened our army. Federal gunboats were up and down the Mississippi all of January, throwing shells into our encampments.

The Federals won Forts Henry and Donelson in Tennessee. Their General McClellan may be a fool, but they've got somebody named Grant who isn't. He's to be reckoned with."

"Nobody talks much about our losses here."

"Of course, they don't. But we also lost Roanoke Island in North Carolina and now the Yankees have control of the Pamlico Sound, a first-rate base on the Atlantic Coast for operations against us. And when they took Elizabeth City down there, we lost an important inland waterway to Virginia. And they're occupying Nashville as we speak."

"Then it's bad, isn't it?"

He smiled wryly. "Our generals are still better than theirs. But ours are all like Alex. They'll never give up. Which means the South will impoverish itself first. And that's why I do what I do."

I blushed at the mention of Alex's name. He saw it.

"You haven't asked for him," he said. "He sends you his best regards."

I nodded. "How is he?"

"He's well. The army left Manassas on March sixth. Don't let it kill you, Oscie. You're not still carrying the torch for him, are you?"

"I love him one minute and hate him the next," I confessed.

He got up and went to peer out the window. "Exactly the way I feel about the South."

Silence, except for the sound of rain on the window panes. We had each made a painful admission. Alex is the South, I wanted to say. But instead I gave the conversation another turn.

"How long are you staying this time?"

"At least a month. Long enough to get in your hair and make you miserable." He turned to grin at me.

His face, in the candlelight, seemed tired. I felt something stirring in me, some sadness and sympathy and affection for this man. The candle was going out in the South and he knew how hopeless it all was. And he'd made a clearing for himself in the midst of all the pageantry and horror of the war, like some bantam rooster in the barnyard, determined to do anything to take care of those who belonged to him.

I respected him more that night than I had in a long time. And I think he felt about me in kind. I'd met his challenge and was still somebody to be reckoned with.

He stayed the month. We became a family again. He gave permission for Maria and Michah to become betrothed, providing they wouldn't marry before the war ended. Julia Stratton-Wilcher had run off to marry her Yankee soldier, he told us. He'd have none of that. Or he'd be after Maria and Michah with a shotgun. I think he would, too.

Spring came to Charlottesville. When we saw him off at the depot at the end of April, he told us that in his travels he would look for a new home for us.

"Where?" Willie and Lula asked.

"I don't know," he said. "Somewhere away from the war. I don't think I ever want to see another soldier again. Present company excluded, Michah," he added.

"I swore never to take up arms again, Sir," Michah told him.

Will McLean said nothing, but there was a knowing look in his eyes. Within the week, Maria confided that Daddy Will had told her not to be surprised if Michah rejoined the army.

Within the month, Mama told me she was again with child.

Chapter 20

January to May 1863

I stood in Mama's room waiting for Maum Hanna to hand me my new little sister. Nannie McLean came into the world as the clock struck twelve on a night of howling winds and plummetting temperatures.

The doctor from the university who had attended Mama had just left. Nannie's birth had been quick and they'd allowed me in the room part of the time. Between pains all Mama talked about was the new house Will McLean had bought for his family. A good property, she'd told me. An attractive price. Two stories. Brick. A fireplace in each room.

Now Mama was sleeping. Maum Hanna handed Nannie to me, to hold just a little while before I went to bed. I sat in the rocker before the fireplace, with Alex's buffalo robe around me.

I felt a sense of peace. All I could hear was the fire crackling and the snow against the windows. Maria had taken the children to the McGuffey's hours ago.

Will McLean had not come home for the birth of the baby. And I'd fought with Maria over that. "He doesn't care!" she'd shouted at me. "He's been home

176 Literature Connections

only once since last spring."

That much was true. McLean had traveled the whole South since last spring. "He's in Jackson, Mississippi, on business," I told Maria.

"Business! That's all he cares about!" she'd said.

I'd taken up for Daddy Will, telling Maria that she didn't complain when he sent her new frocks he got from the blockade runners. Neither Mama nor Maria knew that he'd gone to see General Pemberton because he was having trouble getting his cargo of sugar released from a warehouse in Vicksburg, Mississippi. Because everyone was saying Vicksburg would soon be under siege and they needed provisions.

The baby made mewing sounds at me. Oh baby, I thought, all around us there is suffering. What a time for you to be born. In the middle of a silly war.

Yes, we won at Second Manassas. But that just shows you what it's all about. First Manassas wasn't enough for everybody. They had to do it a second time. That baby looked at me out of bright eyes. McLean's eyes. She understood. I know she did.

Maria's just upset for worry about Michah, I told her. After the battle of Port Republic last June, when we were flooded with wounded again, Michah got nervous and went to rejoin the army. Just like your daddy said he would.

And yes, we won at Antietam last September, I told her. And for a while in Kentucky. But the Yankees are plaguing us in Arkansas and all along the coast of the Carolinas and Georgia. And there's always the blockade, so we can't buy anything, no matter how much money your daddy sends us. And we have to use raspberry leaves for tea and plant okra or use yam potatoes and burnt corn to make coffee.

And there was a great battle in Fredricksburg in December. And though the North withdrew across the Rappahannock, everyone is criticizing Lee for not counterattacking.

But at least we all love Lee and Jackson. Mr. Lincoln keeps replacing his generals. He replaced McClellan with Burnside, then Burnside with Hooker.

Then, just before you were born, what does Mr. Lincoln do? He freed the nigras, baby, that's what. Gives it a fancy name. Calls it the Emancipation Proclamation. And nobody knows what all it means.

It was a fine May morning. The air was like silk and everything was in bloom. Nannie was sleeping peacefully in her cradle. Will McLean must have gotten his sugar out of that warehouse in Vicksburg, I conjectured, because the talk at breakfast was all about the furnishings we'd need for our new house. Until Willie spoke up.

"They let us off from school today to see Jackson's body when it comes through on the train. Can I go? Can I?"

At nine, Willie was very bloodthirsty. Mama hesitated.

Stonewall Jackson, the hero of the Shenandoah Valley campaign, had been wounded a few days ago and died on May tenth. When we received word in Charlottesville, people just came out of their houses and stood looking at each other and crying.

Jackson, who sat his horse at First Manassas like a stone wall. Jackson, the hero of Front Royal and Cross Keys, wounded at Seven Pines last May. Jackson, who traveled fifty-one miles in two days with his men to destroy General Pope at Second

Manassas, who saved Lee from being overwhelmed by Yankees at Antietam, was dead.

"You can't go alone," Mama said.

"For heaven's sakes, Willie, he's dead," Maria said. "Why does everyone have to troop down to the depot to see him? What's wrong with people, anyway?"

Michah had been with Hooker in winter quarters across from Fredricksburg. She hadn't heard from him for a while. Then she learned he was with the Yankees fighting against Jackson at Chancellorsville.

"This is all so stupid, this war." Maria glared at Willie. "Bread riots in Richmond last month. And our wonderful President Davis tossing the women and children coins from his pocket, then setting troops on them! Don't let him go to the depot, Mama. He doesn't have to see a dead body, does he?"

She started to cry. "I'm sorry, Mama. But nothing makes sense anymore and I'm frantic with worry about Michah."

"Michah is a smart young man, he'll come through," Mama promised.

"Jackson was a college professor," Maria reminded her.

"They say he was shot by his own men by mistake," Willie put in. "They took off his left arm and he died of pneumonia."

"Stop it, Willie," I ordered. "I'll take him to the depot, Mama," I offered. "I'll get him out of everybody's hair."

"I wanna go," Lula said. "Wanna see the dead general."

"No, darling, I want you with me today," Mama said brightly. "We're paying a call on the Mosbys. Will you come along, Maria?"

"I hate Virginia Mosby," Maria said vehemently.

"All she talks about is her darling John. I hear Mosby's Rangers are a vain lot of dandies, with their plumed hats and scarlet-lined capes. And they go on drinking binges, too."

"Captain Mosby does not drink," Mama stated. "Virginia is constantly finding fresh-ground coffee for him. He carries a pouch of it with him always. He is one of the South's newest heroes, Maria. And heaven knows, we need heroes. He and his men strike at Yankee pickets and outposts and go constantly behind Union lines."

"Yes, and they strike out at Michah," my sister said.

Mama sighed. There would be no winning with Maria today. She wasn't giving anybody any quarter.

Willie and I waited with hundreds of people for the train that would bring General Jackson's body through Charlottesville. People had come with their nigra servants, with babies in arms, with little children in tow. Mama should have let Lula come, I thought. This is something to remember. Everyone was in their Sunday best, too, bearing flowers, everything from Queen Anne's lace to early roses.

People greeted their neighbors and inquired after family members away at war. Then, when we heard the chug-chug-chugging of the train in the distance, everyone fell silent. And all of Charlottesville's church bells started to toll. Then the singing began.

The nigras were singing about climbing Jacob's ladder. Shivers went through me. The train came slowly into the depot. The coffin bearing Jackson was on a bier in the baggage car. You could see it through the windows.

A guard of honor was at the head and foot of the coffin and the whole car was filled with flowers. The train inched its way through the depot. Then it stopped. People filed by, viewing the body and handing flowers to the officers who stood on the platform.

The officers looked fine in their gray uniforms and polished boots, their mustard-colored sashes and sheathed sabers. They reminded me of Alex. But they looked tired and sad. And I wondered how Alex looked these days.

Willie and I handed them our roses. When everyone had finished, the whistle shrieked, the steam rose, the iron wheels grated, and we stood in respectful silence until the train was out of sight.

"He looked dead," Willie said. He sounded disappointed.

"He was dead," I said.

"I couldn't see that he had only one arm."

"No. He was in full dress uniform."

"What do you think they did with the arm they cut off?"

"I don't know. I suppose they buried it."

"We won at Chancellorsville," he boasted.

"Yes, but nearly 13,000 on our side are killed, wounded, and missing."

We went home. In July, Daddy Will arrived and, after three months of siege, Vicksburg fell to the Yankees. In August, Captain John Mosby was wounded and came to Charlottesville to recover. Mama went to meet him. I never did. I was busy packing.

The first week in September we took the train south. We were all excited, because we were going to our beautiful new home. The war would never find us there, Will McLean promised.

"Neither will anybody else," Maria wailed.

"If you're talking about Michah," Daddy Will told her, "he's a soldier. Trained like a fox hound to find what he's after."

"I can't even remember the name of the place," Maria said.

"It's Appomattox Court House," Will McLean told her.

Maria sniffed. "Who ever heard of it," she said.

Chapter 21

September 1863

A week after we moved into our new home at Appomattox Court House, Maria and I set out to the store. It was a sweet September afternoon and the first chance we'd had to explore the town, although Willie had been all through it and already had a bosom friend in a little boy named Eddie Tibbs.

We each had baskets on our arms. We were in search of dress patterns and, since the store was also the post office, mail. Though mail service was in a sorry state.

"I would think people would have called," Maria said as we went down the wide front steps of our two-story brick house. "What kind of a town is this, where people don't call when you move in?"

"You heard what Daddy Will said," I reminded her. "They don't cotton to strangers."

"I wish he hadn't gone away again so soon. I think the only reason he bought this place is because of the good railroad connections. You know how the Yankees love to cut railroad lines. The last time I heard from Michah he was in Tennessee helping to destroy the rails between Chattanooga and Virginia."

Sun filtered through the leaves of the locust trees in our front yard as we went down the brick walk. A turn to the right and we were facing the brick court house, surrounded by a grass square and white fence and encircled by the Richmond-Lynchburg stage road. To the left was Meek's store. Most of the village was a stone's throw from our house, the buildings all neatly laid out in patches of green, hem-stitched with white fencing.

"I'll wager people have found out that Will McLean's a merchant," Maria said. "Didn't you hear Mary Ann say there are all kinds of shortages here?"

"I heard." We walked in silence. "But I'd just as lief never hear another thing Mary Ann has to say. I near to died when I saw her waiting on that porch for us last week when we arrived. I wish Daddy Will had given *her* her freedom, instead of Paula and Fanny and the others."

Maria sighed. "Don't know what got into him, giving all our servants their freedom."

"He was always an abolitionist at heart," I told her. "Mama knew that way back before the war started. Now that we have no more plantation, he has no need for so many nigras. Says he brought Mary Ann because her Allie ran off to join the Yankees. And she has no place to go. Says Allie has to know where to find her when the war is over."

"Mama says he offered Maum Hanna and Hiram their freedom too," she whispered. "Imagine. Has Will McLean gone plum crazy?"

"I 'spect the war's made everybody a little crazy, Maria." I poked her. "Look at you. In love with a Yankee."

We giggled over that. Then we mulled over the idea of either Maum Hanna or Hiram taking their freedom.

"Where would they *go?*" Maria asked.

We considered that for a moment, shaking our heads. "I'm glad they stayed," I said fervently. Home wouldn't be home without Maum Hanna and Hiram. Maria agreed with me.

But I was sure my sister knew nothing about Mary Ann's lost babies. Or about Will McLean's speculating. Those were my secrets to keep and keep them I would. Our family had been through enough as war refugees, just now finding a home.

We all loved our new house. It had a parlor and main bedroom on the first floor, children's rooms on the second, and a lovely warming kitchen and dining room on the underground level. Best, though, the log kitchen and servants' quarters were out back. Which meant that Mary Ann, being in the kitchen, didn't have to come into the house much at all.

Will McLean had shipped down all our furniture, as well as ancestral portraits, Mama's porcelain from China, her crystal and silver, Maria's piano, and the portrait he'd had done of me and Maria and Sarah back at Lang Syne.

The parlor had been crammed when we arrived, with crates and boxes holding many new items, too, velvet draperies, marble-topped tables, a chessboard with figures carved out of ivory, and the makings of winter clothing for us all.

We found the best wool and grosgrain, cashmere, taffeta, and silk, in those boxes. Along with whalebone for crinolines and stays, lace to trim our drawers, all purchased, no doubt, from blockade runners. For Mr. Lincoln's blockade was drawing a noose tighter and tighter around the neck of the South.

But apparently Will McLean knew how to secure the goods. And apparently he was doing well enough in his speculating to be able to pay the inflated prices.

Four or five people were gathered around the stove in Meek's store, discussing politics. They stopped talking as we entered. From behind the counter an elderly man eyed us over spectacles.

"Kin I do something for y'all?"

"I . . . that is, my mama wanted to know if you have any dress patterns," Maria said.

"Not as many as I used to." He searched the shelves. I noticed how his hands trembled as he set three patterns down on the counter. "Y'all are the McLean girls, right?" he asked.

"Yes and no," I said.

His pale blue eyes regarded me sternly. "Either y'all are or y'all ain't. Seems to me y'all old enough to know."

"Our name is Mason," Maria said. "Our mama is married to Will McLean. We kept our daddy's name."

The people around the stove stared at us as if we'd just said we were spies for old Abe Lincoln himself. One was a young girl our own age. She was dressed in a plain frock. Her eyes appeared lively and interested. And I was warmed by the faint smile on her lips.

Mr. Meeks nodded. "These patterns are old," he said. "Don't have all the geegaws on 'em the fancy ladies like today. Not much call for dress patterns. People hereabouts don't have the cloth to make dresses with."

"You know we have cloth, Mr. Meeks," the young girl said. "Why, lots of women have gotten their old spinning wheels down from their attics and taken to making their own cloth."

"Mind your own business, Ellen Bryant. I know from what I'm sayin'. These are fancy ladies. Not much interested in homespun."

"Our Maum Hanna knows how to spin if she has to," I said. "And we have an old spinning wheel from our great-great grandma."

He eyed us doubtfully.

"You seem to have a goodly supply of other dry goods on your shelves," Maria said.

"Not like there used to be. But we still have rail service, leastways. They toted my son, Lafayette, home on the rails after he was killed at First Manassas."

That silenced Maria, but after a moment I spoke up. "I'm sorry about your son, Mr. Meeks."

He took an old pipe down from a shelf and lighted it. Then he propped one foot on a low barrel, rested his arms on the raised leg and considered us. "Your stepdaddy told you 'bout the shortages in this town? How we don't have coffee, sugar, spices or medicines?"

"He did, yes," I said.

"Y'all got sugar up to your house?"

There it was. Everyone was eyeing us. I held my breath. They *knew* that Will McLean was speculating in sugar.

"We may have a bit we brought down from Charlottesville," I allowed.

He nodded. "Sugar's scarcer than hen's teeth in these parts. The county authorities give salt out on salt days. Bring it up from the southwest part of the state. Each family gets a box. Don't suppose y'all be needin' any, though. Hear tell y'all got everthin' needed up to your place."

"Oh?" I raised my chin. "Where did you hear that?"

"That skinny nigra gal of yours was sashayin' around here t'other day, braggin' 'bout how well you folks is livin'."

"You mean Mary Ann?"

"That's the one. She's been makin' friends hereabouts since she first got here, 'bout a month ago."

Mary Ann again! The dark shadow in our lives. What was she telling people? Most likely that Will McLean traveled and could get everything he wanted in the way of goods and supplies. I'd have to tell her to keep quiet.

"My stepdaddy practically gave our place to the Confederate army at Manassas." I put as much of an edge in my voice as I could. "He gave over our house to General Beauregard. He gave our barn for a hospital. He gave our crops, everything. And he worked for nothing for the Confederate Quartermaster."

"That right?" Mr. Meeks said. "Well, folks down here have done a little sacrificin', too. Lost a goodly number of sons and brothers in Company H of the Eighteenth Virginia. In Pickett's Charge at Gettysburg."

Gettysburg! I fell silent. Gettysburg had been a real hog-killing, with over 20,000 wounded, killed, and missing on our side. The Yankees had lost 23,000.

"I'm sorry our family didn't have a son old enough to get killed at Gettysburg, Mr. Meeks," I said. I was near to crying.

"Now, Mr. Meeks, you've baited them long enough." Ellen Bryant stepped forward and took my hand. "We have plenty of dress patterns at our house. I'd be honored if you'd stop by with your sister." She embraced me.

I was trembling. "Don't pay mind to that old ram," she whispered in my ear. Then she embraced Maria. "Welcome to Appomattox Court House. I'm afraid we've all forgotten our manners. I wanted to call, but figured on letting you all get settled in."

Mr. Meeks muttered something and turned away. The shop door opened and someone came in. "Hello, Thomas Tibbs," she said. "Come meet our new neighbors."

I turned. And it was well worth the effort. For the young man in the shop doorway was a sight to behold. He was tall and fair of hair and blue of eye. He sported a thin mustache and his hat was pinned up on one side with a plume of a feather. He was dressed all in gray. His boots were polished as for a quadrille. He wore gauntlets and a sword and though it was not an official getup, I knew it was a uniform.

He immediately swept off the hat, bowed, and reached for my hand to kiss. Then he kissed Maria's. It was done so effortlessly, I scarcely had time to blush.

"I hope you all are being properly cared for on your first visit to our store," he said.

His voice was husky, with just enough of a drawl to ice over the note of authority.

"They aren't." Ellen sighed. "Mr. Meeks is being . . . well, he's being Mr. Meeks."

Thomas Tibbs scowled. "Have the young ladies been assisted in their purchases?" he asked Mr. Meeks.

"They don't see anything that suits their fancy," he growled.

"We'd like the mail," I said.

Mr. Meeks shuffled over to the mailboxes, took some letters and handed them to me.

"Ladies, may I walk you home?" Thomas Tibbs inquired graciously. "Ellen, will you join us?"

In the next moment we were outside in the bright September sunlight. Thomas and Ellen looked at each other and burst into laughter. Oh, they're sweet on each other, I thought. And I felt a stab of disappointment.

"Are you the Thomas Tibbs who is brother to Eddie?" Maria asked.

"I suppose I have to claim that responsibility," he said.

"Your little brother told ours that you're waiting to get into Mosby's Rangers," Maria said.

He nodded, assenting silently.

"Did you know that John Mosby's parents lived in Charlottesville, and we met them?" Maria pushed.

"I know everything there is to know about John Singleton Mosby," Thomas Tibbs said in a reverent tone. "Except when I'm going to get the call."

"I heard they're a vain lot of dandies," Maria teased.

"Well," and Ellen nudged Maria, "just look at that plume in Tom's hat. And the shine on his boots. He's been a dandy-in-training for months now."

"Are you two sweethearts?" Maria inquired.

I blushed for my sister. How could she be so bold? I hadn't said a word since leaving the store. I was tongue-tied, suddenly.

Ellen and Thomas hooted with laughter. "Hardly," Tom said, "she's like a sister. Always at my house, plotting with my sister Elvira about beaus."

"I never plot over beaus," Ellen retorted. "Because all the young men are in the army and I'll never give my heart to a soldier. It would impoverish my spirit."

"I could tell you how it impoverishes the spirit," Maria said with wisdom beyond her years.

"We *heard* you were betrothed to a Yankee," Ellen whispered. "Your Mary Ann told us."

"Is there anything Mary Ann *hasn't* told about us?" I asked. "No wonder people hereabouts hate us."

"They don't hate you," Tom explained. "They're hurting from losing so many boys at Gettysburg. And with the final surrender of Vicksburg to Grant at the same time they're beset with hopelessness. And shortages. And like at our house you all have got nigra servants. Many of the nigra servants hereabouts have been drafted into public service."

"They can have our Mary Ann," I said.

"Your Mary Ann's made friends with Claibourne Humbles, the free nigra shoemaker. And some of the other free nigras around here," Tom said.

"Free nigras?" I asked.

"Sure. We got a few. Like Mary Christian. She owned her own husband for a while. Set him free ten years ago, she did. You two sure don't know much about this place. Haven't you met anybody else in town but us?"

We both admitted we hadn't.

"Well then, I'm inviting you to Ellen's house of an evening. She plays the harp like an angel. She teaches music to the little ones hereabouts. I'll bring my fiddle."

"I play the piano," Maria said.

She and Ellen talked about music. And I was glad

Maria had found a friend. With Michah so far off in the fighting, she often became despondent. Though I was jealous, too.

At our front gate Thomas looked down at me. "I hear tell your little brother is to attend the local one-room school with my brother. Mr. Isbell is a good teacher, but my mama wants my little sisters tutored at home. Your stepdaddy said you'd done some tutoring. Do you think you could do it? We'd pay real handsome like."

I looked up at him. He reminded me of someone. Alex, I decided. He had that same tall and gallant presence, that same dash, that same mix of stately tradition and boyish charm. But there was something different about him, something all his own, that set him apart from Alex.

I could not think what and, truth to tell, it didn't concern me right then. I only knew that for the first time since I'd said goodbye to Alex, I felt alive in the company of a man.

"Can you take a fence on a horse?" I asked.

He laughed. "You can't get into Mosby's Rangers unless you can ride without stirrups, charge, slash at an opponent with your saber while hanging half off your horse, and fly over fences."

I smiled. "Perhaps you could come to tea tomorrow with your mama and we can discuss my tutoring your sisters. You come too, Ellen."

That evening I sought Mary Ann out in the log cabin kitchen. "You've got to stop roaming all over town telling people our business," I told her quietly and firmly. "I'm sure Will McLean would say the same thing if he were here."

She was kneading some bread dough. To my surprise, she was submissive. "If'n he talked to me," she said. "Massa Will put Mary Ann in the house afta y'all left Yorkshire. But he never talk to me."

So. I absorbed that in silence and nodded. "He's a merchant," I told her, "and people hereabouts are suffering from shortages. You're only harming us telling our affairs."

She nodded. "Still gonna see my friend, Claibourne Humbles."

"You can see him all you want," I snapped. "Just don't tell our business!"

Chapter 22

September to December 1863

In the next three months we became so entrenched in life at Appomattox Court House it was hard to believe we'd ever lived anywhere else. The little village had its own rhythms and shadings of light. We fell into routines. Willie attended school; Maria took to teaching music with Ellen Bryant. I tutored the Tibbs girls, who were eight and six, along with Lula.

Every morning Thomas came to fetch me. Many nights Lula and I were invited to supper at the Tibbs house. Afterward, Tom would bring out his maps and we would study them.

"Mosby's renewed operations against the O and A Railroad," he told us one October night. "It's become the lifeline of Yankee General Meade's army, along the Rapidan River."

He showed us where Mosby and his men were scouting—as far as Falls Church, near Alexandria. He traced my old home territory at Manassas on the map, where Lee's Army of Northern Virginia was pushing Yankee General Meade back.

His mother, Nancy, would just sit there with her needlework and listen. His father, Jacob, the white-haired patriarch, was indulgent with Tom, who at twenty-four was his father's joy. But his father clearly was not entranced with Mosby or the war. The elder Tibbs called Mosby "a marauder with a license to kill." And sometimes they would argue.

Tom would say that Mosby was just like Francis Marion in the American Revolution.

"Are Abraham Lincoln's sons on the battlefield?" old Jacob asked one night.

"His son Robert goes to Harvard," Nancy Tibbs said.

"No president's sons go on the battlefield," Jacob Tibbs insisted.

But it was a good family, despite these disagreements over war, which I supposed every family, Northern or Southern, was having these days. I liked the rough and tumble household, which consisted of Tom's brother Elburton, twelve; John, eighteen; the two little girls; and Elvira. I liked the constant presence of the white-haired father, the quiet strength of the mother.

Nancy Tibbs thought the cruelest trick of the war was the law the Confederacy had allowing planters with twenty slaves or more to be exempt from serving in the army. "If you want a way of life, you should be willing to fight for it," she said.

"The war isn't over slavery, Mama," Thomas told her. And oh, where had I heard that before?

"Son," Nancy said, "go with Mosby if you must. I understand they are gallant men for all the controversy surrounding them. Have your adventure. Your father dreamed of going West in the '40s and never did and always regretted it. But don't tell me this isn't a fight over slavery. And don't tell yourself that, either."

The Tibbs had eleven nigras working the corn and tobacco fields.

Since August, the Yankees had been bombarding Fort Sumter in Charleston Harbor. By Christmas, when the guns were still bellowing against Sumter and hope was lessening in the South, three things happened in our household.

Maria wanted to run away. Button somehow got a letter through to us. And Mary Ann came to me with a problem.

> My dear Oscie, *Button wrote,* The days and months have flown by without my putting pen in hand for my own pleasure. But this does not mean I do not think of all of you.
>
> The War Department has finally decided to take responsibility for the sanitation in this city. We are beset by *smells.* I blame the lack of sanitation for the outbreak of smallpox last winter. They say that the president himself had a light case. I think disease is now a greater threat to us than war. But we nurses have been using our influence to get the Sanitary Corps and local physicians to take heed of what we say. And now, finally, municipal garbage wagons are carting off the piles of hideous waste that have accumulated.
>
> But I am so weary of this war, dear Oscie. I am tired of young men dying in front of my eyes. How much longer will it go on?

I am glad to know you all are established in your fine new home. Can you remember those days when we sat in the schoolroom at Yorkshire and discussed the life of Elizabeth Barrett and Robert Browning? My dear, it was another world. Hold fast, that is all I can advise. We will all create a new world again when this is over. And know our dream of being able to see one another again . . .

I was interrupted in my reading of Button's letter by a commotion downstairs.

Maria was sobbing. The same mail that had brought Button's missive had delivered one from Michah.

"You must let me go! You must! I'll write to Mrs. McGuffey. She'll go with me." Maria was carrying on like a banshee in the parlor.

"I can't do that, Maria," Mama said. "Travel is dangerous, no matter who goes with you."

"I'm going to *marry* Michah!" Maria sobbed. "And he needs me now, Mama, please."

At Maria's feet on the red-and-green ingrain carpet, were the pages of the letter. I picked them up.

Michah had been wounded in the shoulder, fighting at Missionary Ridge in the battle for Chattanooga. No bones were splintered, however.

I put my arms around my sister. "Button is a nurse. She has told me that wounds are not so bad if the bones aren't splintered."

"Button! Who cares what she says?" She pulled away from me. "Can't you take my side for once and convince Mama to let me go? You've got your Thomas!"

Her request seemed as unreasonable to me as her

statement about Thomas.

"He isn't *my* Thomas," I said.

She turned on me like a cat in the barnyard. "You could at least be honest! And not deny you're smitten with him. It's the same as it was with you and Alex! At least I'm honest about my feelings, Oscie. And sooner or later, you're going to have to be, too!"

"You're hurting Mama," I reminded her. "You know she can't allow you to go running off to Tennessee."

"When Daddy Will comes home for Christmas he'll let me go!" She ran from the room. For the next two days she refused to come out. She screamed at Maum Hanna who brought trays of food up. She slammed doors and kept the household in turmoil, and I wished Will McLean would come home soon. He wouldn't hold with such behavior.

It was up to me then to do something about it. So I asked Ellen Bryant to come to our house and talk to Maria. She allowed Ellen into her room and Ellen stayed there for a while. Then they came out together. And Maria joined the world again. She went back to her music teaching, wrote endless letters to Michah, but spoke no more of going to Tennessee. And although she didn't speak much to the rest of us either, the crisis subsided.

Only to be replaced by another one.

The very day Maria came out of her room, Mary Ann sought me out. I'd just come in from tutoring, with Lula in tow. It was an ungodly cold day, for that winter turned out to be the coldest they'd ever had in Appomattox. Lula had the sniffles and I turned her right over to Maum Hanna to be put to bed and doctored.

I had the devil's own headache and all I wanted

was something hot and to go to bed myself. But as I was taking my cloak off in the hall, Mary Ann glided in. She handed me a cup of hot chocolate and took my wrap.

She seldom came in from the servants' quarters out back. I was grateful for the hot chocolate, and a little embarrassed at her solicitude, too.

"Talk to you," she said. She still had that old shawl wrapped around her. It was all threadbare now. Like our hopes, I thought dismally.

"Now? I'm weary."

"There be no more sugar," she said.

I knew our sugar supply had been diminishing. Then two days ago the stationmaster at the depot had sent a note saying a shipment of goods was waiting for us. It had come from Lynchburg.

It fell to me to see that our family got the goods, of course. But I'd put the matter off. Because I also knew the shipment would include all the necessities people were going without around here. Not only sugar, but coffee, tea, writing paper, and some medicines.

Daddy Will had written to Mama telling her of the supplies and advising her not to share them with anyone.

How could I now bring home this vital bounty and not share it? Before coming here I never really understood what it took to keep a family fed. McLean had always taken care of this. But now I saw people truly suffering.

Mrs. Tibbs frequently got bad headaches that only strong coffee would cure. The Tibbs had so often shared their table with me and Lula. And what of Ellen Bryant? Her family was doing without, also.

Mary Ann stood there, placid, waiting. She read

my thoughts, I wagered. She knew more about what went on in the village than I, since she spent all her spare time with that free nigra, Claibourne Humbles.

"Christmas comin'," she said. "Your mama and the chillens got a right to what Massa sent."

"I don't need you to tell me that, Mary Ann."

"You best git to the depot an' pick it up. Mary Ann go wif' you, if'n you like. Claibourne will come, too."

"I don't need Claibourne."

"You best take somebody."

"Why?"

"Doan wanna ask Claibourne, ask Thomas." She smiled. "He be sweet on you. Claibourne say . . . "

My face flamed. "Mind your own business about Thomas," I snapped.

She fell silent. And the memory of Alex rose between us.

"We'll go for the shipment tomorrow," I said. "Hiram can drive us. You may come, if you wish. But don't tell anyone else, you hear?"

"I hears," she said.

Chapter 23

December 1863

Hiram drove the next morning, Mary Ann sat beside me. There was a hint of snow in the air. We had just passed Benjamin Robert's house, with the depot in sight, when I saw the crowd at the depot.

"Is a train due, Hiram?" He knew the schedule.

"Not that I knows of, Miz Oscie."

"I tol' you, we shudda brought Claibourne," Mary Ann said. "Or your Thomas."

I turned to her. "Did you know all these people were going to be here?"

She shrugged. "Mary Ann didn't tell nobody 'bout the shipment. Claibourne, *he* says the stationmaster did."

"Why didn't you let me know?"

"Mary Ann try to tell you what Claibourne say," she murmured. "You tell me to mind my own business."

So I had. I sighed.

There were at least a dozen people on the platform and, as they turned to look at us, I saw they were angry. I didn't know any of them, but I recognized some faces. Many times they'd passed us on the street without so much as a hello.

"We might as well go and get this over with," I told Mary Ann and Hiram. "Just let's tend to our business. Don't act afraid."

Hiram guided me with a hand under my elbow, up the steps. The crowd formed two lines for us to walk through. I could see our shipment at the other end of the platform.

Everyone was glaring at us, stonily. To the side, behind one of the lines of faces, were several nigras.

"They be Mary Christian an' her people," Mary Ann whispered. "They help us if need be."

With Hiram guiding me and Mary Ann on the other side, we walked through the double line, to the stationmaster's window.

"I heard tell," one man said as we passed, "that there be some medicines in that shipment. You could use some for your patients, couldn't you, Doctor Bernard?"

"Sure could," came the reply.

"What 'bout you, Obediah," the same voice inquired. "Couldn't you use some sugar or coffee in your house?"

"Some of us ain't so lucky as to have family members who kin get anything at any price," came an answer. "And who drive the prices up by speculating."

Oh, I thought I would die! It reminded me of the ugly crowd at the dentist's office in Alexandria! How I wished Will McLean were here with his brass-handled revolver! My legs trembled beneath me.

But Hiram and Mary Ann stood close. At the stationmaster's window, the man peered out. "Come for your goods, Miss McLean?"

"Name's Mason," I said. "I have come for my mama's shipment. Her name is Virginia McLean."

He pushed the manifest through the bars at me. "Sign. And you'd best get it all out of here right quick, before a riot starts. You got help to get it on the wagon?"

There were at least four large crates. "Couldn't you have put them at the other end of the platform?" I asked.

"Could of, I suppose." He grinned wickedly.

I surveyed the crates dismally. Had Will McLean sent half the dry goods and foodstuffs in Lynchburg? I looked at Hiram, then at Mary Ann.

"We'll manage," Hiram said.

But I knew that Hiram was too old, Mary Ann too skinny, and I not strong enough. It was then that the elderly Mary Christian and her friends stepped forward.

"People of Appomattox Court House," she said in a soft voice, "This child and her family are new to us. Can't we help her?"

She was a frail woman, who looked as if she'd seen all there was to see in life. But she had a dignity about her.

The man named Obediah stepped forward, brandishing a gun, blocking the way of the five darkies with Mary Christian who'd stepped forward to help. "Back off there, nigger," he said to one of them. "All the rest of you, too. You may be freedmen, that's your affair. This is our affair. This little gal's stepdaddy is a speculator. Thanks to people like him, a woman on the street in Richmond paid $70.00 for a barrel of flour t'other day. And we can't get some goods, even with money. We look like vagabonds. Yet in the cities, the thieving quartermasters and speculators look sleek and well-fed."

It was quite a speech. The darkies backed off.

"I'd suggest you be the one to back off, Mr. Jenkins."

The familiar voice pulled me out of a swoon, just as I thought I would faint. I turned. Coming up the platform steps was Thomas Tibbs, like some medieval knight in one of Sir Walter Scott's novels. His boots were shined to a fare-thee-well, his Colt revolver drawn, just as Daddy Will's had been that day so long ago in Alexandria. Thomas's hat was cocked at just the right angle.

With him was Claibourne Humbles.

"Jesus be praised, thought they'd never get here," Mary Ann whispered.

Thomas moved across the platform, parting the double line of people, like Moses parting the waters. "Put the gun away, Obediah," he ordered quietly.

The man called Obediah did so. Then Thomas came to stand beside me. "Anybody else want to stop Miss Mason from claiming what's hers?"

"You ought to be ashamed, Thomas," one woman shouted. "You're about to join Mosby. And now you stand with people who are making money on the Confederacy!"

"I stand for people's rights," Tom said quietly. "We've come to a pretty pass here in the South when we have to keep from our neighbors what's theirs."

"I heard that Mosby and his men divide up all the booty they capture," another man put in.

"That's right," Tom answered. "Mosby shares his spoils. But these aren't my spoils to share. They belong to Virginia McLean, a fine lady. She and her family gave generously to the Confederacy back at

First Manassas. Now, there will be no further discussion. Disperse!"

Some of them moved, some didn't.

"Suit yourselves," Tom said. "You can stay here 'til hell freezes over. But if anyone makes a move to stop these good people from loading this shipment, you'll answer to me."

Oh, I was so proud of Thomas! And there on that train platform he stood with that Colt revolver drawn as Mary Christian's people and Claibourne Humbles loaded the crates onto our wagon. Then he turned to Mary herself.

"Thank you, Mother," he said. "Your presence here has been gratifying. Go home now, before it snows."

Mary and her husband and friends got into their own wagon. I ran over to it as they were about to depart. "I'm beholden to you," I said, looking up at Mary.

Her hair, under the gray blanket, was white. Her clothing was shabby, but of better quality than that worn by slaves. Her eyes entranced me. They were so young in such an old face.

"We did what we thought was right," she said.

"I want you to have some coffee. And sugar. May I bring some to your house?"

"We didn't do this for reward," she said.

"But I want to show my appreciation. Please?"

She smiled and nodded. "If it makes you happy, child. Mr. Humbles knows where we live."

I watched them drive off. Thomas was standing on the edge of the platform. Claibourne Humbles was on his horse at the foot of the steps, holding the reins of Thomas's horse.

"Thank you ladies and gentlemen of Appomattox Court House," Thomas said. "Your performance here today was most entertaining." Then he took off his hat with the plume and bowed.

Oh, he was so dashing!

Then he was on his horse accompanying us home. Snow was starting to fall. Tom suggested we not look back, for some people were still gathered on the platform, staring after us.

"I'm beholden to you and Claibourne for your help," I said, as our wagon pulled away from the depot. Then I noticed Claibourne wasn't with him. Neither was Mary Ann.

Tom smiled. "They've gone off. Wouldn't have known enough to come if your Mary Ann hadn't told me. Claibourne got word the locals were planning trouble. He told Mary Ann and she got word to me and Mary Christian and her people."

"As soon as I get home, I'm making the biggest pot of coffee and inviting you in," I said. "And I'm sending some coffee home to your mama."

"Your stepdaddy may not like that," he advised.

"Well, he'll have to. Especially when I tell him what happened today."

I had made my mind up. Will McLean had left me in charge, more or less. It wasn't right that I should have the responsibilities and not the freedom to make my own determinations.

I'd made my mind up about something else too. I had to make amends with Mary Ann. She'd tried to tell me trouble was coming and I'd shut her up. If not for her, there would have been what-for to pay at the depot today. If she hadn't asked Tom, Claibourne, and Mary Christian and her people to help, we probably would have lost our shipment of goods.

I was going to have to eat humble pie with Mary Ann. And thank her. I'd do it tonight, I decided.

That afternoon, after Thomas unpacked the shipment for us, I made up a package of supplies for his family.

"I like taking a stand," I told him. "Didn't know it could make a body feel so good. Makes me wonder why people don't take stands more often. It feels right sharing these supplies with good people."

We were saying goodbye in our front hall. "You've discovered what men have known for a long time," he said.

"It's unfair for you men to have all the sport in making decisions and leave us women out."

"Ah, but isn't that what the South is all about? Us men taking care of our womenfolk?"

"Sometimes I don't know what the South is about anymore, Tom."

"A lot of people are of the same mind these days."

"And you? Do you know what the South and the war are about?" I asked.

He nodded gravely. "I'm out for the adventure of it, before it ends. That's why I'm joining Mosby. As for the South," he shook his head. "Our way of life is fast disappearing, Oscie. I can't bother my head wondering if it's right or not. It's all I've ever known, and I'll defend it long as I can. That's why I want to hunt Yankees. Want to make them sorry they ever came down here spoilin' for a fight. I want to wear gray and rise out of the mists to charge at them when they least expect it."

I gazed up at this handsome young man. And for the moment I saw Alex again, wearing gray and rising out of the mists to charge at the Yankees. I shivered.

"Do you think we can win the war, Tom?"

"Don't know about that. Let the generals worry it. Just know I want to give the Yankees something to remember, even if we don't win. Just want to be a part of it all while I can. This war could be the last great adventure we all get a shot at. What happens afterwards, happens. Why worry about it now?"

There was the difference between him and Alex. Tom knew we were lost, too, but he was taking part for the honest adventure of it. I'd just as lief be around that kind of person when the losing came, as anybody. Because, like Will McLean, he had no illusions about the South. He'd be able to face whatever came next. And as for giving the Yankees something to remember, why something told me that Thomas Tibbs could give as good as he could get.

"You've never said a word to me about my stepdaddy's speculating."

"None of my business, Oscie. This war has done strange things to people. Man's lost his plantation to the war. He's taking care of his family, is all. How he does it, makes no never mind to me. And it sure doesn't change the way I feel about you."

I stared up at him.

"You must know how I feel by now," he said.

"You never told me, Thomas."

He blushed. "I'm not quick with girls."

"I don't like men who are quick with girls."

"Oh, Oscie, I've been smitten since the first day we met."

"Well, Thomas, you could have fooled me."

"I hung back from the telling. Mary Ann says you're languishing over that Alex fellow up to Manassas."

"I did love Alex," I allowed. "Still do, a bit, I

guess. I don't know, Tom. I'm all confused. You remind me of him to a point. But then after that point, the real you comes through. More than the real Alex ever did."

He laughed. "Do you think you could love the real me, if you put your mind to it?"

He had to put down the sacks of sugar and coffee then. Because, though he could hold off a mob at the depot with no trouble, even he couldn't kiss a girl with his arms full of contraband.

After everyone was in bed that night, I sent for Mary Ann. I told Maum Hanna to have her come downstairs to the warming kitchen.

She came. This time I had the hot chocolate all ready. She stood in the door of the kitchen shyly, that old shawl wrapped around her. I invited her in, lighted candles, and bade her get two cups out of the corner cupboard. Then we sat. From the pantry I also produced some large round sugar cookies which Lula had baked late that afternoon.

"The cookies are good," she said. "Lula should be proud."

I nodded and watched her sip her chocolate. She knew I wanted something but was wary, waiting.

"I want to thank you for asking Tom and Claibourne and Mary Christian and her people to come to the depot this morning," I said.

She nodded.

"Why did you do it? You didn't have to. You could have had me hanging there at that depot, like a possum hanging from a tree, with dogs yapping underneath."

"I wuz in that tree, too," she said.

Our eyes met, solemnly for a moment. Then in the

next moment we both laughed.

"Still, I owe you," I said.

She shook her head. "No. I owes you. Fer Sarah. And fer tellin' Massa Will 'bout Alex. If'n I cud make up for it all, I would."

"What about what I did to you, keeping my mouth shut when I knew you were having a baby?"

She shrugged. "Massa wud a sold me."

"I could have talked him out of that. All I had to do was tell him Mama didn't want it."

We both sat there pondering the whole of it, like some old quilt we'd just taken out of an attic, faded and worn, with patches that were added every whichway, without pattern or reason.

"Trust doan come easy," she said. "We both done mean things to each other."

"I was supposed to know better, Mary Ann. But we started out wrong. When you came to Yorkshire, I had so many fears. I was still missing my daddy. And Will McLean came along. I didn't want him around. But I couldn't do anything about that, so I took everything out on you."

"No matter. What's done is done." She spoke with great dignity. Her hair was almost all white now. How old was she, I wondered? "We've both seen a lot," she said. "I 'spect we're gonna see lots more. Better if'n we're friends. Kin help each other."

I sighed. "We need all the friends we can get in this place."

"I ain't tol' your mama 'bout your givin' some of the goods away," she offered.

"It doesn't matter. I'll tell Mama. And Daddy Will."

"You kin trust me. 'Bout time you learned it."

I swallowed a mouthful of hot chocolate. I ached

with tiredness. It had been a full day. But something was happening here and I had to pay mind to it. "I know that now," I said.

We sat for a moment in silence. Then she smiled. "I wuz right 'bout Thomas, wasn't I?"

I blushed. "Yes. I don't know where my eyes were concerning Thomas."

"Sometimes we is the last to know when somebody loves us," she said. "He be a fine man. Claibourne holds him in high esteem."

"Claibourne is a fine man, too. But I must ask you something, Mary Ann. Don't you still consider yourself married to Allie?"

She shook her head, no. Then from under her apron she pulled out a letter. It was old and wrinkled. "This wuz written to me last June. Finally caught up wif me here, last October. Mary Christian read it to me."

I read the letter quickly. It was from a Confederate officer. It told how Allie had been killed in General Grant's second assault on Vicksburg last May.

"Vicksburg?" I asked.

She nodded. "Everybody say Allie run away from me. He run, all right, but not from me. He run at First Manassas, when he wuz sent out from Massa Will to go look for forage. Went to join the Yankees. They used him to build forta-cations."

"Fortifications," I said.

She smiled. "He wuz wif Gen'l Butler in Hampton, Virginia, in August of '61. That's the last I heard from him. Confederates said Yankees were usin' town for runaway slaves an' burned it. They took Allie back as a slave. I wuz still at Yorkshire. The rebels, they made him work the same way. Buildin' forta-cations. An' that's what he wuz doin' for them at Vicksburg, last May, when he wuz killed."

"I'm sorry, Mary Ann," I said.

"Coupla months after I got here I knew I wuz a widow. At first Claibourne was just a friend. Then he be more."

"Are you going to marry him, Mary Ann?"

She shook her head. "Hafta get permission from Massa Will. Claibourne want to buy me."

"You mean own you? Like Mary Christian owned her husband?"

"Tha's right."

"Will McLean would never sell you, Mary Ann. But he might set you free now."

"Massa Will, he won't even talk to me," she said sadly.

"I'll ask him for you, if you want."

"Thank you. But Mary Christian say be better if Claibourne buys me. Wuz safer wif her husband that way when he wuz young. Onliest reason she set him free wuz cause he be so old now, no white man gonna want him no more."

I nodded. I was tired, cold, and couldn't think. But I knew one thing. This was my chance to make up to Mary Ann for everything I'd done to her. No, I couldn't get her babies back. Nobody could do that. But she needed me now, like I'd needed her earlier this day.

"I'm going to visit Mary Christian tomorrow," I said. "I'll talk to her about it. And I'll see that Will McLean does right by you, Mary Ann. I promise."

Chapter 24

Mary Christian was waiting for me on her front porch. "Glad to see you," she said.

Inside her house she introduced me to her aged husband, Stephen. Then the other members of her "family." I recognized them as the people who'd helped us yesterday on the platform.

I gave her sugar and coffee. She put the coffee right on and took a fresh cornbread out of the oven. After we'd eaten and the dark smiling faces went off to other parts of the house, I looked at her.

"Mary Ann wants to marry Claibourne Humbles," I said. "I could ask my stepdaddy to free her."

She nodded. "For a nigra to take freedom at the wrong time could be bad. I bought my husband in 1850 and didn't free him 'til he was too old to be of use to any white man."

"That's what Mary Ann told me."

"Let me tell you about slavery," she said. "In March of 1862, the Yankee Congress forbade their military to return runaway slaves to their masters. Slaves were runnin' to the Yankee Army. Nobody know what to do with 'em. Then the Yankee Congress said no more slavery in Washington City. Then they said persons of African descent could go into the military. Then Mr. Lincoln makes his Emancipation. But freedom don't come from words on a piece of paper. Freedom's got to come from inside the slaves themselves."

I listened carefully.

"Slaves gotta understand this freedom. Be ready to take it at the right time. The right time is different for everybody. Some places, deep in the South, where master is away fighting, the slaves face their mistress and demand she pay wages or set them free."

I was downright astonished. Things *were* changing.

"Some places in deep South, when rebel owners of plantations flee before Yankees arrive, the slaves stay and set up their own households and farm the plantations. The slaves knew this freedom was coming. Just waiting for the right moment, is all."

"Yes," I agreed.

"In many places in the South, nigra men are sent away by the government to work on fortifications. Like Mary Ann's Allie. These men have never been off their plantation before. They know nothing of freedom. They've been kept *ignorant.*"

She spat the word out. "So they go up to Richmond or Manassas to fortify and dig and work. They meet other nigras. They *learn.* They come home and wait."

"Yes," I breathed, understanding now.

"Allie should have come home and waited. He didn't. Took his freedom at the wrong time. Confederates took him again. Mr. Lincoln made his Emancipation, but it didn't hold here in the South. Won't hold 'til Yankees win the war. If Mary Ann is free, she could be sold back into slavery by some mean and vicious white Confederate. Even free papers don't help, if she's in the wrong place at the wrong time."

"So Will McLean should sell her to Claibourne," I said.

She smiled. "Thas' right. Now you're learning." She stood up and patted my head. "I been free since 1840. The burden of being free and nigra is to know. And to teach others. If I don't do that, I don't deserve my freedom."

We went out onto her porch. Before I got back into my wagon she looked at me. "Mary Ann said your stepdaddy came here to get away from the war," she said.

"Yes."

"Nobody can do that. This war too big to hide from. No human being alive can hold back the tide sweeping the slaves toward freedom."

I shivered. She peered at me intently, drew me to her and kissed me. "Thank you for coming. If you know something, you are prepared. Thank you for the sugar and coffee. But thank you more for your visit."

Just before Christmas, Thomas was called up by Mosby. He would leave the first week in January. It was a bittersweet time for us. He was so happy, yet sad at leaving me. And I couldn't bear to think of him going. But his happiness was so true that I wanted to share it with him.

"When your stepdaddy comes home for Christmas, I'll speak with him and ask permission for us to become betrothed," he promised.

Will McLean came home on Christmas Eve. We had a family reunion supper. I'd helped Maria and

Willie and Lula to decorate the house with greenery and holly berries, ribbons, lace, and popcorn. Will McLean had brought gifts: foodstuffs in cans, delicacies like canned sardines and oysters, French mustard, jars of hard candy, Yankee cheese, and pickles. Yankee soup in cans, too.

And real needles, which were so scarce now that women were making them from hawthorne bushes. He brought tea, fresh fruit, a new rag doll for Lula, dolls for Nannie, a toy train for Willie, ribbons and books and parasols for Maria and me.

"The *Banshee* ran the blockade and put into port before I left Richmond," he told us. "She was in from Bermuda, where she'd taken Southern cotton. As part of her return cargo, she brought 600,000 rifles. These goods I bought, helped make her trip financially possible."

But Will McLean brought something else with him, too. On Christmas morning, at breakfast, he handed Maria a letter from Michah.

Miraculously, it had come with him and the mail on the same train, to Appomattox.

Maria read it to us, in a clear, unfaltering voice, leaving out the personal parts, of course. And we sat in silence as Michah's words brought the war into our peaceful Christmas morning dining room.

". . . around Chattanooga, a barrel of flour is going for $250.00. A pair of shoes for $800. You all heard about Chickamauga? I was there in September. Your General Bragg hit us hard. President Lincoln's brother-in-law died in that fight. He was a Confederate general. So there we were, bottled up in Chattanooga afterward and the bad rains came.

"One soldier said they weren't any shilly-shallying Presbyterian rains, but a gen-u-ine Baptist downpour. We had little to eat. We were on half rations. And then Grant came."

Maria paused. Maum Hanna was dishing out eggs and ham and biscuits. Hiram was serving hot coffee. We all looked at each other, then Maria continued.

"I've got this cough still, from those bad rains. Everybody in camp has it. Sounds like drumming when we wake in the morning. Well, things got better when Grant came. He had a pontoon bridge laid across the Tennessee River and set up a 'cracker line,' to get food to us. It was sixty miles long."

I saw tears in Mama's eyes as Maria read this.

"Battle of Chattanooga began in late November. Your General Bragg's line extended for six miles on the crest of the ridge, but we Yankees wanted to avenge our losses at Chickamauga. You see, we took an awful beating there. So we fought our way through pits and up the summit. 'Bout sixty Yankee flags advanced up that ridge. We were all screaming, 'Chickamauga! Chickamauga!'"

Maria had to stop and wipe her eyes. She could not

go on. She handed the letter to me and I continued reading.

> "We took four thousand Reb prisoners, but it's not over yet. Your Lee is so determined. Do you know, my dear Maria, that Lee owns no slaves? Do you know that Lincoln gave a two-minute speech at Gettysburg last fall and they still had dead horses on the battlefield? Do you know that Reb soldiers are deserting all over the place? They just pick up and go home. Get letters from home saying there's nothing to eat, so they just skedaddle. Can't blame them."

I stopped reading and looked at the bounty of food laid out on our table. Maria reached for the letter and I handed it back.

> "On Missionary Ridge at Chattanooga," *she read*, "there was this crazy lieutenant from the 24th Wisconsin. No more than eighteen. Ran right up that ridge with his unit's colors, screaming, 'On Wisconsin!' Said his name was Arthur MacArthur Jr. They say the whole family's just as dedicated.
> "Why am I telling you these things, Maria. Not to worry you. I am fine after my shoulder wound. I am mending in all but my heartsickness for you. I . . . "

Here Maria broke off and put the letter down. "Dear God," Mama murmured. "What are we doing fighting this war? Does anybody know?"

I waited outside the parlor. It was the day after Christmas. Inside, Will McLean was talking with Thomas, who had come to ask permission for us to become betrothed.

Maria came down the stairs. "Oh, Oscie, I hope he says yes. I want us all to be happy."

I stared at her. A certain peace seemed to have come over Maria since she received Michah's letter. "How can you be happy when you haven't seen Michah in so long?"

"He was wounded twice, Oscie, and survived. So I just know it will be all right. He said in the rest of his letter that now that the Yankees won at Chattanooga, they can move into Georgia and divide the Confederacy. Oh, Oscie, I know Tom's a Confederate, but the only way we'll all be happy is if it's all over soon!"

I hugged her and agreed. I wanted that, too. Her innocent sentiments struck right at the chord of my misery and we held each other. Then the door opened and Thomas came out.

I could tell right off that Will McLean had said no. I looked past Tom. "Daddy Will?"

"Come in here, both of you."

When the doors closed, he spoke quietly to me. "I like your Thomas, Oscie. And I've told him so. But I don't like Mosby."

I struggled to understand. "What does *Mosby* have to do with this?"

"Yankee General Sherman says that men who fight guerilla warfare are the most dangerous set of men that this war has turned loose on the world," he recited quietly.

The fire in the hearth crackled. I felt sick.

"Sherman says war suits them. That they are fine and brave riders and bold to being rash. He says they don't bother their brains about past, present or future."

Thomas held my hand.

"I know your Thomas isn't like that," Will McLean went on. "But he'll have to *become* like that to stay alive."

I found my voice. "He'll always be my Thomas," I said.

Will McLean smiled wryly. "I want to believe that, Oscie. But there is another reason and I've told it to Thomas. You must consider your family. You must do what is right and good for all."

I looked from McLean to Tom, then to McLean again.

"The Yankees are beside themselves with fury because of Mosby's actions against them," McLean went on. "They take that fury out on local citizens who are in any way in league with Mosby. When things turn bad for us here in the South, there will be reprisals against those connected with Mosby."

My mouth went dry. I was trembling.

"I brought my family here to get away from the war, Oscie. It came to our very house at Manassas. I don't want it here."

I strangled back a sob. "Tell him, Tom, about Mosby's fairness and how he protects civilians and sometimes is the only law in some places. Tell him!"

"Your stepdaddy is wrong about Mosby," Tom said softly. "But not about the way Yankees feel about anybody connected with him. We love each other, Oscie. In our hearts, we're promised. That's all that matters."

What was he saying?

Then, right in front of Will McLean, bold as a brass-handled monkey, he put his arms around me and kissed me. "Hold your fire for now," he whispered, using the phrase I'd told him Button had once said.

I could not speak for a moment. But I did not have to. Tom's kiss said everything for both of us. I stole a glance at Will McLean. He was lighting a cheroot, pretending disinterest.

Then Thomas stood, drawing himself up in full military fashion. "I only want what's best for Oscie, sir."

"Thank you," Will McLean said. "I have no wish to hurt her. But I think if you two love one another, it will hold."

He walked Tom to the door, reminded him he was coming back for supper, and came back into the room to move the logs in the fire with a poker.

"I don't care what you say," I told him. "In my heart I'm betrothed."

He came to me and took my cold hand in his big warm one. "It isn't like last time when I asked you to break with Alex completely," he said. "See Tom while he's here, love him, write to him when he goes, Oscie. But wait and see if you still love him when the war is over."

My chin quivered with emotion.

"Men who band together for guerilla warfare soon lose the veneer of civilization. They lose their individual conscience to the group."

"Tom won't."

"I pray you're right, Oscie. And I know what I've asked of you. I wouldn't have asked it, if I didn't believe that we're doomed here in the South. We're being pressed back. It's only a matter of time until disaster. I'm trying my best to keep that disaster from touching our house."

"Mary Christian says the war is too big for anyone to hide from."

He eyed me, waiting.

"She said no human being alive can hold back the tide sweeping the slaves toward freedom."

"Speak your piece, Oscie Mason. What are you getting at?"

"I'm always giving in for the good of the family. Always the one told to bide my time and do the right thing. Well, all right. But I think you ought to do the right thing now, Will McLean."

The pupils of his eyes became blacker. "To what are you referring?"

"Mary Ann."

"Good God!" he muttered. "That again?"

"Yes. I want you to sell her, but now my reasons are different." And so I told him.

He listened, then gave a weary sigh. "All right," he agreed finally, "I'll draw up the papers tonight. I never did feel right having her around, creeping in the halls and hiding in the shadows. You can tell her yourself."

"She creeps and hides because you haven't spoken to her since before First Manassas. But I think you should tell her that you're selling her to Claibourne, Will McLean."

He glowered at me. "You're going to make me pay for not allowing you to become betrothed, aren't you?"

I smiled sweetly. "No sir, it's not that. But like you said, we must do what is right and good for all."

Chapter 25

April 6, 1865

My very dear Button:

I was so happy to get your letter, though I see by the date that it took a month to get here. Willie wants to know more about the baseball game you attended on the old Potomac grounds. And Mama can't quite believe ladies in Washington are wearing light silks and tulle bonnets. Why, it seems like a different world!

We still have some bolts of silk left over from the batch Daddy Will brought home last fall, but Mama says she is saving it for us for when the war is over. I was most interested in the visit of the poet, Mr. Longfellow, to your hospital.

Our cousin, Dr. John Cleary, wrote in December of '64. He served at the battle of the Wilderness last May and told of how the trees and underbrush caught fire and he hunted the wounded who were lying in the burning woods all night. He is now at

Petersburg where soldiers have been living in the trenches for months.

He writes that if we lose the war, he will never accept defeat, but will practice medicine in Brazil. Oh, how I shall miss him!

Daddy Will traveled most of last year, but has been home since Christmas because rail travel is impossible now. Mama is once again to have a baby, her last, she says. She will be forty-seven in May. The baby is expected in September.

Nannie is two now, a cunning child with endless amounts of energy. She is just starting to talk. Her dark eyes grow round with wonder each time she says a word. Lula will be eight in May. Willie turned eleven in January and talks of going off to fight with Mosby. All he had to hear was that some drummer boys are ten and eleven. We try our best to discourage him.

Maria will be twenty-one this year and keeps busy teaching music to the local children and stitching linens for her dowry. The last she heard from Michah he was in the trenches at Petersburg. But that was late November. He wrote that Mr. Lincoln proclaimed a day of Thanksgiving and their cooks made over 100,000 turkey dinners. And only miles away, the Confederates had no food, but held their fire all day out of respect for the Yankee Thanksgiving.

I find myself looking more and more to Maria for strength now that my Thomas is gone. She has such patience and stamina, and sometimes I have neither. I sit here, betrothed and yet not betrothed, because I cannot put the family in danger by letting it out that I am spoken for by one of Mosby's men. Sometimes I think this is so unfair! I cannot even write to Thomas because I never know where he is. But his letters do get through.

Mosby's men are always on the move, attacking Yankee supply lines. Thomas cannot release military information to me, but he did write that on one occasion he was sent into a Yankee camp under a flag of truce to ask for a prisoner exchange. But the Yankees refused.

We cannot understand here in the South why your Mr. Lincoln will not allow the exchange of prisoners. Especially when we hear how men on both sides are dying by the thousands in horrible prison camps.

Oh, Button, we are on different sides of the question. And I don't even know anymore what the question is. Does anyone? I look forward to the end of the war for many reasons, one of which is to sit down and discuss all this with you. You always made things seem so clear.

I lie awake nights, pondering. And missing Thomas. And wondering what "safe house" he is staying in. And if some Yankee cavalryman is aiming a rifle at him.

We hear so much that makes the blood run cold. And then we hear the good things. Like how, in the siege of Atlanta last summer, a Georgia sharpshooter played ballads on his cornet every evening. And how both armies would stop shooting long enough to hear his playing.

It hasn't been a good year for the South, in spite of our victories last year at the Wilderness in May and Cold Harbor in June. I am sure you know how Yankee General Phil Sheridan stormed into the Shenandoah Valley last summer, his men burning barns filled with wheat and slaughtering tens of thousands of livestock. How can men do such things?

Now your General Sherman marches through Georgia, destroying everything in sight. And we read that 25,000 nigras are following him. Mary Christian, our free nigra neighbor, says the women follow Sherman with babies in their arms. What will the Yankees do for these people when the war is over? Will they care for the women and babies when they are sickly, like Mama always nursed our servants?

We know, of course, that General Sherman gave Mr. Lincoln the city of Savannah for a Christmas present. But I mustn't call Sherman yours, because I know you wouldn't want to lay claim to him.

Mary Ann is happily married to Claibourne Humbles. And you will never guess! She is to have a baby! She still works for us, helping Maum Hanna. But Will McLean pays her now.

Our General Lee has asked that our slaves be armed to defend us and in March our Congress finally agreed. Can you believe this?

It is spring here. The peach orchards are all in bloom, the wheat is already a foot high and the cherry and plum trees are full of white blossoms. The land has come to life again and the weather has been a balmy blessing.

But what a sad spring! Our General A.P. Hill was shot through the heart at Petersburg, by two Union men. But we hear that Richmond is burning! Our capital! I can't abide it, but Daddy Will got word from merchant friends that mobs there are plundering shops and the Confederates are blowing up what is left of our fleet on the James River.

And now Lee's army has come here, where Daddy Will promised us the war would never find us. We heard that Lee was at Amelia Court House, only thirty miles away, expecting to find supplies. He found none. So now his men are foraging the countryside for food. And the Yankees are closing in on them.

Yankees! Here! Even as I write this, word has come to us of fighting at Saylor's Creek. Oh, Button, I am so afraid. Of the Yankees, yes, but I fear for Mama bringing a new baby into the world. Sometimes I am afraid of everything, it seems.

I don't think we are going to be poor, because Daddy Will has provided for us. I know he is in constant contact with merchants in Richmond, Lynchburg, and

Mobile. And that he has connections with Montgomery Exporting and Importing. Many times he has handed me letters to such places, to give to Hiram to get them to a courier.

If Mama knows of her husband's speculating, she never speaks of it. But what will Will McLean do when the war is over?

You once said that courage is putting on a brave face over our fears. Well, then, I am courageous, Button. But I long to see you. I wish you were here to face the end with us. But I shall try to do as you would do.

Your loving friend and former student, Oscie Mason.

Chapter 26

April 8, 1865

"Woman, do you aim to feed this whole army?"

I came up behind Daddy Will as he said this. He was standing in the doorway of the warming kitchen. It was early on Saturday morning and I'd smelled coffee and bacon cooking.

I excused myself and went into the room, surprised at what I saw. Why Maum Hanna, Mama, and Mary Ann must have been up half the night cooking. A side table was covered with freshly-baked bread and pies. On the black warming stove, two large pots were bubbling with stew. My little sister Nannie was ensconced in a rocker, wrapped in a shawl and eating a large sugar cookie. Lula was hopping around, helping. So was Maria.

I took a cup and poured myself coffee. Mama looked up from the table. "I'll feed as many of them as I can," she said. "They're starving."

Will McLean was scowling. He stood there in trousers and a clean shirt which was open at the neck. He smelled of witch hazel, which meant that he'd either just finished shaving or had interrupted his morning toilet to have this confrontation.

And it was a confrontation. I perceived that in a moment. For he never called Mama *Woman*. Always it was either *Virginia* or *Love*.

"The whole South is starving," Will McLean said.

Mama directed Mary Ann to take the next batch of bread to the log kitchen out back and put it in the beehive oven.

"Woman, have you taken leave of your senses?" Will McLean stepped aside to let Mary Ann through. "You can't feed an army! We haven't the provisions!"

Mama's eyes were bright. She moved deftly around the kitchen, in spite of her "condition." She was well into her fourth month by now.

"Virginia, you can't do this. I'm asking you not to do it, please." Will McLean's voice dropped several decibles and he now used a tone he might use on Lula when she insisted on bringing her rag dolls to the dinner table. "Don't you remember what happened back at Manassas?"

"Of course, I do," Mama answered. "We had many dinners for Beauregard and Alexander. We opened our home to them, as is our custom. We are still Southerners, aren't we, Will?"

Will McLean looked bleary-eyed. He ran his hand through his hair. "Virginia," and he stepped into the warming kitchen. "Please."

Mama had been all movement, like a hummingbird. She stopped in her flight.

"I won't have here what happened at Manassas. I am finished with armies, Virginia. I don't want any part of what's going on out there."

"Will McLean, for heaven's sake, are you saying we can't feed the hungry stragglers coming through the village? Why Ellen Bryant was by early this morning to say such men were taking turkeys, hogs, and chickens as they passed through, all night long. If we feed them, they won't take our animals."

He took her wrists in his hands. "I will personally stand on the porch with my revolver and make sure they don't take anything."

Mama was aghast. "I don't want that, Will. I *want* to feed them!"

"The advance of Lee's army will be through town today," he said, "on their way to the depot to find trains with provisions. Do you know what men in their starved condition will be like?"

Mama raised her eyes to him. "What are you saying, Will?"

"I'm asking you to honor my wishes."

"Exactly what *are* those wishes, Will?" Mama's face seemed to have gone white, suddenly.

"To lock the doors and keep our family in the house until the army passes. And if they return, to seek out their commanding officers, on whatever side, and secure a guard for the house."

Mama closed her eyes. Everyone in the kitchen waited, as if frozen in some tableau. I thought Mama was pondering her husband's request. Or praying on it. But then, in the next moment, she slumped against him and fainted.

Instantly, everyone came alive. Will McLean picked her up, shouted something to Maum Hanna, then to me, to keep the children in the kitchen, told Hiram, who'd just appeared with an armful of wood, to lock the doors, and took Mama up the stairs.

She did not come out of her room all day. For the first time in my recollection, my mama took to her bed and stayed there without caring what happened in the household.

Maria and I and the children went upstairs after a while. But the clocks in the house chimed twelve noon before Will McLean came out of their bedroom.

"Your mother is fine," he told us. "Just overtired. Oscie, I told you to keep the children downstairs." He looked terrible, like a man who'd taken leave of his senses. His hair was mussed and his face was drawn.

"We were worried," I said.

"Maria, take the children down to the dining room for their noon meal," he ordered.

My sister did so. I stood there. "May I go to her?"

"You may as well," he mumbled. And, as he went across the hall to the parlor. "She won't have anything to do with me."

I went into their bedroom. Mama was lying in the large four-poster, fully dressed. Her eyes were open. I could see she'd been crying. A handkerchief was balled up in her fist. "Mama, can I get you anything?"

She smiled and patted my hand. "I've said terrible things to my Will," she told me.

"He knows you didn't mean them, Mama."

"Oh, but I did. That's just it. And now I'm hiding in here because I feel so guilty."

"Don't be guilty, Mama. I'm sure he understands."

"I was flat-out righteous to him," she said. "I picked away at his conscience. That's never a good thing to do to a man, Oscie."

"You have the right to your thoughts, Mama."

"But what were my thoughts? They were for me, Oscie. Do you know why? Because I wanted my Will to be the way he was before the war. Back before Manassas. He isn't, you know."

I said nothing.

"He's changed so, Oscie. You think I don't know he's been speculating in sugar and making money on the war? He never speaks of it to me. He keeps it all inside. That has cost him, Oscie, keeping it inside. I know it was selfish of me, but in that kitchen before, I wanted my old Will back. The one who gave our barn and crops to the Confederacy. The Will McLean who worked for the Quartermaster Department for nothing. What happened to him, Oscie?"

I sat down on the bed and smoothed the tendrils of hair from around her forehead. "We're none of us the same as we were before the war, Mama."

"It was so sweet the way it was before," she told me. "I would give anything to go back to the way it was when we were married and you girls were small and I was expecting Willie and the world was so rich and bountiful. And nobody was questioning our way of life. My Will was so sure of himself then, so believing."

She blew her nose and went on. "Now he's so careworn. He doesn't believe in things anymore. I wonder what he did on those travels. I wonder what agreements he made with his own conscience to keep his family fed and cared for."

I let her cry a bit. I just held her hand in my own.

"Oscie, I was raised to be docile and supportive of my husband, never to question his decisions. But it came to me before in the kitchen that right now, when our world is falling apart, we have to hold onto what we were. And the only way I knew to do that was to feed the starving soldiers coming through town."

"I know, Mama," I said.

"I was doing it more for us than for the soldiers," she said. "I was offering my Will the chance to still be his old self, one more time. And he refused it."

"Mama, don't get overwrought. It isn't good for you."

"Oh, I don't know what I think anymore. I've hurt my Will, Oscie. I told him right here before in this room, that all I wanted was to believe in him again."

She burst into a fresh onslaught of crying. I tried to quiet her. Maum Hanna came through the door with a drink. Mama took it obediently. It must have had some potion in it, for as she lay back on the pillows she immediately became calmer.

"Needs a good rest, poor chile," said Maum Hanna. "Been up half the night cookin'."

"I'll stay until you fall asleep, Mama," I offered.

She nodded. "I told him I wanted him to do something so I could believe in him again," she murmured. Her eyes closed. I stayed with her. She soon went off to sleep.

I went across the hall and knocked on the parlor door. No answer. I knocked again.

"Who is it and what do you want?"

"It's Oscie. I must speak with you."

"Go away."

"Please. It's about Mama."

A moment passed. I heard footsteps within, the door opened a crack. I peered up into his face, tanned from the spring sun, but with an anguished pallor showing through. His eyes were narrowed. "Is your mother all right?"

I could smell brandy on his breath. He was drinking! In the middle of the day! "She's resting."

"Then go away." The door closed.

"I won't go away, Will McLean. There's things that need saying between us."

"Then stand there all day if you haven't anything better to do."

"Well, I could take Mary Ann and Maum Hanna and bring some of that stew and bread into the center of the village for any stragglers who come through."

Footsteps across the floor again. Once again the door opened. "You heard what I said about staying inside the house."

"I'll go out if it pleases me."

"You'll answer to me if you do. I'm still head of this house. I won't be dallied with. Try me if you care to. I'm up to it." He glared at me with gimlet eyes.

"This isn't fostering conversation between us."

"There's nothing we have to talk about." The door started closing again. I had to snare him.

"There's your speculating," I said. "And the fact that Mama knows about it. And what it's done to you."

That snared him, all right, like a rabbit in a trap. In the next instant, the door opened wide, he reached out and grabbed my wrist with a hand that felt like a claw, and pulled me into the room.

Outside our house that day events were conspiring to bring an end to the war that had raged over the land for four years. Most of those events we didn't know about yet, but would be told of later.

Armies were converging, marching, setting up tents, planning. Stragglers from the Confederate army were throwing down their muskets, dropping out of lines and heading home.

Yankee cavalry was scouting in the woods. Local families were digging holes to bury everything from silver to kegs of brandy.

Yankees from the 152nd New York and the 7th

New Jersey found ham and pork, flour and meal at the village of New Store, fifteen miles away. Yesterday, our General Lee had hoped to cross the Appomattox River from Farmville and burn all the bridges behind him, so the Yankees couldn't follow. Lee, with his starving army, was hoping to join our General Johnston in North Carolina.

But the Yankees cut him off south of Farmville. So Lee moved north to Cumberland Heights.

Lee was hoping to find rations at the depot at Appomattox Station. Meanwhile, General Sheridan's Yankee cavalry was coming down the South Side Railroad. And General George Armstrong Custer was closing in with his cavalry, his destination being Appomattox Station. Confederate commissary trains were waiting there, three train loads of supplies just arrived from Lynchburg, with badly needed shoes, shirts, jackets, blankets, medical remedies, and food.

A squad of Confederate cavalry was defending the train. But General Custer would get there that evening, capture the trains in a battle that would drive our artillery back to our village and dash Lee's last hope to save his ragged army.

In the spring darkness, on the eastern edge of our little village, Lee's army would dot the fields with their white tents.

We knew nothing of this on that Saturday, of course. Nor could I have conjured up the scene I was to learn of in a few days, the scene taking place on the Stage Road, six miles northeast of our village. There the First Corps of the Confederate Artillery was making camp. And its commander, General Edward Porter Alexander, was setting up quarters in the house of Joseph Abbitt, a little down the road from his men.

"Let go of my wrist," I told Will McLean.

He released me. I rubbed my chafed wrist. He turned away in embarrassment, realizing he'd hurt me. He ran his hand through his mussed hair and murmured an oath against himself.

Hearing that oath, I knew what I was up against. A man trying to avoid his conscience, who, at the same time, prided himself, at least in his manner towards women, in being a Southern gentleman. And I stood there holding a mirror to his soul, something no Southern woman should ever do. No wonder he had wanted to hurt me.

"Speak your piece," he said.

"It's more than the food you won't allow Mama to share with the soldiers. It's more than that."

He turned to me. "Explain yourself."

"Do I have your permission to speak plain?"

"Since when have you ever needed my permission for that?"

"Mama knows about your speculating. She's always known. She said a good Southern wife never questions her husband's decisions or business practices."

He stared at me stonily, over his brandy glass. His expression didn't change, but I thought I saw his shoulders slump. "Go on," he said.

"You know why she wanted to feed the army today? Because she knows what it must have cost you, making money on the war to care for your family."

Silence. The pupils of his eyes were black with emotion. He nodded that I should continue.

"She wanted, just this morning, for you to be the way you were before the war. The way you were back at Manassas. She wanted . . ." my voice faltered, but

I kept on, "she said she wanted her old Will back."

He turned on his heel. He did a complete whirl. He threw the empty brandy glass against the brick hearth. It smashed into pieces and I jumped at the sound. He raised his arms in despair. "Oh, I see. A small favor. A simple thing. To be as I was before the war started." His voice was rich in sarcasm.

"Yessir," I said. "That's what she wanted."

"Well tell me, Oscie Mason. Which of us is the same as we were before the war? Are you?"

"Nosir."

"Is Maria?" His voice was rising.

"Nosir."

"Are the servants?"

I shook my head, no.

"Is your mother?" He shouted it at me.

I could only shake my head like the village idiot. Oh, he had such a temper when roused. He picked up the decanter of brandy, found another glass, poured the dark liquid into it, and drank it in one gulp.

"She wants me to be like I was before the war?" He threw that glass against the hearth, too. I jumped again and started to leave the room.

"Stay!" And he was by my side in an instant. "You started this. Now finish it, like Lee's army is finishing what they started out there today."

"I won't stay. You're drunk."

"I am not drunk. It will take considerably more to put me in such a state and I can't afford that luxury today. I am being rude and overbearing. And tomorrow I will have to ask your forgiveness. But we're speaking plain now. Do I have that privilege around here? Or just you? Never mind, just let me tell you something."

He stepped back. *"I never was the man your*

mother thought I was back at Manassas before the war!"

My eyes went wide in amazement. "Yes, you were."

"No, I wasn't. I didn't marry your mother for her money. I loved her. But I was in debt. My store failed because the economy was bad. Everybody was in debt and using credit. And my customers didn't pay. I had to sue them to get what was mine. Your mother put her holdings in trust, so her property couldn't be seized for my debt. As much as for what people were saying about us."

I just stared at him.

"I was never comfortable in the role of slave owner. You knew me for what I was. And I told you in the beginning that change was coming."

He halted. All my senses were crowding me.

"The war brought out the real Will McLean, Oscie. And he stands before you now. All the rest is pettifoggery."

"Pettifoggery?" I asked.

"Yes. All the impeccable manners and genteel ways. They belong to your father's world, not mine. They won't put food on the table today. Go downstairs to the dining room where the noon meal is laid out. The food on that table comes from my speculating, Oscie. Everything we have now comes from it. The world, from here on in, when this war ends tomorrow or the next day, will belong to people like me. Not the Will McLean your mama thinks she left back at Manassas."

I had to sit down then. Because he meant it. I saw the pupils of his eyes get even blacker. "I don't like such a world, Will McLean," I said.

"Nobody will like it," he said sadly.

"But what's to become of you and Mama?"

"We've just had a set-to. A good marriage can stand it."

"But, if you could have seen the look in Mama's eyes before."

"I *saw* the look. I spent the morning seeing it."

"Well then?" I stood up and went to him. He was staring at the carpet. I looked at the top of his bent head, the hair still full but tinged with gray. I minded the wide-footed stand of him, the hands thrust dejectedly into his trouser pockets. He was still a fine-looking man, as fit and good-looking as when Mama had married him. "Well then, can't you *do* something, Will McLean?"

He laughed. It was more of a grunt. He still stared down at the carpet. "What would you have me do, Oscie Mason? Put on my white frock coat and planter's straw hat and waltz upstairs with a bouquet of cherry blossoms and invite her for a stroll back at Yorkshire?"

"No," I said. "I know we can't go back to Yorkshire."

"What then?" His head snapped up. "Your mama will have to accept what's happened to her world. Like everybody else."

"I won't hold with that, Will McLean," I told him.

He shrugged.

"I've abided every other restriction you put on me. But I won't abide this for my mama."

"Oh, and I've really hog-tied you with restrictions all these years, haven't I?"

"Sometimes you did and sometimes you didn't," I said. "Don't care about that now. I care only about Mama. And I want you to do something so she can believe in you again."

He turned away. "I can't feed the army, Oscie," he said wearily. "Don't ask me to. I can't open that door and allow the army in our house again."

The words had a sadness about them that made me determine he didn't like what he was all about right now. And a thought seized me. "Then do something else to make her believe in you again! You're her world, Will McLean!"

He shook his head. "I've had enough of this. Go now, Oscie. I'm weary of it."

"No." I went to stand before him. "You just said the war would probably end here in our village today or tomorrow. Mama will love you, Will McLean, whoever you are. But her belief in you is just kind of tuckered out right now. Still, if you did something, while this war is ending today or tomorrow, to make her come round, I'm sure she'll accept anything that happens after."

"Like what?" he snapped.

I was taken back. "I don't know. But couldn't you just ponder on it? A body would think that if you loved her you'd ponder on it."

His handsome face contorted with anger. Oh, I had gone too far! "May I go now?" I asked.

"I would advise you to, yes." His voice was cold enough to put the fire in the hearth out. I turned and fled from the room.

Chapter 27

Hiram had closed the curtains and, as the afternoon waned, lighted the candles. The house was deathly quiet. Maria read to the children. Mama slept. I wandered about like a nervous Nellie and helped Maum Hanna set the table for dinner. Maria brought the children into the dining room.

"The Confederate army passed through town this morning," she whispered as she passed me.

"When?" I asked.

"When you and Daddy Will were in the parlor having it out. Sit children," she told them. "We'll wait for Daddy Will."

We all sat around the table. Maum Hanna brought in a tureen of steaming soup, dished it out and left us. Hiram waited by the sideboard, getting the wine ready. Still we just sat. Maria gave Nannie a cracker. Then came the sound we were waiting for. Footsteps coming down the stairs.

Will McLean came into the dining room. He was meticulously groomed, elegantly turned out. In an instant Hiram was at his side, pulling out his chair.

"Thank you, Hiram." McLean took the linen napkin Hiram offered and put it in his lap. "Has anyone said grace?"

Maria spoke up then. "No. But since tomorrow is Palm Sunday, I've selected some verses I thought would be fitting," she said.

"Very good, Maria. I'm sure we could all use some appropriate Bible verses right now. Be quiet, children, and listen."

Maria read: I knew enough of my Bible to recognize that it was snatches of John, Chapters 13 and 14: Before the feast of the Passover.

"A new commandment I give unto you, that ye love one another. As I have loved you, that ye also love one another."

Maria flipped a page and continued in her clear, confident voice. *"Let not your heart be troubled. Ye believe in God, believe also in me. In my Father's house are many mansions, if it were not so, I would have told you. I go to prepare a place for you. And if I go and prepare a place for you, I will come again, and receive you unto myself: That where I am, there ye may be also. And whither I go ye know, and the way ye know."*

Will McLean was staring at her across the table, as if he'd never heard these words before. His eyes seemed blacker than ever and I thought I saw tears in them.

He cleared his throat. "Thank you, Maria, that was very appropriate. Now eat, children."

Guns boomed in the distance as we took our soup. The children behaved. Will McLean was solemn, but his langorous ways, his impeccable manners, his compliments to Maum Hanna, and his concern for the little ones had a quiet and steadying effect.

But Willie wouldn't eat.

"What's wrong, son?" his father asked.

"Saw the soldiers come through town today. They were in tatters. Some had bleeding hands and feet."

"Our army is retreating, son. When an army retreats, the men don't wear full dress uniforms."

Willie was eleven, growing fast to manhood, almost as tall as I was. He glared at his father.

"They are on their way to get provisions, son. They'll eat tonight," his father promised. "Starving yourself won't help."

All through the meal those guns boomed. It was most unsettling. Thank God for little Nannie who kept us smiling with her baby antics.

There was chocolate cake for dessert, but Willie even refused that. His father didn't badger him, but watched him carefully when Willie wasn't looking. Then, when Maum Hanna poured the coffee, Will McLean took his napkin from his lap and flung it down on the table.

"Is this a wake? Will somebody tell me who died?"

Nannie got her hands into Maria's cake then and came away with chocolate all over her face. Everyone laughed. "Give that child to me," Will McLean said. He reached for his daughter, almost gratefully. And he sat with Nannie on his lap through the rest of the meal.

Then, just as it was over, he looked at Maum Hanna. "Get some tallow candles and set them in the front windows," he directed.

"Yessir, Mister Will."

We all stared at him. "What for?" Willie asked.

"Son, this night Lee's army camps on the slopes of Appomattox Creek. There are men out there who are old friends of mine. The candles are a sign that we are here if they need us."

Maria caught my eye and I looked at my plate.

I go to prepare a place for you.

Had Maria read those verses intentionally? If so, I was still underestimating my sister.

"Now, I want you children to go to your rooms. You may play quietly or read until Maum Hanna says it's bedtime. If you hear anyone knocking on our front door, stay upstairs."

"Maybe I'll take some food to my room," Willie said.

"Why don't you do that, son?"

When the others left, I stayed. "Thank you for the candles in the window," I said. "Mama will like that."

His shoulders slumped. He stared into his coffee cup.

"What do you think is happening down at the depot?"

"The Yankees are attempting to capture the Confederate commissary trains."

"Will they?"

"Yes."

"And then what?"

"Then if Lee has any brains, he'll know the seriousness of his situation. If not, well his officers will tell him. He's got good men around him. They know the army is finished and the killing can't go on anymore. You can't run an army without food. The merchant in me has known that a long time."

"Do you think anyone will see the candles and come to our door?"

"If they come, they're welcome."

That where I am, there ye may be also.

Was he thinking of those words, too? I dared not ask. I said goodnight. He admonished me to keep the children upstairs, no matter what happened. I said I would.

Chapter 28

April 9, 1865

People came to our house that night. Soldiers.

Maria and I peered out the upstairs hall window when we heard knocks on the front door. We saw Confederate cavalry horses out front and then we saw a sentinel taking his place in our front yard by the well.

"Who is it?" Willie came to stand with us.

"Confederate officers," I whispered.

"I'm glad Daddy put the candles in the windows," Willie said. "So his friends would be welcome. I'd do it for my friends, too."

The next morning when we gathered in the dining room for breakfast at seven-thirty, the guns started booming in the distance again. But they seemed closer, to the west.

Nannie was fitful, growing afraid of the guns. Maria was feeding her. Lula clutched her rag doll close to her. Willie was dressed as if to go out. He ate hurridly, stuffing cornbread into his pockets.

"Where are you off to?" I whispered.

"Out. To see what's going on."

"You daren't. Your father will wear you out if he finds you left the house."

He gulped his hot chocolate. It left a ring around his mouth and my heart lurched, minding how young he was. And, when he stood, how tall he was. A man soon, I thought. Dear God, let the war end this day.

"Always says he'll wear me out, but he never does."

"There's always a first time, Willie," I warned.

Just then Will McLean came into the dining room, dark circles under his eyes, but freshly shaved and wearing a white shirt and silk cravat. Everyone spoke at once, demanding to know who'd been here last night.

McLean smiled wryly and sat, took the coffee Hiram poured, sipped it, waited until we settled down and then spoke. "I shall tell you and then expect to be left in peace. My old friend, Major General Thomas Lafayette Rosser, was here last night. He's cavalry, and a good friend of Custer, though Custer is Yankee. We talked until two in the morning."

"About what?" Willie asked.

"About old times. I knew him well at Manassas. The others who came were our General Gordon and General Fitz Lee, nephew of Robert E."

"What did they want?" Willie persisted.

"Want, son? To talk. To be inside a real home for the first time in months. To set a while. To confer about plans for today's battle."

"They're out there fighting now," Willie said almost reverently. "Hear the guns."

"Yes," his father agreed. "Gordon's infantry and Fitz Lee's cavalry. They're trying to push the Yankee cavalry aside and find a way through the Yankee line. If they can do this and General Longstreet can hold back the Yankees, why they might yet save the day."

"And if they don't?" Willie asked.

We all waited. As did Maum Hanna and Hiram, in the background.

"My dears," Will McLean said, "then a flag of truce will be sent out. Two days ago General Robert E. Lee's most trusted officers approached him about asking Grant for surrender terms."

A gasp went around the room. Maum Hanna let out a little cry. "Sweet Jesus!"

"Yes," Will McLean said. "We'll all need to pray to Jesus if that happens. Grant and Lee have been sending letters back and forth for two days. Last night I got the feeling that neither Gordon nor Rosser wanted to fight this morning. I think they know it's over."

"Then why are they doing it?" Willie persisted.

"Because they are soldiers who obey orders and who are bound to make this last charge of the war with a spirit worthy of our army," Will McLean explained. "Because they are good men and will do their jobs to the end. Now, if you children are finished eating, please go and find something to do so I can have my breakfast in peace. Maria?" he looked at her.

"Come on, children," she commenced to usher them from the room. But Lula stopped next to her father's chair.

"Are the guns coming closer?"

Will McLean looked down at her quizzically, saw her fear and took her on his lap. "No, sweet, they won't come to the village. Are you frightened?"

"Betty is frightened." She held up her rag doll.

"And Nannie is terrified. But I'm not."

"You're my brave girl. Now run along with Maria. When the war is over, I'll buy you another rag doll."

They left the room. I stayed. "Is Mama coming down?" I asked.

"No." He swallowed a mouthful of his breakfast. "Apparently I have not yet sufficiently redeemed myself in her eyes. I offered to saddle up Eagle and ride with Fitz Lee this morning to try to get through the Yankee line." He shrugged and continued eating. And I knew he was making jokes to cover up his feelings. I also knew he'd slept on the sofa in the parlor last night. Perhaps because he hadn't wanted to wake Mama so late after the men left. And perhaps because it was bad with him and Mama, worse than I'd thought.

"What are you going to do?" I asked.

"I guess I'll just have to let Fitz Lee get through the Yankee line alone."

"I mean about Mama."

"I can only worry about one war at a time," he said.

I started to leave the room. His back was to me, his head bowed dejectedly over his coffee. So, Mama was holding out. The tallow candles weren't enough for her. Her Will wasn't yet the man she'd known back at Manassas.

"Mama must know you'll do something to redeem yourself before this is all over," I said.

"Then she knows more than I do." His voice had dropped to a whisper.

Perhaps she does, Will McLean, I thought. Perhaps Mama knows, better than any of us, what kind of man you are.

By nine that morning Maria and I knew that Willie had sneaked out of the house. Will McLean was in the parlor again, with the doors closed. Maria and I searched the house for Willie.

"Well, at least the shooting has stopped," Maria said.

I stood stock-still. "You're right, Maria. I haven't heard guns for the last hours. It's so *quiet!*"

We stared at each other. "I think we should find Willie," Maria said. "I think we should go outside and find him."

We crept out the back way. We knocked on the door of the privy, searched the servants' quarters, the log cabin kitchen, the icehouse, the smokehouse, the stable. On this fine morning Eagle and the carriage horses, Mirabella and my Cottonwood who were old now, and Willie's Maggie were all in the pasture.

We looked in the well out front. No Willie. My eyes scanned the village. The silence mocked us. Reluctantly, we went back inside, but before doing so I peeked behind two rain barrels and checked under the front porch steps.

By ten o'clock Lula dragged me to a window in a bedroom on the second floor. "Look," she said pointing, "soldiers!"

They were gathered in front of the Court House down the street, right past Mr. Meek's store. We could see blue uniforms. And butternut and gray.

"Yankees and ours," I said. "Oh, Maria, do you think Lee and Grant are meeting in the Court House?"

Even more of them rode up to loiter and talk in the square. As they dismounted, they approached one another hesitantly, sometimes saluting. I saw a flask being passed around. Then I saw one man in a gray overcoat with a cape, too warm for the weather.

"It's probably the only clothing he has, if he's ours," I said dismally. And I wondered where Tom was at this moment. And what clothing he had to cover him against the night fogs.

"The war must be over," Maria said. "They appear so friendly." She put her hand on my arm. "Oh, Oscie," she murmured.

I looked at her and I knew she was thinking of Michah. I hugged her. My sister, Maria. We'd grown up together during this war. It had marked our youth in ways we had yet to work out. It had made us grow up before our time. And it had brought us together, yes. Our embrace was a long one. No words were necessary.

Then we heard running footsteps downstairs and Will McLean's voice. "*Where* have you been, young man!"

In a flash Lula and Maria and I were running down to the first floor. Willie stood there, just inside the front door, looking up at his father. His hat was off, his shirt rumpled, his boots dusty.

"It's over," he said.

"What's happened?" his father demanded.

"I was with Eddie. In front of the Court House, officers are meeting. From both sides. All the important ones."

Willie's words tumbled out of him, he was so excited. His face was red, his eyes fairly popping out of his head. "They just started coming to the Court House. They all know each other. They were shaking hands and clapping each other on the back and saying 'how goes it?' And that kind of thing. I saw Yankees. Up close! I saw Ord and Sheridan and

Gibbon and others. Our General Longstreet was there. So was your friend Gordon. I got close up to their horses, from behind a tree! I could see their swords and pistols!"

"What were they saying?" his father asked.

"Sheridan, the Yankee? He's not too happy. All the others are. They were joking and passing around the whiskey. Sheridan said he was fired on by some Rebels as he was coming to the Court House under a flag of truce!"

"There's a truce?" I asked.

Willie nodded his head vigorously. "From ten o'clock this morning until two this afternoon. They agreed on that. They said they were waiting for Lee's answer to Grant's terms of surrender."

"Jesus be praised!" Maum Hanna was behind us, crying. Maria started crying too. She went to Will McLean and he put his arms around her. I stood frozen, hearing Willie out.

"They're *friends*," he said derisively. "All of them. I heard them say that if Grant and Lee don't stop the war today they would tell their men to load with blank cartridges so no more on either side would be killed. Ask Eddie Tibbs. He heard it, too."

Maria was sobbing now, unashamedly.

"They're *friends!*" Will spat the word out. "How can they be friends when all along they've been killing each other?"

"They knew each other at West Point, son," McLean said sadly.

Willie looked up at his father. "Are we gonna surrender?"

"I think so, yes, son."

"Damn!" Willie threw his hat on the floor.

"That's enough, young man," Will McLean said

severely. He took Willie's arm and gave the boy a good shake. But Willie just peered up at him.

Tears were coming down my brother's face. "I'll wager if Captain Alex was here, *he* wouldn't surrender."

"We don't know that he isn't here." His father knelt down in front of Willie. "It'll be all right, son. We'll be one country again. You don't remember how it was when we were one country, Willie, but it was a good thing. It was a fine thing."

Willie wiped his face with the back of his hand. "I wanna go back out. Eddie's waiting for me."

"No," his father said. "I should whup you good for going out this morning."

"Don't care if you do. It was worth it. Lemme go. I gotta go back out. The Yankees are making a signal station at Eddie's house. They're *in Eddie's house right now!* They're watching the Confederate cavalry. Old Sheridan said that our cavalry might dash away during the truce. I gotta go. Promised Eddie I'd be back."

But Will McLean had a firm grip on him. "The Tibbs will be fine." He was pulling Willie into the parlor. "Come on in and we'll talk about it. I want to hear it all again."

"You gonna whup me?" Willie asked.

"No, son. I need a man to talk this over with." Will McLean winked at us over Willie's head and I breathed a sigh of relief. He wasn't going to punish Willie.

In the hallway we all just stood and looked at each other, dumbstruck. Then, as if on cue, we hugged each other, Maria and I, Lula and Nannie, and Hiram and Maum Hanna.

As I was hugging Maum Hanna, two things

happened. I thought of Alex suddenly, saw him as clearly as I had on that day he'd first come to Yorkshire when he jumped our fence on Dixie. It was more than a thought, it was a feeling. It was as if he was standing there next to me. I shook the feeling off. It was just because of what Willie had said, I told myself.

Then, over Maum Hanna's shoulder, I saw Mama. She'd opened the door of their room a crack and had been listening! She saw me, waved me away and closed the door.

I moved away from Maum Hanna and went to the door of their room, knocked softly, and went in.

Mama stood there in her blue robe de chambre.

"How are you, Mama?" I inquired.

"I'm tolerable, thank you, Oscie."

"Did you hear the news?"

"I heard." She walked away from me, crossed the floor to stand in front of her dresser in the corner and look at herself in the mirror.

"Will you be coming down for our noon meal then?"

"I think not, Oscie. I'm not ready yet to rejoin the family."

I walked over to her. "Mama," I said. "He's trying. He put the tallow candles in the front windows last night. Some officers came. He let them into the house to discuss things."

"I know that, Oscie."

"He looks awful, Mama. He's suffering."

She smiled at me. "You taking up for Will McLean, Oscie? My, things have changed, haven't they?"

"Mama, please." I reached out and took her hand and held it in my own. It was so cold. "Mama, what do you want from him?"

She held both my hands in hers and smiled wanly at me. "My Will is capable of so much, Oscie," she said. "He's lost sight of what he is. I want him to find it again."

"But how, Mama?"

"He'll know when the time comes, Oscie," she said. "He'll know."

I cast a look at their four-poster as I left the room. Mama's side of the bed covers were back, used. Will McLean's side was neat and unslept in.

I don't know if Will McLean did what he did that day because of Mama. Or if he did it for his own reasons. Or if he ever intended to do what he did at all.

There are people who say that he was just walking in town when he met Colonel Charles Marshall, aide to General Lee, who came riding along. And that Marshall talked with my stepdaddy because he was the first man Marshall met.

That's what people say. But I know what I think. And it's so plain, I don't understand why people can't work it out. I think Will McLean went walking in town that day to meet somebody, yes. But it wasn't Marshall. It was the Will McLean he wanted to be. The one my Mama thought she left back at Manassas. And the one my Mama knew he'd find, sooner or later.

He told us at our noon meal that he was going out. He looked around the table at his children and his eyes gleamed, like black jewels.

"I'm going to find a Yankee officer to place a guard in front of our house," he said. "You all are to stay inside."

I followed him into the hall, up the stairs, and into the first floor hallway where he stood in front of a mirror adjusting his cravat and putting on his jacket. He nodded at me and went out the front door. I watched him go down the porch steps and through our front yard on the brick walk. There was a set to his shoulders, I minded, that I had not seen for a long time.

When he came back, half an hour later, his face was very white and he looked enormously weary. He called all of us into the center hall. "What do you think of such luck?" he said to us. "Generals Grant and Lee will soon be here to talk over terms of surrender."

"You mean in our village?" I asked.

"No. Here in our house. Most likely in our parlor."

We just stared at him. His words hit me like a thunderclap.

And if I go and prepare a place for you, I will come again, and receive you unto myself.

I stared at Maria. Her eyes were filled with tears. She hugged him. Willie yipped. Lula and Nannie caught onto his sleeve and Will McLean called for Hiram and Maum Hanna and told them to see to the parlor, that the generals were coming.

And, as they'd taken a thousand other orders from him, Hiram and Maum Hanna said "yessir" and set to work.

I felt the thrill of it in my bones. Yes, I thought, this is right. I went to the front door and opened it a crack and peered out. Not a soul was in sight.

"Oscie!" Will McLean called out sharply.

I shut the door. "No one is around."

He laughed. "There are whole armies out there.

Two armies poised at either side of our village. Waiting."

Waiting. Not to fight this time. But to move toward each other and come together finally, as one people. All kinds of people, but together as one country again. One country, with room for all kinds of people.

In my Father's house there are many mansions.

"Do you children realize that the first battle of this war took place on our front lawn back at Yorkshire?" he was saying. "And the surrender will take place in our parlor?"

They listened.

"Now you must all go down to the warming kitchen and stay there and be quiet. And not come up, no matter what happens."

They started downstairs. I just stood there staring at him. His black eyes met mine.

"Are you thinking something I should know about?" he asked.

"You've done a good thing."

"It didn't start out that way. When Marshall approached me in the village and asked me to show him a house where Lee and Grant could meet, I took him to the old Devon place."

"But it's falling down! Eddie Tibbs and Willie play there all the time. It's deserted."

"I was stalling for time, Oscie. I needed to think. All I thought of was Manassas and how we lost our plantation."

"So what changed your mind, then?"

"I don't know. I started remembering the good times at Manassas. Do you recall when the army first came and we opened our house to Beauregard and Alex? It was another world then."

"I remember," I said.

"Well, I minded how good we all felt about things then, Oscie. and I thought it fitting if we could all feel that way again. Just for a little while."

I smiled weakly at him.

"And then, of course, there were those verses Maria read yesterday at the table. Brought it home to me, what it's all about." He scowled. "You don't suppose your sister selected those verses for any reason, do you?"

So I was right. There *had* been tears in his eyes when he listened to those verses. I felt a stab of jealousy, that Maria had been the one to move him. "Nosir," I said. "I suppose she just read them for Palm Sunday."

"So I told Marshall that perhaps my house would do." He sighed. "My house. The first time they used it to start tearing each other to pieces. Now they'll use it to start the healing. Only fitting, don't you think?"

"Yessir," I said. "Only fitting."

He winked at me. "Then of course, when you told me that if I loved your mother I'd ponder on what to do about things, why I pondered, Oscie," he said. "I just pondered."

Chapter 29

"You met Lee?" Willie was thunderstruck.

Will McLean had come down to the warming kitchen to grab something for his noon meal. It was almost two in the afternoon. Mama was beside him, in her best summer calico, a lace shawl covering her in front to modestly hide her condition.

"Yes," McLean said. His eyes were grave, but there was a contained excitement in him.

"What does Lee look like?" Willie pushed.

Will McLean and Mama sat at the table to take some refreshment. "He looks worn," Daddy Will said. "His face is very bronzed from the sun and his beard and hair are very white. He must be over six feet and he bears himself magnificently. He is dressed in a spotless gray uniform and his linen is snowy white. He is wearing a beautiful sash and sword, but no insignia except three stars on his coat collar. His boots are shined to a fare-thee-well. Marshall came in first and sat and waited for Lee and Babcock. He told me that Lee was dressed since one o'clock this morning, because he thinks he is going to be Grant's prisoner."

The quiet words fell on us like soft rain. Daddy Will continued, "Marshall borrowed a dress sword and a pair of gauntlets and a clean shirt from a friend. But all our officers make a fine appearance. We've nothing to be ashamed of."

"Did Lee speak to you and Mama?" Maria asked.

"We welcomed him to our home." Daddy Will set his cup down. He and Mama exchanged a private glance and he took her hand in his. "Then Lee went into the parlor and in two seconds he was asleep."

"Asleep!" Willie was mortified.

"Yes, son, the man is exhausted. Your mama left the room and I waited and spoke softly for a while with Babcock and Marshall. Then your mama and I went out onto the porch to wait for Grant. He came about half an hour after Lee. We welcomed him and his officers, also."

"What's Grant like?" Willie asked.

Will McLean rubbed his chin thoughtfully. "He wore a slouched hat, no decoration on it, a common soldier's blouse, and his trousers are baggy and tucked into muddy boots."

"Did you talk to him?" Maria asked.

"We said hello. He nodded and mumbled something. He wears no sword but he looks like he has the world on his mind. We stayed in the front yard a while. It's filled up now with Yankee officers. And Grant brought a few to the meeting with him. I hear tell that Grant's secretary is a full-blooded Indian."

"How long are they gonna be in our parlor?" Willie asked.

"I don't know, son. This is all so different. Nothing

like it has ever happened before. Two armies, one people."

At this point Lula started to sniffle and screw up her face. "I left Betty in the parlor. Will the soldiers hurt her?"

"Of course not," Mama said. "They won't bother her at all."

"Can you go up and get her, Daddy?"

"No, darling, I can't. We'll get Betty later. I promise."

Mama and Daddy Will took themselves off to other parts of the house. Maria and I kept the children busy and quiet in the warming kitchen. Willie peered outside and kept us informed about the "blue soldiers" in our front yard. They gathered in groups, talking. At one point Daddy Will went out and showed them the well and spoke with them for a while.

At three o'clock Willie called us to the front windows of the warming kitchen which looked out directly on the lawn. "Lee's leaving!" he said.

We watched. We saw an aide bring up the general's stately gray horse, watched Lee mount it and look down at the shabby-looking man who stood looking up at him. Lee touched the brim of his hat in a salute.

"That must be Grant," Willie whispered.

Lee rode off. Daddy Will came into the room. He was agitated and indignant. "Is your mother here?"

We said no. "Those Yankee soldiers are removing my fence rails," he told us. "I was promised there would be no damage to the place. Grant is still upstairs, overseeing the writing of orders. Dammit, I have to find somebody who's in charge."

He went out again. It was just about four o'clock,

after Grant left, that the trouble started.

Mama had come to sit with us and confer with Maum Hanna about supper. We heard a commotion going on upstairs. Mama became worried. "Will did this for me," she whispered to me, gathering her skirts in one hand and heading out of the kitchen. "Dear God, I pray it doesn't turn out badly."

We followed her upstairs. Lula and Nannie clung to her skirts. Daddy Will was in the middle of our parlor, which seemed full of blue soldiers in knee-length tunic coats with double rows of brass buttons. One man, who was short with dark hair and a downward-curved mustache, was holding our small oval marble-topped table.

"How much you want for it, McLean?"

"It isn't for sale, General," Daddy Will said.

"I mean to have it." The man withdrew some gold pieces from his pocket and thrust them into Daddy Will's hand.

"It isn't for sale!" My stepdaddy threw the gold pieces down. They rolled across the red and green carpet.

"It's a valuable souvenir. Don't be a fool, McLean."

"The contents of my house are not for sale!" They should have known to skedaddle then. Will McLean was using his best no-nonsense voice. The other blue officers, who were examining the room's furnishings, stopped and stared at him.

"I may be a fool, General Sheridan," Daddy Will said, "but I do not indulge in petty larceny. Yet, what can I expect from the man who laid waste to the Shenandoah Valley and reduced the populace to starvation."

The silence in the room was heavy. Sheridan smiled. "War is hell, McLean. Here, Custer, take this with my compliments. A gift for your charming wife." He handed the table to a tall blond officer with long golden ringlets, sad eyes, and a drooping mustache.

Custer took it. He was cavalry. I'd heard Tom speak of him. Third Cavalry, Custer was breveted for gallantry at Gettysburg. Tom had said he was the youngest general in the Union army. I noticed the air of dapper elegance about him.

"Grant wrote the conditions of surrender on that table," Sheridan said. "I've given you twenty dollars in gold, McLean. Good Yankee money. Take it or leave it."

He and Custer walked out, right past us in the hall, as if we weren't even there. I heard a low moan out of Mama. I took her hand to calm her. Inside the room a handsome blond officer had picked up another marble-topped table.

"Sir," he approached Daddy Will respectfully, "I'm Major General Edward Ord."

"I know who you are." Will McLean said coldly.

"I offer you forty dollars for this table on which Lee signed the surrender."

Will McLean stood eyeball to eyeball with Ord. "Keep your money," he said.

Mama rested her head against me. "Oh, I'm so proud of him, Oscie," she said.

Ord walked to the mantel, put the money there and left the room with the table in hand.

Another officer approached Will McLean, with brass candlesticks in hand and held out money. Daddy Will simply shook his head, no. The officer dropped the money on the carpet and left. And so it went on, like some kind of a macabre parade, with the blue soldiers walking up to Daddy Will, who never changed his stance or manner. All held out money.

For the stone inkstand, the chair in which Grant sat, the chair Lee had occupied.

Daddy Will stood like a rock. Some of them dropped money on the floor, some just walked out and no coin of the republic was even offered.

And then we heard a piercing scream from out front. Unmistakably, it was Lula. We all ran to the front porch. "Lula!" Mama called, "Where are you?"

The front porch, steps, and yard were full of blue soldiers. In a moment the screaming Lula came running to us, hair flying, skirts flapping. She ran up the steps to her father. "They've got Betty. *They're taking her away!*"

A blue soldier had the rag doll in his hands.

"In heaven's name," Will McLean said, "it belongs to the child!" He'd picked up Lula, who was clinging to him and sobbing.

The Yankee officer had been about to mount his horse. He hesitated and saluted. "Lieutenant Colonel Thomas W.C. Moore," he said in polite gravity. "And I've something to keep the little one happy. I was bringing it home to my own little girl." He reached into his saddle bags and withdrew a French china doll, handed it to his young aide, who brought it to Daddy Will.

"Sir?" He saluted smartly and held out the doll.

"I don't want it! I want my Betty!" Lula's sobs rang out in the yard. "Please give me back my Betty!"

The blue soldiers all fell silent.

"She doesn't want the fancy Yankee doll," McLean said. "You heard what she said."

The young aide set the French china doll down on

the porch steps and walked back to mount his horse.

Lula sobbed out her grief on her father's shoulder.

"Enjoy your booty, men," Daddy Will said. "I understand your General Grant's surrender terms were extremely generous. It's too bad you couldn't have upheld the spirit and compassion shown by your commander."

They rode off. Some glanced back cautiously. Some saluted.

"I'm sorry, Will," Mama said. "I'm beholden for what you did for me. And I'm sorry it turned out this way."

"I did it for myself as much as for you," he said.

Mama nuzzled him and Lula. "Were we wrong then, for making a place for them here?"

"There was nothing else we could have done, if we want to live in peace with ourselves," he said. "They were wrong."

"They don't think so," Mama said.

"They're soldiers," he said simply. We went into the house. Maria came over to me and hugged me. "I hope he doesn't start brooding over this," she whispered.

"It'll be all right," I said. "He's at peace with himself." I didn't say it, but I was thinking that if Maria was going to read any verses tonight at supper, they should be the ones about the money changers in the temple.

The next day, on the tenth, three blue soldiers came back to our house, along with three of ours. They brought their own camp tables. Except for our sofa, our parlor was stripped bare.

It was raining. We went about our business in the rest of the house. They were hammering out details of the surrender, Will McLean told us. That same day Elvira Tibbs came to our back door with a letter for me from Thomas.

"He's wounded," she told me, "but he's all right."

My heart beat inside me like a wild rabbit. I invited her up to my bedroom. In the hall on the first floor we almost ran into a Yankee officer.

My dear Oscie:

Don't fear for me. I am wounded, a flesh wound in the shoulder. It is not grave and I am in a safe house in Facquier County. We were bivouacked in Southern Loudoun County in late March, where we skirmished several times with Yankees. Then Mosby withdrew into Facquier. On March 30, I was with five other Rangers, scouting around Berryville in the Shenandoah Valley. We tangled with the 30th Massachusetts Infantry in a barnyard and I was shot. We lost three comrades and rode deeper into Confederate territory.

I am on the mend. It seems that March was nothing but chilling rain. But I have the warmth of a cheery fire. Yet we don't know what is happening. Guns seem to be silencing all across the Confederacy. We know Atlanta is in ruins, Savannah and Mobile occupied, and Richmond burning. Everyone seems to want peace now and some people are no longer interested in supporting us.

I have enclosed the address of where I am. I miss you so. My heart cries out to see you. The thought of you keeps me whole. I will ride again when I am ready, if Mosby needs me. But people are saying it will soon be over. I cannot entertain that thought. But whatever happens, I will do the right thing, you can count on it.

Your beloved Thomas.

Will McLean was half slumped at the table in the warming kitchen, having coffee. Candles flickered on the table. The soldiers had left and the rest of the family was in bed. I showed him the letter from Thomas. He read it and set it aside. When he spoke, his voice came cautiously. And he did not speak of the letter or Thomas.

"When Fitz Lee was here, the night of the eighth, he told us that if Lee surrendered he would take to the woods and not come back."

Ah, yes, I thought. Fitz Lee is cavalry. McLean is trying to tell me something here.

"Fitz and his men fear being taken prisoner, shot, or hanged."

"But you said Grant was kind in his terms of surrender."

"He was. Just today Grant told Lee at a meeting in the field that our men will be allowed to keep their horses and mules for spring plowing. That's downright generous to these men who are going home to starvation."

I nodded and waited respectfully. It was time, as Button had once told me, to hold my fire.

"When Lee told Grant his men were starving, Grant sent food over to their camps for the men and horses. But before that, Yankee soldiers were visiting the Confederate camps and sharing their own food."

Silence in the kitchen. He sipped his coffee. "Of

course, Mosby and his men have no way of knowing any of this."

He dropped that observation into the silence, like a stone into some water. And I felt the ripples of alarm.

"If Mosby decides to take to the woods, Thomas will have to ponder what he wants to be. Does he want to become an outlaw? Or a citizen of the United States again?"

I speculated on this.

"This is one reason I would not allow you to become officially betrothed."

"He said in the letter that he'll do the right thing," I reminded him.

He raised his eyes to me, black and unblinking. "The right thing according to whose conscience," he said.

It was not said with unkindness. But he lowered his eyes again when he said it.

All night I saw Thomas in my dreams, a ghostly figure on horseback, forging through mists. Sometimes I saw him jumping fences. Then he turned into Alex. My dreams were all bad.

I awoke to more chilling rain the next morning, the eleventh. It dripped from the eaves of the house. I could hear it making pinging sounds as it hit full rain barrels outside. It pattered on the porch and against the windows. When I went down to breakfast, I peeked into the warming kitchen to see Mary Ann sitting in a corner, stitching up a new rag doll for Lula. She nodded to me.

"Where is everyone?"

"Your mama and chillens be across the hall in the dinin' room. Mister Will, he said I should tell you to stop by the parlor afore breakfast. Somebody up there he wants you to meet."

"Who?"

She shrugged. "Can't remember the name. Fitz somethin'."

I ran upstairs. A man with a bushy beard, in the uniform of a Confederate officer, was sitting in the parlor with Will McLean, on a sofa out of which pieces of the haircloth upholstery had been cut by relic seekers. The two men got to their feet as I went in. The officer was well over six feet.

"General Lee, this is my Oscie," Will McLean said.

"Welcome, General," I said.

He bowed. "Why don't you just call me Fitz. Everybody else does."

"You have come back." I beamed up at him. He must have thought me demented, poor man, but he was most charming.

"Good heavens, I'd have returned sooner, if I'd known I'd get such a welcome from such a pretty girl."

"Oscie is betrothed to one of Mosby's Rangers," Will McLean explained. "She is concerned that they will take to the woods rather than surrender."

"Ah." Fitz Lee's smile was reassuring. "Well, Miss Oscie, I wanted to make for the bushes myself. Fully intended to. Then I decided I couldn't live the life of an outlaw. Couldn't do that to my uncle or family. If our army can surrender tomorrow, so can I."

"I am so glad you came back," I said again. I couldn't think of anything else to say. I didn't want to say anything else. And he understood.

"Mosby is a good man," he told me at parting. "My uncle trusted him. What is your young man's name?"

"Thomas Tibbs. He's from this village."

"He'll return, Miss Oscie. I guarantee it. We all say we'll run and never surrender. Especially if we're cavalry. We're free spirits. But win or lose, the South is still ours. And we can't let the Yankees take it away now, can we?"

Oh, I thought, he is the most wonderful man. Tears came into my eyes. I curtsied. "Thank you, sir. You have made me most happy."

Fitz Lee stayed in our parlor all that day and night. He slept on the floor, rolled in his blankets, like a child. Hiram fed him and kept the fire going for him.

That very afternoon we had still another visitor. I was upstairs, reading to Nannie before her nap when Hiram came to say that Will McLean wanted me in the dining room, immediately.

It was a summons, nothing less. And it sounded ominous, though I couldn't imagine what could happen next that could prove more ominous than the events of the last few days.

As I went down to the lower level of the house, I heard voices from the dining room. And there, in the half-light of a dismal afternoon, with all the world falling apart around us, there stood Alex.

It was Alex and it wasn't. The man who stood in front of the sideboard with Will McLean, was hatless and his hair was still blond and streaked with sun. His face was bronzed. He wore that same sword and sash, though, like Fitz Lee's, his uniform was the worse for wear. But this was an older Alex, with lines around his mouth that had not been there before. And eyes that were deeper set for having seen so much.

I felt my legs go weak, the color drain from my face. And standing there I witnessed a whole complement of feelings I had thought were long since gone.

Will McLean was pouring him a small glass of liquor. Some movement from me must have caught Alex's eye. He looked up. We stared at each other. He opened his mouth as if to speak, decided against it, set the glass down and his blue eyes went over me in the way a man's eyes go over a woman, but only for an instant. In the next moment the Southern gentleman, still very much present, took over.

He came forward, bowed, took my hand and kissed it. I wanted to touch the sun-streaked top of his blond curls. He was a vision, surely, some ghost come to haunt me. Then he straightened up and gave me a long and searching look. For a moment I felt panic. I had been in love with this man. I had once made a brassbound fool of myself over him. Now what was I to do?

Then I saw his eyes and I knew he expected nothing from me. He was weary. And quietly resigned to things. And shaken. And filled with a huge sadness. He had come as a friend, nothing else.

"You're alive, Alex," I said.

He smiled and I saw that the boy was gone in him, forever. "Yes. I came into the village to confer with General Gibbon about surrendering my artillery. I passed your yard and saw this man here," he smiled at Will McLean. "I said, 'Hello, McLean, what are you doing here?' I had no idea you people lived in this place. 'Alexander,' he said, 'what the hell are you fellows doing here?' And so!"

"I'm glad you came," I said warmly.

"You're all grown up, Miss Oscie." His voice was reverent.

Embarrassment flooded me. McLean was slipping out of the room. "She's betrothed, Alex. But I'll let her tell you."

"Indeed!" Alex's cheer was genuine. "Who is he?"

We went to the table and took chairs facing each other. "Thomas Tibbs, from this village. He rides with Mosby."

"I'm happy for you. Where is he now?"

"Wounded and recovering in a safe house in Facquier County."

He nodded and it became awkward between us. "Were you wounded?" I asked.

"Yes. At Petersburg. But I'm fine now."

"Do you still have Dixie?"

"Yes. She took me all through the war. I see Fitz Lee is asleep in your parlor."

"He was going to run away. But he came back."

"So was I." He smiled at my amazement. "I wanted to take to the woods. Just before General Lee decided to surrender, I went to him and suggested he order the army to disperse, each man for himself."

"What changed your mind, then?"

"Lee. He's a grand old man, Oscie. He said he would have none of that, he was too old to go bushwhacking. He told me it was the end of the Confederacy, yes, but as Christian men we couldn't choose pride over personal feelings. He showed me the situation on a plane to which I had not yet risen. So tomorrow I shall surrender my artillery."

"Oh Alex, it's so awful!"

"I know, Oscie. It seems as if our world has fallen apart. Then, just when you think that, the old graces come forth in strange ways. Riding about this past day, I've seen evidence of honor from both sides to gladden the heart. Yankees came into our camps, sharing food. And to meet old friends."

I was startled to realize how familiar his voice was to me. Yet I had not thought of him for months at a time. Where had I hidden these memories?

"What's awful for so many of us, of course, is that after we surrender, our guns will be gone, our country will be gone. We will no longer be soldiers. We will have no orders to obey, nothing to do, and nowhere to go."

"You will miss it, Alex," I said.

"Yes. I will. I know I am fortunate to have lived through the war. So I wonder if there is something ailing in me to say such a thing."

He sipped his brandy. A silence fell between us. Once he glanced at me and smiled and I responded in kind. But there was no awkwardness now. We always had been able to be silent in one another's company, I recollected. It was a sign of true friendship. Then he began to talk.

"I was at Gettysburg, Oscie. I commanded 140 cannon, in the center of the Union lines. I can't describe to you what it was like."

"Like a hog-killing?" I asked.

"Yes, that's it. Guns booming in the distance. Men shouting. Horses screaming, the sound of preachers praying over men before they went into battle. Drums rolling. I was supposed to keep the Yankee cannon on Cemetery Hill quiet so Pickett and his division could take the hill. General Longstreet was relying on me."

I sensed he had to tell me this. It was gnawing at him. Someday he might tell his wife, but now he had to tell me.

"Pickett was riding around whooping it up like a schoolboy. He wore long curls. He couldn't wait to fight. God, what is wrong with us? Then I saw him and his men come out of the woods, with over a mile to walk in the open, under Yankee guns. The Yankees had Hancock up there, commanding the Second Corps. And I knew Hancock was good. Just like I knew Pickett would never make that charge without losing a good number of men. We all knew it, Longstreet, maybe even Lee. But nothing could have held us back, Oscie, nothing!"

"We heard what happened," I said.

"Yes." He paused to clear his throat. "I managed to silence some Yankee artillery, but not enough. The smoke was so bad, you couldn't see where to fire. Our brigades, commanded by Kemper, Garnett, and Armistead, were all cut to pieces, those good officers killed. And then Pickett came down the hill, crying. Lee asked him to re-form his division. He cried. 'I have no division, General,' he said. I saw him crying, Oscie."

I shivered. He smiled weakly at me. "That's when I knew we were finished. After Gettysburg. Not because we couldn't fight, but because we loved fighting so. I knew what fools we were, but I still continued to love it, Oscie."

"You knew we were finished back at Manassas," I told him.

He shrugged his broad shoulders under the tunic and looked down at his glass. "The killing was awful, Oscie. And we all came to love the war. What's wrong with us?"

I wanted to take his head against my shoulders, not in any romantic way, for in these moments alone with him I had determined there was no more romance between us. But I wanted to comfort him. "You were trained to be a soldier, Alex," I told him. "You did what you were trained to do."

He looked at me hopefully. "That's it, Oscie. Simple as that. But what will people like me do now?"

"You will turn your abilities into something fine, Alex. You will go home and help the South. It needs you just as much now as in war. You must work out what to do." I was starting to sound like Button.

He got to his feet. "I'm an old man and I'm only twenty-eight."

"No." I stood also. "You just need food and rest. Like Fitz Lee."

"But I'll never again be the dashing soldier boy you knew back at Manassas."

So that was it. He'd come to me, because he knew I remembered that dashing soldier boy better than anyone. So then, it was up to me to release that young cavalier, to let him go.

"Manassas was another world, another time, Alex. We're none of us the same. We all left part of ourselves back there."

"It was a fine world. Do you remember the day we rode over to Mrs. Henry's?"

"I have thought of it often."

"She died in her house. It was struck by an artillery shell."

"She was too old to live for what would come, Alex. We aren't."

"You've a great deal of wisdom, Oscie. You have become a woman."

I said nothing to that.

"I suppose, if I were honest with myself, it's the camaraderie of war that I'll miss. The working together for a cause. Not the killing."

"Then be honest with yourself, Alex. As I recall, back at Manassas you told me that you knew the risks, but you were willing to take them, because if you couldn't do that, you weren't much good."

"You remember that?" His blue eyes crinkled with a smile.

"I remember it all, Alex."

He sobered and took my hand in his own for a quiet reflective moment. "We stole something back there at Manassas, Oscie. Something neither of us had a right to. Something bright and precious. I have thought of it often in the middle of the killing."

I nodded, tongue-tied now.

He sighed and grinned at me. "However, we must put it and the war in proper order in our minds. You are betrothed now and I go back to my beloved wife. But do you think it would be proper if we each remembered it on occasion?"

"I fully intend to keep the memory alive," I said.

He looked down at my hand which he still held in his own. "You're betrothed to a soldier," he said. "I told you not to give your heart to a soldier, Oscie."

"They keep hearts best," I said. "Or so I've found."

He was struck speechless then. He raised my hand to his lips and kissed it. "I wish you a long and beautiful life, Oscie."

"And I you, Alex."

He released my hand, drew himself up to his full military bearing and bowed. I thought I saw tears in his eyes. I couldn't be sure, for the tears in mine blurred everything. I watched him take his leave of the room, knowing he took that young girl I was back at Manassas with him.

Chapter 30

April 12, 1865

The morning of the surrender dawned gray and chilled, as if the very heavens sympathized with our ragged army.

We did not have to go far to watch the proceedings. Yankee soldiers were lined up on both sides of the Richmond-Lynchburg Stage Road, from the northern branch of the Appomattox River, all around the Court House, and to the front of our house.

The Yankees stationed in line in front of our house were the 118th Pennsylvania. Every so often Willie would come into our parlor with Eddie Tibbs to inform us what was going on.

"A Maine man is in charge of the surrender," he said angrily.

His father saw the blood in Willie's eyes. "Major General Joshua Chamberlain is a college professor, son. He speaks seven languages and was wounded four times. Grant personally put him in charge."

Willie nodded and ran back out. Maria and Ellen Bryant were in our front yard, too. Ellen had made friends with a soldier from Pennsylvania who was finding them a good spot from which to view the proceedings.

Maria and Ellen came into the parlor. "Ellen's friend said some troops from the Sixty-ninth Ohio were in the fight on the skirmish line at the Court House on the Ninth," Maria said.

Clearly this was a prelude to something. We waited.

"Michah's people, the Sixty-ninth Ohio. He must be dead or he would have come to us." Her voice was quaking.

"Nonsense," McLean said briskly. "We know the names of everyone killed at the Court House. Maybe he's hurt and been taken to Farmville, where the Yankees took their wounded."

"I must go to him, then!" Maria appealed.

"We can't get out of this village today," McLean gestured to the window. "We'll go tomorrow. I'll take you."

"I'll ask Martin if he'll send an aide to Farmville as soon as possible," Ellen consoled my sister. She looked at us, smiling. "My friend is a colonel in the 121st Pennsylvania."

"Always good to have a colonel for a friend, Ellen," Will McLean said. "Thank you."

I shall not forget that day if I live to a hundred.

It was the silence that most impressed me. It was almost terrifying, given the presence of so many souls gathered in one place. It was so silent during that surrender that you could hear the birds twittering or an occasional cough from the line.

I was drawn outside, finally to stand with Willie, Eddie Tibbs, Ellen, and Maria behind the 118th

Pennsylvania men. We stood in respectful silence as our tattered soldiers passed by, hearing the shuffling of feet and the snapping of orders far down the road.

And there was not a sound. No trumpet, no drum roll, no cheers, no derisive remarks, no motion from any Yankee up and down the line. It was as if everyone were holding their breath.

One Confederate soldier looked at the Yankee in front of me. "What regiment is you-uns?" he asked.

"The 118th Pennsylvania," came the reply.

"Didn't we give it to you-uns at Shepherdstown?" the soldier asked.

"Yes," came the easy answer. "But it took a whole Reb division to do it."

But there was no animosity. Only whispered exchanges like this.

"Come on," Ellen urged us. "Martin said he'd save us a place in the field by the Peers and Kelly houses. That's where we'll see things."

We followed Willie and Eddie Tibbs. The walk was long, but it was worth it. For we did see things, sights I shall remember longer than I live.

Ellen's friend, the Yankee officer, gave us a spot on the hill and advised us to be quiet and not move. He was polite and charming as Ellen introduced us. He pointed out Chamberlain, standing with aides to receive the last remnants of arms and colors of our army. Then he left us.

If we looked west, down past the Court House, we could see the long Confederate line. I recognized General Gordon, Daddy Will's friend who had come to our house after the tallow candles were set in the window. He led the first corps of men who had come to lay down their muskets and flags. He rode a magnificent black horse and he came forward slowly.

But he was riding with his head down and shoulders slumped. Then we saw Chamberlain speak to an aide. In the next moment everything changed. A bugle sounded and the Yankees all changed the position of their muskets, in unison.

"That's the carry arms order," Willie told us. "Chamberlain changed it from order arms. It's the marching salute. Alex taught me that."

Suddenly General Gordon raised his head, saw what was happening in the Yankee line, wheeled his beautiful horse toward the Yankee 3rd Brigade and, uplifted in full military manner in his saddle, he dropped the point of his sword to the toe of his boot to return the salute to Chamberlain.

Then, crisply, he ordered his men to return the Union salute also.

The Confederates came to order behind Gordon. They drew themselves up. They fixed bayonets. And they stepped forward to stack their arms and lay down their flags and cartridge boxes. Many of the men kissed their flags before laying them down. Some of them were crying.

I heard Maria sniffing next to me. Ellen handed her a handkerchief and I had to wipe tears from my own eyes.

Willie and Eddie were speechless. We stayed for a while, watching, then went home. At supper, Willie told his father what we had seen.

"Well," Will McLean said, "It seems Chamberlain knows more than seven languages. He knows the most important language of all. Human compassion."

At dusk I sought out Daddy Will, who was sitting on the front porch. The weather had changed and there was a balmy sweetness in the air. Up to the Peers house where we'd stood watching this afternoon were flickering lights, like firecrackers.

"The remaining Confederate cartridges being set on fire," he told me.

"It's like the Fourth of July," I said.

"Yes. Ironic, isn't it?"

In the gathering dusk you could hear the creaking of Yankee wagons and the snorting of their horses as they passed our house to collect the equipment left by our army. I leaned with my back against the porch railing.

"Well, it's over," he said.

"Yes."

"Something to see today. You children should remember it always. Tell your grandchildren. The Yankees behaved most admirably."

"Some of them cried when they saw our men crying," I said.

"Lots of work to do now. I hear the Yankee army's small printing press they used to print parole papers broke down. I hear they're giving our men free transportation on the railroad to get home."

I had not come to the porch to speak of parole papers. But I bided my time.

"Well," he said, "Maria's happy."

"Yes." A Yankee soldier had ridden in from Farmville late this afternoon. And Ellen's Yankee colonel had found out from him that one Michah Stevens was alive and slightly wounded in a hospital there.

"Will you take her to see him?"

"Tomorrow," he promised.

"Thomas's parents are talking of taking a trip to Facquier County to bring him home," I said.

"They've invited me to go along."

Silence, long and stretched out. He was smoking a cheroot and the tip glowed against the dusk. For a moment I felt the coldness of his silence, something palpable between us, the resistance familiar.

"Does Thomas want to come home?" he asked.

"I don't know," I said.

"Well, I know one thing. If Thomas was my son I'd get myself to Facquier County right quick and beat some sense into his head."

"You never beat anybody, Will McLean," I told him. "You talk a good line, though."

He smiled at me. "It's all I needed to do, talk. It kept you children decent. Speak your piece, Oscie Mason."

"What piece?"

"Ask me what you came out here to ask me."

"Didn't come out to ask anything."

It wasn't so dark that I couldn't see the raised eyebrows. "Oh, are you *telling* me then, that you're going with the Tibbs to see Thomas? Or asking?"

"I'm asking," I said dutifully.

He puffed his cheroot in silence. From inside the house came lovely sounds of Maria playing "Dixie" on the piano. "Well, that's a new wind blowing. You asking my permission for once," he said.

"I've always asked, Will McLean."

"No, you haven't." He flicked the ashes of the cheroot and they blossomed, miniature fireballs in the night. "You went ahead and damned well didn't. You fell in love with Alex without so much as a by-your-leave. And betrothed yourself to Thomas without my permission."

"A person doesn't ask permission to fall in love," I told him. "Not even of themselves."

He grunted. "Everything you ever did was without my permission."

I held my fire, not wanting to plague him.

"Look," he said, "I know Thomas's parents are decent people. And that if you made the trip with them it would be seemly and proper."

"Seemly and proper! Good heavens," I said. "After all we've been through you're still worried about seemly and proper?"

"Yes, I am, my girl." His voice was sharp, with an edge I recognized all too well. "I'm more concerned now than ever. It's more important now that we remember what we are."

I allowed him the rebuke. I didn't mouth him. Nothing made him madder than when I mouthed him. I knew better by now.

"What I was about to say, before you so rudely interrupted, is that I have no qualms about your going. But what will you do if, when you get there, your Thomas doesn't want to come back? Have you pondered on that, Oscie Mason?"

"Yessir."

"And?"

"I'll come back here. To this house."

To my father's house.

He grunted.

"May I go, then?"

"What will you do if I say no?"

I hesitated. He was baiting me and enjoying it. He knew I was up to it. And, though he wouldn't tolerate sass, he expected me to give as well as I was getting.

But something else was happening here, also. I was asking him to let me go. The way a girl asks her father.

And he was getting ready to release me. The way a

father does, when he knows a girl's grown. But it wasn't any easier for him than I suspect it would have been for my own daddy.

Part of being grown up, I knew, meant I had to leave him with something. It wasn't anything he hadn't earned. And he was waiting for it.

"I want to see Thomas," I said carefully, "and if you say no, I'll go anyway, Will McLean. But I'd rather go with your blessing."

"So you want my blessing." His voice was husky.

"Yessir. It'd mean a powerful lot to me."

Maria commenced playing "The Battle Cry of Freedom," slowly. The notes drifted out on the night air, almost a dirge. I knew the words by heart:

The Union forever, hurrah boys, hurrah. So we'll rally 'round the flag, let's rally 'round the flag, singing the battle cry of freedom.

The music found the hurt places in my soul. The Union forever. I thought of Alex's words.

We are no longer soldiers, we have no orders to obey, nothing to do, nowhere to go.

Would Thomas think in kind? My heart was full to bursting. Would Thomas insist on taking to the bushes, to live the life of an outlaw?

"All right," McLean's voice came in the darkness. "You have my blessing. You may go."

"Thank you."

We sat in silence for a while. Then I thought of something. "You told both Fitz Lee and Alex that I was betrothed," I said. "Why did you do that?"

"Because you are in your heart, Oscie. We can't help what's in our hearts. I learned that a long time ago."

I was so moved, I had to get up and go to the railing. Next thing I knew I felt his presence beside me.

"When are the Tibbs leaving?"

"In two days."

"Well, remember who you are. Don't beg him to come home."

"I never beg anybody for anything."

"No, you don't. I can vouch for that."

I peered up at him. Beyond, in the distance, the intermittent flaring of the cartridges provided enough light so I could make out his profile. It was still firm. His shoulders were still strong, his hair still full, though graying at the temples. I felt the strength emanating from his nearness. I always had, I pondered. Ought to tell him so. Must try. My thoughts came in scattered flares of light, like the exploding cartridges.

"I'm beholden to you," I said.

"For what?"

"For all you've done for us."

"I was always just doing my job, Oscie," his voice was wondering. "Like I always promised you I would do."

"I wonder what my daddy would have done about the war if he'd lived."

"Probably would have gone off and done his doctoring. Like I went off and did my business. Like Alex went off and did his soldiering. And Tom went off to do his riding with Mosby. Everybody did what they had to do, Oscie."

"Do you think the war would have changed my daddy?"

"If he was as good a man as I knew him to be, yes. He'd have had to change. Nobody could come through this war and not change. You'd better go upstairs now. You've packing to do."

"Yessir." But I lingered a moment, with his hand

on my shoulder. Then, of a sudden, I hugged him.

He put both arms around me. "Well," he said, "did it take a war to bring this about?"

"Don't joke, Will McLean. You never will learn when to be serious." I sniffed and wiped my face with my hand.

"Tell you what, Oscie Mason, hope I never do, either. A sense of humor is the only thing that keeps intelligent people from hanging themselves. You know who said that?"

"Voltaire," I said. "You see, Button did teach me something."

"She taught you a lot more than that," he said dryly. He drew out a handkerchief and wiped the tears for me.

We stood for a while watching the flaring of the cartridges. Then he patted my shoulder. "You'll be right fine, Oscie. Whatever happens with Thomas. You've got good makings."

I thanked him and said goodnight. I left him there and went into the house. Maria was playing "The Battle Hymn of the Republic."

Author's Note

This is a novel *based* on events in the lives of Wilmer McLean and his family, the man on whose property the American Civil War started, and in whose parlor it ended after he had moved hundreds of miles away in the hopes of "never seeing another soldier again."

As an author of young-adult historical novels, I attempt to separate, in the author's note, fact from the fiction I have written. Ironically, the day this manuscript came back from the copy editor, new research material on Wilmer McLean also came in the mail, from Ronald G. Wilson, historian at Appomattox Court House National Historical Park in Appomattox, Virginia.

This new research, done by Carol Drake Friedman for the Historical Society of Fairfax County, more fully rounds out and explains the character of Wilmer McLean and I was able to incorporate certain facts into the manuscript before it went back to my publisher.

"Where did McLean take his family between the time they moved from their plantation at Manassas until they moved to Appomattox Court House in the fall of 1863?" I had asked Ronald Wilson when I was doing my original research.

"Nobody knows," he told me.

That was true at the time, which was two years before Ms. Friedman's research was available. So, in my novel, working with what research I had, I have McLean taking his family to Charlottesville, Virginia. This was logical to me, since McLean's sister, Hannah Cleary, and her family went to Charlottesville after leaving Washington, D.C., at the outset of the war. As did Howson Hooe, the husband of another of McLean's sisters.

In her new research, Ms. Friedman asks: "Where did the McLeans go? Perhaps to Virginia's [McLean's] house on the north side of Bull Run in Fairfax County."

However, there is no current firm scholarship on this. So I do not feel as if I am flying in the face of history by placing them in Charlottesville.

Ms. Friedman's research also uncovered a fact not available to me at the time of my writing—that Maria Mason, one of McLean's stepdaughters and a main character in my novel, was married to Philip Lee at St. John's Episcopal Church in Centreville on January 20, 1869.

I have Maria marrying Michah Stevens, a Yankee from Marietta, Ohio. I cite this to show how I improvised for the sake of plot, when I ran into dead ends in history. (At this point it was too late to rewrite the novel to have Maria marrying Lee.)

However, I was happy to be able to use Ms. Friedman's research to place McLean's mercantile business in Centreville instead of Alexandria, as previous records had cited. And to be more accurate by telling how McLean's store was a failure because of the bad state of the economy at the time. McLean's courtship of Annabelle Hurst, before marrying Virginia Mason, was another gem this research uncovered for me. As was "Willie" McLean's real name—John Wilmer.

Historical novelists live in fear of exactly this type of thing happening: new research on their topic coming to light after the book comes out. Such instances show that history, what we may regard as a "dead" subject not worth bothering with, is constantly being revived and rejuvenated with the emergence of newly found letters, court records, or diaries, some discovered in people's attics, and others there for the scholar who bothers to track them down in various places.

Who knows? Two years after this book is published, we may have a whole new body of information on Wilmer McLean and his family!

All historical novelists have to invent much of the motivation of their characters in order to take them from one historically accurate event to the next.

Actually, it wasn't until thirty years after the end of the Civil War that the unique role played by the McLean family in this conflict was noted—by General Edward Porter Alexander in his writings. (He appears in my story as Captain Alex.)

So it is safe to say that research on the McLeans started late. Perhaps that is why no one can tell us what Virginia Hooe Mason's first husband, Seddon, died from. Or how the little sister died. Her manner of death is my own invention. As is the character of Mary Ann. McLean's feelings about slavery, Oscie's "romance" with Captain Alex, and the premise that Virginia McLean urged her husband to do something, at the time of the surrender at Appomattox Court House, to salvage the kind of person she perceived him as being—all this is from my own fertile imagination, for the sake of fictional tension.

But we do know that McLean's marriage to Virginia Mason, a widow with three daughters, created gossip in Prince William County, so much so that Virginia postponed the wedding to have her money and property put in trust.

We do know that McLean was orphaned at an early age, that his sister Hannah Cleary had many children, gave four sons to the Confederacy and that one was a physician in Washington, D.C., who raised his own company of Confederate soldiers and went to practice medicine in Brazil after the war, because he could not accept defeat.

From the personal papers of Captain Edward Porter Alexander, kindly shared with me by the manuscripts department of the University of North Carolina at Chapel Hill, we know that Alexander and General Pierre G. T. Beauregard, the hero of Fort Sumter, were wined and dined by the McLeans just before the war started.

Alexander wrote of frequently taking meals with the family, of knowing them well. He noted that his wife was a niece of Mrs. McLean's first husband and that, "This is near enough relationship in Virginia to warrant recognition and family intimacy, especially if there are two pretty daughters as there were in the McLean family." His papers also tell of his background and feelings about leaving the Federal army.

Again, the romance between Oscie and Captain Alex is of my own making. I created it in Oscie's mind, encouraged by the gallantry, courtesy, and dashing appearance of Captain Alexander, whom I saw as the quintessential Confederate officer.

In actuality, Alexander did return to visit McLean at Appomattox at war's end. He came as a general, riding into the village on April 11, 1865, to confer with Union General John Gibbon about turning over his artillery. He is on record as having seen McLean in his front yard and stopping to speak to him. His meeting with Oscie at this time is of my own making. I could not resist it.

It is impossible to recount here all I invented, but I cite the important fictitious events so my readers will not be confused.

McLean did give his house and barn at Yorkshire to the Confederate army. He did donate his time as quartermaster, staying on at Manassas after his family left. What made him change, during the course of the war, from a staunch patriot to a man who speculated in sugar, making money on the war, is not so difficult to imagine, once one realizes how his business in Centreville failed, how he had a family to support, how he lost Yorkshire to the conflict, and saw others speculating.

Research tells us that McLean was not a man to let the opportunity for profit slip by.

What is more mystifying to me than his speculating in sugar is what made Will McLean walk out of his house at Appomattox on April 9, 1865, to meet accidentally Colonel Charles Marshall, General Robert E. Lee's military secretary, who was seeking a site for the surrender.

Historians say McLean went to get a guard put in front of his house. But then, why did McLean offer his house, when he was so turned against the military for what he had seen at Manassas? These are the unanswered questions in history that intrigue novelists, the haunting tunes to which we must find words. I found my words and play this tune with a whimsical ear to bring my story full circle.

My scene with Oscie fetching goods McLean shipped to Appomattox stems from the fact that while the McLeans lived in that village, they did not want for anything, probably due to McLean's connections with Richmond merchants. There was a young girl named Ellen Bryant in Appomattox Court House, who married a Pennsylvania soldier after the surrender. There was a free black woman named Mary Christian, who purchased her own husband, then set him free. Mr. Meeks, who owned the general store, did lose his son at First Manassas.

The Tibbs family also lived in Appomattox, their son Thomas rode with Captain John Mosby and Oscie Mason did marry Thomas after the war.

I have described the surrender as accurately as an ex-newspaperwoman can, combining historical facts with my own perception of scenes that I experienced when, as a member of a Brigade of the American Revolution, I saw the "surrender" of the British army to the Americans as reenacted with a cast of thousands, at Yorktown, Virginia, in 1981. Then I witnessed, recreated, the terrible silence in the presence of so many assembled souls, "no trumpet, no drumroll, no cheers" (as I have written in this novel) from any American up and down the line, while all held their breath as the British lay down their colors and their arms.

I was fortunate to have been at that reenactment of the surrender of the British to the Americans. And like Oscie, I shall never forget it as long as I live. All I had to do to recreate the incredible sense of history was to change the uniforms and the era. Surely the emotions when the South surrendered to the North must have been similar.

In a little-known fact of history, but one I felt

necessary to incorporate in my novel, the Union and Confederate officers did meet at the Court House in Appomattox, reviving old friendships before the surrender. And McLean did put tallow candles in the windows during the night of April 8 to have old friends visit, with Fitz Lee sleeping in the McLean parlor overnight.

The scene in McLean's parlor after the surrender, when Union soldiers started stripping the place for souvenirs, is accurate, right down to Union General George Custer's part in the plunder and the Yankees taking little Lula's rag doll.

Such a story! How can a novelist not be drawn in! I have tried to honor the history that is there. I have connected the dots between the gaps to create my story, with all respect for those who actually lived it and their descendants.

Ann Rinaldi
June 23, 1992

Related Readings

CONTENTS

The War Comes to Richmond Children

by Sallie Hunt

When he hears the news that Confederate forces have fired on 68 Union soldiers at Fort Sumter, Will McLean comments, "God help us all." But the events at Fort Sumter drew a different response from many others in the South. In the following memoir, Sallie Hunt recalls the buzz of patriotic excitement in her hometown. As you read, compare the mood of the children in Richmond with that of the McLean family as the war begins.

ONE SPRING DAY in April, 1861, all Richmond was astir. Schools were broken up, and knots of excited men gathered at every street corner. Sumter had been fired upon, and Lincoln had ordered the men of Virginia to rush upon their brethren of the South and put the rebellion down. Now "the die was cast," our lot was with theirs, and come weal or woe, we would fight for independence. How merrily the sunbeams danced that day! how proud we children were of the great preparation for the illumination that night!—how few recked of the great underthrob of misery, grief and want! Every patriotic citizen had his house ablaze with a thousand lights, and the dark ones were *marked*. I remember distinctly my father taking us to see the Exchange Hotel and Ballard House with the glass balcony, stretching over the street and connecting the two houses, all glittering and reflecting the crystal lights. To us it was a grand spectacle, and our hearts swelled with pride to think we could say to our tyrants: "Thus far shalt thou come, and no further."

The excitement permeated the schools, and those of our number who lived in the dark houses, or the non-illuminators, were dubbed "Yankees," "Abolitionists" and "Black Republicans," and virtually ostracized. Saturdays we would spend in the lecture-rooms of the different churches we attended, where our mothers and grown-up sisters were busy plying the needle, and cutting out clothes for the soldier boys, and indulging in such talk about the vile usurpers as would fire our young hearts with indignation. Snatches of song improvised for the emergency—"Maryland, My Maryland," "John Brown's Body," "There's Life in the Old Land Yet," &c.—grew as familiar as "I Want To Be an Angel." In fact, we had a parody which ran thus:

> *I want to be a soldier,*
>   *And with the soldiers stand,*
> *A knapsack on my shoulder,*
>   *And musket in my hand;*
> *And there beside Jeff Davis,*
>   *So glorious and so brave,*
> *I'll whip the cussed Yankee*
>   *And drive him to his grave.*

But what were our boys doing while the girls were sewing up sandbags to fortify Drewry's Bluff? It seemed the "Demon of Destruction" was possessing the whole land. The boys were keeping their patriotism warm by *playing* "Yank" and "Reb" in mock battles, and so sorely did these young archers wound each other that steps had to be taken by the city authorities toward the suppression of these hostilities. I remember being on Church Hill on one occasion, when the rowdies from Rocketts, calling themselves Yankees, came upon our boys who were unarmed. Immediately our party of little girls flew to a coal-house near, which happened to be open for replenishing, and filling our little aprons with the dusky diamonds ran into the midst of a hot battle, screaming with all the enthusiasm of our young natures, "Kill them! kill them!" We bound up heads and filled pockets with "ammunition" till our nurses, noticing our escapade, came to carry us to our mamas to be punished for soiling our dresses.

The Battleground

by Elsie Singmaster

As the Civil War continued, the excitement of the early days turned to disillusionment as people from both North and South experienced the harsh realities of war. Like the McLeans, the woman in the following story lives in a small town that became the site of a momentous battle in the war— the battle of Gettysburg. Unlike the McLeans, however, she is not able to move away. The story begins a few months after the battle, in which the woman's husband fought and was lost.

Mercifully, Mary Bowman, a widow, whose husband had been missing since the battle of Gettysburg, had been warned, together with other citizens of Gettysburg, that on Thursday the nineteenth of November, 1863, she would be awakened from sleep by a bugler's reveille, and that during that great day she would hear again the dread sound of cannon.

Nevertheless, hearing again the reveille, she sat up in bed with a scream and put her hands over her ears. Then, gasping, groping about in her confusion and terror, she rose and began to dress. She put on a dress which had been once a bright plaid, but which now, having lost both its color and the stiff, outstanding quality of the skirts of '63, hung about her in straight and dingy folds. It was clean, but it had upon it certain ineradicable brown stains on which soap and water seemed to have had no effect. She was thin and pale, and her eyes had a set look, as though they saw other sights than those directly about her.

In the bed from which she had risen lay her little daughter; in a trundle bed near by, her two sons, one about ten years old, the other about four. They slept heavily, lying deep in their beds, as though they would never move. Their mother looked at them with her strange, absent gaze; then she barred a little more closely the broken shutters, and went down the stairs. The shutters were broken in a curious fashion. Here and there they were pierced by round holes, and one hung from a single hinge. The window frames were without glass, the floor was without carpet, the beds without pillows.

In her kitchen Mary Bowman looked about her as though still seeing other sights. Here, too, the floor was carpetless. Above the stove a patch of fresh plaster on the wall showed where a great rent had been filled in; in the doors were the same little round holes as in the shutters of the room above. But there was food and fuel, which was more than one might have expected from the aspect of the house and its mistress. She opened the shattered door of the cupboard, and, having made the fire, began to prepare breakfast.

Outside the house there was already, at six o'clock, noise and confusion. Last evening a train from Washington had brought to the village Abraham Lincoln; for several days other trains had been bringing less distinguished guests, until thousands thronged the little town. This morning the tract of land between Mary Bowman's house and the village cemetery was to be dedicated for the burial of the Union dead, who were to be laid there in sweeping semicircles round a center on which a great monument was to rise.

But of the dedication, of the President of the United States, of his distinguished associates, of the great crowds, of the soldiers, of the crape-banded banners, Mary Bowman and her children would see nothing. Mary Bowman would sit in her little wrecked kitchen with her children. For to her the President of the United States and others in high places who prosecuted war or who tolerated war, who called for young men to fight, were hateful. To Mary Bowman the crowds of curious persons who coveted a sight of the great battlefields were ghouls; their eyes wished to gloat upon ruin, upon fragments of the weapons of war, upon torn bits of the habiliments of soldiers; their feet longed to sink into the loose ground of hastily made graves; the discovery of a partially covered body was precious to them.

Mary Bowman knew that field! From Culp's Hill to the McPherson farm, from Big Round Top to the poorhouse, she had traveled it, searching, searching, with frantic, insane disregard of positions or of possibility. Her husband could not have fallen here among the Eleventh Corps, he could not lie here among the unburied dead of the Louisiana Tigers! If he was in the battle at all, it was at the Angle that he fell.

She had not been able to begin her search immediately after the battle because there were forty wounded men in her little house; she could not prosecute it with any diligence even later, when the soldiers had been carried to the hospitals, in the Presbyterian Church, the Catholic Church, the two Lutheran churches, the Seminary, the College, the Courthouse, and the great tented hospital on the

York road. Nurses were here, Sisters of Mercy were here, compassionate women were here by the score; but still she was needed, with all the other women of the village, to nurse, to bandage, to comfort, to pray with those who must die. Little Mary Bowman had assisted at the amputation of limbs, she had helped to control strong men torn by the frenzy of delirium, she had tended poor bodies which had almost lost all semblance to humanity. Neither she nor any of the other women of the village counted themselves especially heroic; the delicate wife of the judge, the petted daughter of the doctor, the gently bred wife of the preacher forgot that fainting at the sight of blood was one of the distinguishing qualities of their sex; they turned back their sleeves and repressed their tears, and, shoulder to shoulder with Mary Bowman and her Irish neighbor, Hannah Casey, they fed the hungry and healed the sick and clothed the naked. If Mary Bowman had been herself, she might have laughed at the sight of her dresses cobbled into trousers, her skirts wrapped round the shoulders of sick men. But neither then nor ever after did Mary laugh at any incident of that summer.

Hannah Casey laughed, and by and by she began to boast. Meade, Hancock, Slocum, were noncombatants beside her. She had fought whole companies of Confederates, she had wielded bayonets, she had assisted at the spiking of a gun, she was Barbara Frietchie and Molly Pitcher combined. But all her lunacy could not make Mary Bowman smile.

Of John Bowman no trace could be found. No one could tell her anything about him, to her frantic letters no one responded. Her old friend, the village judge, wrote letters also, but could get no reply. Her husband was missing; it was probable that he lay somewhere upon this field, the field upon which they had wandered as lovers.

In midsummer a few trenches were opened, and Mary, unknown to her friends, saw them opened. At the uncovering of the first great pit, she actually helped with her own hands. For those of this generation who know nothing of war, that fact may be written down, to be passed over lightly. The soldiers, having been on other battlefields, accepted her presence without comment. She did not cry, she only helped doggedly, and looked at what they found. That, too, may be written down for a generation which has not known war.

Immediately, an order went forth that no graves, large or small, were to be opened before cold weather. The citizens were panic-stricken with fear of an epidemic; already there were many cases of dysentery and typhoid. Now that the necessity for daily work for the wounded was past, the village became nervous, excited, irritable. Several men and boys were killed while trying to open unexploded shells; their deaths added to the general horror. There were constant visitors who sought husbands, brothers, sweethearts; with these the Gettysburg women were still able to weep, for them they were still able to care; but the constant demand for entertainment for the curious annoyed those who wished to be left alone to recover from the shock of battle. Gettysburg was prostrate, bereft of many of its worldly possessions, drained to the bottom of its well of sympathy. Its schools must be opened, its poor must be helped. Cold weather was coming and there were many, like Mary Bowman, who owned no longer any quilts or blankets, who had given away their clothes, their linen, even the precious sheets which their grandmothers had spun. Gettysburg grudged nothing, wished nothing back, it asked only to be left in peace.

When the order was given to postpone the opening of graves till fall, Mary began to go about the battlefield searching alone. Her good, obedient children stayed at home in the house or in the little field. They were beginning to grow thin and wan, they were shivering in the hot August weather, but their mother did not see. She gave them a great deal more to eat than she had herself, and they had far better clothes than her bloodstained motley.

She went about the battlefield with her eyes on the ground, her feet treading gently, anticipating loose soil or some sudden obstacle. Sometimes she stooped suddenly. To fragments of shells, to bits of blue or gray cloth, to cartridge belts or broken muskets, she paid no heed; at sight of pitiful bits of human bodies she shuddered. But there lay also upon that field little pocket Testaments, letters, trinkets, photographs. John had had her photograph and the children's, and surely he must have had some of the letters she had written!

But poor Mary found nothing.

One morning, late in August, she sat beside her kitchen table with her head on her arm. The first of the scarlet gum leaves had begun to drift down from the shattered trees; it would not be long before the ground would be covered, and those depressed spots, those tiny wooden headstones, those fragments of blue and gray be hidden. The thought smothered her. She did not cry, she had not cried at all. Her soul seemed hardened, stiff, like the terrible wounds for which she had helped to care.

Suddenly, hearing a sound, Mary had looked up. The judge stood in the doorway; he had known all about her since she was a little girl; something in his face told her that he knew also of her terrible search. She did not ask him to sit down; she said nothing at all. She had been a loquacious person, but she had become an abnormally silent one. Speech hurt her.

The judge looked round the little kitchen. The rent in the wall was still unmended, the chairs were broken; there was nothing else to be seen but the table and the rusty stove and the thin, friendless-looking children standing by the door. It was the house not only of poverty and woe, but of neglect.

"Mary," said the judge, "how do you mean to live?"

Mary's thin, sunburned hand stirred a little as it lay on the table.

"I do not know."

"You have these children to feed and clothe and you must furnish your house again. Mary—" The judge hesitated for a moment. John Bowman had been a schoolteacher, a thrifty, ambitious soul, who would have thought it a disgrace for his wife to earn her living. The judge laid his hand on the thin hand beside him. "Your children must have food, Mary. Come down to my house, and my wife will give you work. Come now."

Slowly Mary had risen from her chair, and smoothed down her dress and obeyed him. Down the street they went together, seeing fences still prone, seeing walls torn by shells, past the houses where the shock of battle had hastened the deaths of old persons and little children, and had disappointed the hearts of those who longed for a child, to the judge's house in the square. There wagons stood about, loaded with wheels of cannon, fragments of burst caissons, or with long, narrow pine boxes, brought from the railroad, to be stored against the day of exhumation. Men were laughing and shouting to one another. The driver of the wagon on which the long boxes were piled cracked his whip as he urged his horses.

Hannah Casey congratulated her neighbor heartily upon her finding work.

"That'll fix you up," she assured her.

She visited Mary constantly. She reported to her the news of the war. She talked at length of the coming of the President.

"I'm going to see him," she announced. "I'm going to shake him by the hand. I'm going to say, 'Hello, Abe, you old rail splitter, God bless you!' Then the bands'll play, and the people will march, and the Johnny Rebs will hear 'em in their graves."

Mary Bowman put her hands over her ears.

"I believe in my soul you'd let 'em all rise from the dead!"

"I would!" said Mary Bowman hoarsely. "I would!"

"Well, not so Hannah Casey! Look at me garden tore to bits! Look at me beds, stripped to the ropes!"

And Hannah Casey departed to her house.

Details of the coming celebration penetrated to the ears of Mary Bowman whether she wished it or not, and the gathering crowds made themselves known. They stood upon her porch, they examined the broken shutters, they wished to question her. But Mary Bowman would answer no questions, would not let herself be seen. To her the thing was horrible. She saw the battling hosts, she heard once more the roar of artillery, she smelled the smoke of battle, she was torn by its confusion. Besides, she seemed to feel in the ground beneath her a feebly stirring, suffering, ghastly host. They had begun again to open the trenches, and she looked into them.

Now, on the morning of Thursday, the nineteenth of November, her children dressed themselves and came down the steps. They had begun to have a little plumpness and color, but the dreadful light in their mother's eyes was still reflected in theirs. On the lower step they hesitated, looking at the door. Outside stood the judge, who had found time in the multiplicity of his cares to come to the little house.

He spoke with kind but firm command.

"Mary," said he, "you must take these children to hear President Lincoln."

"What!" cried Mary.

"You must take these children to the exercises."

"I cannot!" cried Mary. "I cannot! I cannot!"

"You must!" The judge came into the room. "Let me hear no more of this going about. You are a Christian, your husband was a Christian. Do you want your children to think it is a wicked thing to die for their country? Do as I tell you, Mary."

Mary got up from her chair, and put on her children all the clothes they had, and wrapped about her own shoulders a little black coat which the judge's wife had given her. Then, as one who steps into an unfriendly sea, she started out with them into the great crowd. Once more, poor Mary said to herself, she would obey. She had seen the platform; by going round through the citizen's cemetery she could get close to it.

The November day was bright and warm, but Mary and her children shivered. Slowly she made her way close to the platform, patiently she stood and waited. Sometimes she stood with shut eyes, swaying a little. On the moonlit night of the third day of battle she had ventured from her house down toward the square to try to find some brandy for the dying men about her, and as in a dream she had seen a tall general, mounted upon a white horse with muffled hoofs, ride down the street. Bending from his saddle he had spoken, apparently to the empty air.

"Up, boys, up!"

There had risen at his command thousands of men lying asleep on pavement and street, and quietly, in an interminable line, they had stolen out like dead men toward the Seminary, to join their comrades and begin the long, long march to Hagerstown. It seemed to her that all about her dead men might rise now to look with reproach upon these strangers who disturbed their rest.

The procession was late, the orator of the day was delayed, but still Mary waited, swaying a little in her place. Presently the great guns roared forth a welcome, the bands played, the procession approached. On horseback, erect, gauntleted, the President of the United States drew rein beside the platform, and, with the orator and the other famous men, dismounted. There were great cheers, there were deep silences, there were fresh volleys of artillery, there was new music.

Of it all, Mary Bowman heard but little. Remembering the judge, whom she saw now near the President, she tried to obey the spirit as well as the letter of his command. She directed her children to look; she turned their heads toward the platform.

Men spoke and prayed and sang, and Mary stood still in her place. The orator of the day described the battle, he eulogized the dead, he proved the righteousness of this great war; his words fell upon Mary's ears unheard. If she had been asked who he was, she might have said vaguely that he was Mr. Lincoln. When he ended, she was ready to go home. There was singing; now she could slip away, through the gaps in the cemetery fence. She had done as the judge commanded and now she would go back to her house.

With her arms about her children, she started away. Then someone who stood near by took her by the hand.

"Madam," said he, "the President is going to speak!"

Half turning, Mary looked back. The thunder of applause made her shiver, made her even scream, it was so like that other thunderous sound which she would hear forever. She leaned upon her little children heavily, trying to get her breath, gasping, trying to keep her consciousness. She fixed her eyes upon the rising figure before her, she clung to the sight of him as a drowning swimmer in deep waters, she struggled to fix her thoughts upon him. Exhaustion, grief, misery threatened to engulf her, she hung upon him in desperation.

Slowly, as one who is old or tired or sick at heart, he rose to his feet, the President of the United States, the Commander in Chief of the Army and Navy, the hope of his country. Then he stood waiting. In great waves of sound the applause rose and died and rose again. He waited quietly. The winner of debate, the great champion of a great cause, the veteran in argument, the master of men, he looked down upon the throng. The clear, simple things he had to say were ready in his mind, he had thought them out, written out a first draft of them in Washington, copied it here in Gettysburg. It is probable that now, as he waited to speak, his mind traveled to other things, to the misery, the wretchedness, the slaughter of this field, to the tears of mothers, the grief of widows, the orphaning of little children.

Slowly, in his clear voice, he said what little he had to say. To the weary crowd, settling itself into position once more, the speech seemed short; to the cultivated who had been listening to the elaborate periods of great oratory, it seemed commonplace, it seemed a speech which anyone might have made. But it was not so with Mary Bowman, nor with many other unlearned persons. Mary Bowman's soul seemed to smooth itself out like a scroll, her hands lightened their clutch on her children, the beating of her heart slackened, she gasped no more.

She could not have told exactly what he said, though later she read it and learned it and taught it to her children and her children's children. She only saw him, felt him, breathed him in, this great, common, kindly man. His gaze seemed to rest upon her; it was not impossible, it was even probable, that during the hours that passed he had singled out that little group so near him, that desolate woman in her motley dress, with her children clinging about her. He said that the world would not forget this field, these martyrs; he said it in words which Mary Bowman could understand, he pointed to a future for which there was a new task.

"Daughter!" he seemed to say to her from the depths of trouble, of responsibility, of care greater than her own. "Daughter, be of good comfort!"

Unhindered now, amid the cheers, across ground

which seemed no longer to stir beneath her feet, Mary Bowman went back to her house. There, opening the shutters, she bent and solemnly kissed her little children, saying to herself that henceforth they must have more food and raiment; they must be given some joy in life.

A Dark Indefinite Shore

by Bruce Catton

Like other civil wars in history, the American Civil War was a bitter struggle that tore the nation apart. But did it differ in any way from other civil wars? In the following essay, noted historian Bruce Catton considers the unique nature of this war and gives his answer to the question: "Was the war worth its cost?"

I began my work on the Civil War by trying to figure out what made the old veterans tick when they were young men. It was as simple as that. I was trying to turn the old men I had known into vigorous, young soldiers. That carried me quite a distance, but it could not have taken me through years of endeavor because, after all, that feeling you could satisfy quite easily.

The trouble is, as I got deeper and deeper into the war, there were more things I wanted to know. I wanted to know what motivated the people on both sides; why both North and South carried such terribly heavy burdens throughout the war, with really a minimum of complaining. When you read about a battle like Spotsylvania Court House, for instance, with its perfectly appalling tales of suffering, bloodshed, and death on both sides, all concentrated into one rainy summer morning along the edge of a second-growth forest, you are bound to be stirred by certain questions: What motivated the men on both sides? What drove them into that? What kept them at it? What prevented them from running away? I'm not sure that I know the answers yet, but have come to the conclusion that the American man is a pretty good man, no matter what part of the country he comes from. When he sets himself to do something, he will stick with it as long as he can stand on his feet and breathe.

But you must go beyond even that. You conduct your own examination into the war and you arrive, finally, at the questions: What did it do for us, what did it accomplish? Was it simply a waste, a needless, violent episode that broke our country apart? Was it something that should have been avoided or did we get something out of it? I suppose it took me a long time to fumble my way through questions like those, but I did finally come to the conclusion, and I grow stronger in it every day, that the war was worthwhile, that it did accomplish something. It gave us a political unity in the sense that it kept the country from fragmenting into a number of separate, independent nations. The North American continent was not Balkanized; the geographic unit that made possible the wealth and the prosperity of later days was preserved. Beyond that, the country made a commitment during that war; a commitment to a broader freedom, a broader citizenship. We can no longer be content with anything less than complete liberty, complete equality before law for all of our people regardless of their color, their race, their religion, their national origins; regardless of anything. We all have to fare alike. We are fated to continue the experiment in peaceful democracy, and

I don't think any people were ever committed to a nobler experiment than that one.

So I can't help feeling that the war was worth its cost. We have not yet reached the goal we set ourselves at the time, and I'm not sure we ever will be satisfied with our progress. But at least we keep going. We have to continue on the path that was laid out for us at Appomattox, and it is a very good path for any people to follow.

That surrender at Appomattox was one of the most important moments in American history. A great deal of emotion attaches itself to the scene we see there, particularly in the South. When Lee left Appomattox Court House to ride through his surrendered army and the men tried to cheer him and broke into tears instead, he rode straight into legend. He took the army with him, and to this day, Lee and the Army of Northern Virginia live in legend to an extent that none of the Northern soldiers or armies succeeded in doing.

It seems to me that that fact is one of the best things that ever happened to the United States, for this reason: The men of the Southern Confederacy had fought a four-year civil war; they had fought it to the limit of their ability; they had lost. Some of the things Northern armies did on Southern soil were not calculated to make the Southern people love them. All in all, the people of the South had been through a hard, bitter experience.

A civil war is, of all wars, the kind most likely to leave angry feelings; irreconcilably angry feelings. In Ireland, in France, in practically any place you name, an extended civil war has left a very uneasy peace. Often enough, it has left a peace that is not really a peace at all, with shootings at crossroads by night, with violence breaking out here and there, with the populace not in the least reconciled to defeat, and grimly anxious to carry on the struggle against the hated foe, in any way possible.

That did not happen in this country. There was bitterness in the South, to be sure. There was a feeling that still sends echoes across the body politic from time to time, but there was nothing like the incurable hatred and enmity that are ordinarily left behind by civil wars.

The Southerners were not going to resign themselves to defeat. They wanted to go ahead in any way possible, and yet, in the end there was peace.

I think the chief reason for this is the legend of Robert E. Lee and the heroic Confederate soldiers. For this legend was the channel through which pent-up emotions could be discharged. The essence of the legend of Lee and the dauntless Confederate soldiers was that they suffered mightily in a great but lost cause. The point is that this very phrase accepts the cause as having been lost. There was no hint in this legend of biding one's time and waiting for a moment when there could be revenge. This was the lost cause; something to be cherished, to be revered, to be the outlet for emotions, but not to be the center of a new outbreak of violence.

In that sense, I think the legend of the lost cause has served the entire country very well. The things that were done during the Civil War have not been forgotten, of course, but we now see them through a veil. We have elevated the entire conflict to a realm where it is no longer explosive. It is a part of American legend, a part of American history, a part, if you will, of American romance. It moves men mightily, to this day, but it does not move them in the direction of picking up their guns and going at it again. We have had national peace since the war ended, and we will always have it, and I think the way Lee and his soldiers conducted themselves in the hours of surrender has a great deal to do with it.

As it happened, Abraham Lincoln did not live to see the war end. He did know about Lee's surrender, and he knew, of course, that the war would very soon be over. He did not, however, see it end.

On the morning of April 14, Lincoln had a cabinet meeting in the White House. Everybody was feeling relaxed because Lee had surrendered, and Lincoln remarked that they were going to get big news somehow in the next twenty-four hours. His Cabinet members wanted to know what made him think so. He said he had had a dream. It was a recurrent dream that he had frequently during the war, and every time he had it, it foreshadowed some great event—a huge battle, a big victory, a political move of some kind. Well, of course, people wanted to know what the dream was like, and Lincoln said it was rather mysterious. In this dream, he was on some sort of boat, moving rapidly forward over a dim, hazy sea toward, as he put it, a dark and indefinite shore. In the dream, he had never actually reached the shore, but when he woke up, he knew that big news, a big development of some kind, was about to take place.

He was quite right. That night, he went to Ford's Theatre, and less than twenty-four hours after he told about his dreams, he was dead. He had, presumably, reached that dark, indefinite shore. He left his country with the war won, moving likewise on a mysterious vessel across a mysterious sea, toward a dark, indefinite shore. There was no chart for that shore, because nobody had ever been there. We still don't have a chart, but we are still on our way. We are crossing the seas on which the Civil War put us afloat. Like Lincoln, we are moving toward a destiny bigger than we can understand. The dark, indefinite shore is still ahead of us. Maybe we will get there some day if we live up to what the great men of our past won for us. And when we get there, it is fair to suppose that instead of being dark and indefinite, that unknown continent will be lit with sunlight.

When Freedom Came

by Julius Lester

At her mother's urging, Oscie persuades Will McLean not to sell Mary Ann. This way, Mary Ann and her husband can stay together. But what if McLean had ignored Oscie's request? Many married couples and families were in fact torn apart in the days of slavery. The following story looks at the plight of one such family when freedom came at last.

BONG!
BONG!
BONG!

The slaves looked up at the sound of the bell. None of them could remember ever hearing the bell in the afternoon. It always woke them in the morning, and the only other time it would ring was after they came from the fields and massa wanted them to come to the big house to see someone get a whipping.

"What you reckon he called us out of the fields for, Jake?" Sarah asked the tall black man next to her.

Jake shook his head. "Don't know. You suppose what we heard about us being free is true? Maybe he's calling us to the big house to tell us we free."

Sarah laughed. "You better get that notion out of

323

your head. If we was free, you don't think he'd ever tell us himself, do you?"

"I suppose not. Well, let's go see what it is. He probably done sold all of us and our new massa is waiting to take us."

"That's more like the truth."

As Jake and Sarah started to leave the field, the other slaves followed slowly. There were only ten of them on the Brower place now. The older ones, like Aunt Kate who worked in the big house, could remember the days when there were more than fifty slaves on the plantation. But that had been a long time ago. And even Jake could remember when there had been a lot more than there were now. A lot of them had been sold, and with the coming of the war some had run away. And those who remained were hoping to get away at the first opportunity.

When they gathered in the yard at the big house, Massa Brower was standing on the porch, his hands gripping the railing tightly. "Well, I guess you must be wondering why I called you out of the fields in the middle of the day." He grinned nervously at the ten expressionless faces below him, faces that were trying to prepare themselves not to feel any emotion when they heard whatever the bad news was. "I don't rightly know how to tell you this. And I guess the only way to say it is just to come out and say it. The South done lost the war. I just heard the news yesterday that General Lee surrendered to the Yankees. So that means that all the slaves is free." He paused a moment, waiting for a reaction, but there was none. "That's right," he repeated. "All the niggers is free now. You can do what you want to. You don't have to work for me no more."

The slaves stood motionless, hearing what he had

said and yet being uncertain that there wasn't some trick to it. So no one said anything. They simply waited to hear the rest.

"Well, what you standing there for looking up at me?" Brower said impatiently. "You free! Free as a white man!"

And perhaps it was that "free as a white man" that let them know it was true, because suddenly someone shouted, "Praise God! Praise God!"

"Hallelujah!" someone else yelled and started dancing around in a circle.

"Gonna hoe my own row from now on," came another voice.

Others couldn't say anything, still unable to believe what they had heard.

Brower turned red in the face as he saw the jubilation on the faces of those who, a minute before, had been his property. He had hoped that they would have thought well enough of him to have shown some regret. After all, he had been a good master. None of them had ever had to worry about a thing. He had taken care of all their needs. When they were sick, he had a doctor come, unlike other slaveowners he knew. He made sure that they'd had new shoes once a year and some meat to eat a couple of times a month. But he guessed he shouldn't expect them to show any gratitude for all he had done for them. They were only niggers. You couldn't expect niggers to be grateful for all the worry and care someone took with them.

"You was right, Jake," Sarah said. "You hear what he say. We free, Jake! We free!"

Jake nodded. "I had a feeling, Sarah. I just had a feeling."

"Ain't you happy? You always look so solemn-like."

He nodded again. "I'm happy, Sarah. Ain't wanted nothing more than to be free since I can remember. I guess since I done thought about it so much, I know that when the rest of 'em stop shouting and carrying on with jubilation, it's suddenly going to hit 'em."

"What's that?"

"Being free ain't easy. It'll hit 'em in the morning when they wake up. Where they gon' get food for breakfast? Where they gon' work at that day? We free, but free don't mean that much if you ain't got a piece of dust in the world to plant a seed in."

"You talk like you think it was better being a slave."

"I ain't saying that, Sarah, and you know it. But you just mind what I say."

The freed slaves went back to their shacks and danced and sang all afternoon. They didn't return to the field but left their hoes lying in the yard at the big house where they had dropped them when they'd heard the news. But that night, when their spirits quieted a little, they began to wonder, What are we supposed to do? No one knew. A couple of the young ones wanted nothing more than to go, and they didn't care where. "I'm just getting away from here," said one. "Maybe I'll go up North. Maybe I won't. But I'm going!"

The older slaves, however, didn't find leaving so easy. "Where am I going to go?" one said bitterly. "Been a slave for fifty years and slaving is all I know."

"You can learn something else, can't you?" one of the young men said.

"Learning ain't easy when you my age."

"Hush up your mouth!" Aunt Kate said sharply. "You ain't old as I is, Jeremiah, and I'm getting away from here so fast in the morning, massa'll think a whirlwind is coming through."

"Where you going?" someone asked.

"Don't make no difference, chile. I'm going. Free means I can come and go as I please and that's something I ain't never been 'lowed to do. I'm going to sleep all day and stay up all night just to see what it feels like." She laughed. "Sho' am. And if a white man tells me to squat, I'm gon' stand. If he say run, I'm gon' walk. If he say jump, I'm gon' roll. Whatever a white man tell me to do, I'm gon' do just the other. Free means I'm gon' do what I want to do when I want to do it and how I want to do it!"

"Talk it, Aunt Kate!" one of the young men said.

"Yes, son. I'm free now and I dare any white man to say a word to me. I just might spit in his face."

Everybody laughed.

When the laughter died, Jeremiah said, "But what you gon' do for food, Aunt Kate? How you gon' eat? Where you gon' work at?"

"Just hush your mouth. That's what's wrong with niggers. They want to know what's gon' happen before they get out of bed in the morning. Listen, Jeremiah. If the Lawd could take care of the Israelites for forty years in the wilderness, He can sho' put a little bacon rind and greens in front of Aunt Kate every once in a while. Now ain't that so?"

"That's right!" a voice assented.

"I ain't worrying about what I'm gon' eat. The Lord'll make a way. I know He will."

Jeremiah wasn't convinced, but Aunt Kate's speech had stopped the worries of the others, and all of them agreed that the next morning they would leave.

"And I tell you something else I'm gon' do," Aunt

Kate continued. "I'm gon' change my name."

"How come?"

"I'm free, ain't I?" she responded indignantly. "I can be anybody I want to now. Ain't never had a name of my own. Every time I was sold, my new massa come giving me his name. I'm gon' name myself now. Sho' 'nuf. And you better change yo' name, 'cause you know these white folks. They might decide next week that us niggers should be slaves again. And Massa Brower'll come looking for us. He'll be going through the countryside asking folks if they heard of Kate Brower. Well, the way I figure it is if I'm Kate Williams or Kate Jones, then he won't never find me. I just might change my name every week for a while, 'til I'm sure these white folks ain't gon' bring slavery back."

Nobody could sleep that night. Even though they were tired, they didn't want to sleep away their first night of freedom. And why go to bed if you didn't have to? Jake stayed apart from the celebrating. He sat on the steps of his cabin and watched and listened but said nothing. Finally Sarah came over and sat down beside him.

Sarah was much younger than Jake. She didn't know exactly how old she was, having been sold from her mother when she was still a baby. But Aunt Kate said that she wasn't more than five when she came to the Brower place. If that was true, she was about twenty-five now. She had been purchased to be the servant of Mary Lou, Master Brower's daughter, but Mary Lou had died of typhoid fever a little more than a year after Sarah had come. There was no work in the house for her after that, so she was put to work in the fields. She guessed she had fallen in love with Jake the first time she had seen him. He was much older than she, married, with several children. But even as a little girl she had known that she felt something special for him. She was more than happy to work in the fields, where she could see Jake's strong back glistening with sweat in the hot sun. He scarcely noticed her, though. Not until his wife and children were sold. That was six or seven years ago. She hadn't known what to do for Jake, particularly since she was the same age as his oldest child and that was how he thought of her. She hoped that her constant presence beside him made him feel better. He never said. But she always told herself that neither had he ever told her to go away. Now that they were free, she hoped that Jake would finally see that she was a woman, a woman who would be good to him.

"Anything the matter, Jake?"

"Just thinking."

She looked at him, wanting to reach out and hold him in her arms, but Jake looked closed up inside himself. It always made her sad to see him like that, as if he were locked up in a jail and no one could find the key. Many times she had asked him what he was thinking when he looked that way, but he'd never told her.

Jake was glad that Sarah was there. It seemed that ever since Mandy and the children had been sold, Sarah was there. At first he had been annoyed. Surely that young girl didn't think she was going to replace Mandy. But Sarah never acted as if she could. It was obvious, even to him, that she didn't have eyes for anyone on the place except him and would've married him if he had said the word. But she didn't try. After a while Jake understood that she was leaving the choice up to him. She was there and whenever he asked, she would say yes. Jake, however, couldn't see himself marrying a girl the same age as one of his children. Too, she could never have been the help and companion Mandy had been. He'd never known another woman and not a day had passed in the last seven years when he hadn't felt the pain he'd felt that day the overseer came over to Mandy and the children in the field and said that Massa Brower wanted them at the big house on the double. He started to go with them, but the overseer had pushed him back. "Didn't nobody call your name." Just as he had known today that Massa Brower was going to tell them they were free, he had known that day, as they left the field, that he would never see them again. Massa Brower had been selling niggers all spring. He must've been in some kind of money trouble, Jake figured, because he sold almost twenty that year. All that spring he and Mandy had talked about what they would do if they were separated. And all he could say was, "Someday I'd find you. That's all. I'd run away and come to you, Mandy."

He remembered waiting in the fields, waiting as he went down the rows with his hoe, waiting to see them out of the corner of his eye walking back. But they didn't. At sundown, as he left the fields, he hoped that maybe they were at the cabin waiting for him. He knew they couldn't be. No slaves were allowed at their cabins during the day unless they were sick. But he hoped. No one said a word to him as they left the fields, their hoes across their shoulders. He felt someone walking beside him, like a puppy. It was Sarah. But he paid her no attention, being unable to feel anything except a hurting like he had never known before. He walked down the slave row, and it was quiet, like a cemetery. He kept trying to see someone running out of his cabin or hear some noise inside, but there was nothing. When he walked inside, the pallets where they had slept the night before were gone. He looked all around the room and there wasn't even a thread to indicate that Mandy and the children had lived there. It was as if they had never existed.

His face took on the solemn look that made Sarah nervous that day. Everybody did what they could for him. During the next few days, every slave on the place came up to him and expressed their sorrow. He thanked each one, but their concern didn't help. Nothing would ever help, not even finding Mandy one day. Being with her again wouldn't erase that pain of standing helpless while another man took his family away from him. No man would let another man sell his wife, except a nigger. Yet he knew that all he could've done was to try and kill massa and gotten killed himself. And what would that have accomplished? Massa still would have sold them. Yet sometimes he thought it would have been better to have done something. Instead he'd just continued hoeing.

A week or so afterward he'd run away to look for them. But he hadn't gotten far before he was caught, brought back, and whipped. After that he hadn't tried again. Now, however, he was free, and before he could do anything else, he had to find Mandy. After that he would worry about what to do with his freedom.

He looked at Sarah, wondering how he could tell her. He didn't want to hurt her, but he hadn't encouraged her to love him. But he guessed he hadn't discouraged her either. Maybe if Mandy had died, he could think about marrying such a young girl. But as long as Mandy was someplace in the world, he couldn't look at another woman. He just knew that somewhere Mandy was free now, too, and she would be standing by the road looking for him.

"Jake?" Sarah said softly, breaking the silence.

"Hm?"

"What you gon' do now that we free? You gon' leave like everybody else?"

"I reckon I will."

"Where you going?"

"To look for Mandy." He said it as gently as he knew how.

Now that he had said it, Sarah noticed that she really wasn't surprised. In fact she had been expecting him to say that. "And what if you can't find her?"

"I'll find her. I'll keep looking till the day I die."

"But what if you find her and she done married another man?"

"You'd better watch your mouth, girl!" Jake said angrily.

"I didn't mean nothing," she said hastily.

"You just saying that to get me to marry you. You been after me ever since they took Mandy away. You just hoping she's dead or married to somebody else. If she's living, Mandy's waiting for me, just like I been waiting for her all these years. And I don't want to hear you saying nothing about it. You hear me?"

She had never seen him angry and it frightened her. "Jake, please, I didn't mean nothing by it. I was just thinking about you, not wanting you to be hurt. That's all."

"What you know about hurt? A young girl like

you. Nothing but a child. You don't know what hurt is, Sarah."

"If hurt is loving a man who don't love you, maybe I know a little of what it's about."

Jake nodded slowly. "I'm sorry, Sarah. I had no business saying all them things. I guess you just hit a sore spot, that's all. It done occurred to me that Mandy might be married to another man. But I can't believe that. I just can't, Sarah. I told her that if we was ever separated, I'd find her. And she said she'd wait."

"Well, for your sake, I hope she did. I hope she did, Jake."

Daybreak found the slave quarter alive with activity. Everyone, including the frightened Jeremiah, was packing his few belongings and preparing to go. Sarah was sitting on the steps of her and Aunt Kate's cabin waiting for Jake to come out. When he did, she walked over to him. He smiled when he saw her. "Sarah, I'm sorry for all them things I said last night. And I just want you to know that I wasn't unmindful of you. It was just nice knowing you was there all the time, walking by my side. I guess it wasn't easy for you, and I would've been more mindful of you if my mind hadn't been somewhere else."

"I know, Jake."

"But you too pretty a girl to be waiting on an old man like me. There's a lot of young boys around here will make you a good husband."

"You mind your business, Jake. Don't be telling me how to run my life."

Jake chuckled. "Okay. Where you going?"

She shrugged. "Don't know. Aunt Kate say she going and don't much care where. So I'll just go along with her. I expect this time next week she'll be tired of going and we'll settle somewhere. White folks are still gon' need somebody to cook their food for 'em and Aunt Kate can't do nothing else. And I don't reckon white folks going to be ready to get out in them fields and work to make a crop either. So we'll stop when Aunt Kate gets tired, and she'll go back to the kitchen and I'll go back to the fields. We don't know nothing else, do we, even if we is free?"

He nodded. "Well, maybe you'll learn something else. Maybe now you can go to a school and get some learning."

"Maybe."

"Well, Sarah. I'm off."

"Good luck to you, Jake."

"Thank you, Sarah. Thank you."

He knew Sarah was watching him as he walked up the slave row to the big house, but he didn't look back. He was leaving and when you left a place, you only looked to where you were going. And all he could see was Mandy standing by a road somewhere, looking for him.

He walked past the barn, the pig trough, and the well into the backyard of the big house. Stepping on the back porch, he knocked on the door. After a moment Massa Brower opened it. "Morning, Jake. You leaving me, I guess."

"Yessuh. I just want to know where you sold my family to."

"Oh. I been meaning to tell you how sorry I was about that, Jake."

"Yessuh."

"Owning niggers wasn't easy, you know. And I, for one, am glad it's all over with."

"Yessuh."

"I didn't want to sell Mandy. She was a good nigger. Hard worker."

"Yessuh."

"But I had to. You understand, don't you? I was in a whole lot of debt and had to raise some cash in a hurry."

"Yessuh."

"If it hadn't been for that, nothing on earth could've made me sell her."

"Yessuh. I just wants to know where you sold them to."

"They probably ain't there no more, Jake. What with the war and all. Ain't nobody where they was. Everything's turned upside down and every kind of way."

"Yessuh. I reckon the best place to start looking is the last place they was at."

Brower nodded. "Well, a man named Allen bought 'em. William Allen. From Pulaski, Tennessee, he said he was."

"Yessuh. Which way is that?"

"Well, it's east, but, Jake, that's a long ways off."

"Yessuh." And Jake walked away.

Pulaski, Tennessee, was more than five hundred miles from Pine Bluff, Arkansas. Jake wished he was a bird and could have flown those miles in a couple of days. But he had to walk them, one step at a time, one foot in front of the other. And he couldn't walk every day, because he had to stop and work to get at least enough to eat. Sometimes he got paid in money, and for a few days he could travel and buy enough to eat.

There were a lot of ex-slaves traveling the roads. Some were also looking for children, wives, husbands, or parents who had been sold. It helped him to know that he wasn't the only one. Some he talked to hadn't seen their mothers since they were children. He knew how they felt. It helped a man to know where he was from if he knew where his mother was. His mother lay in the slave burying ground on the plantation.

He wondered sometimes how many people looking for loved ones would find them, including himself. In a way it was a foolish thing to do. But there was no way not to do it. Every day someone asked him if he knew such-and-such a person or if he had heard anything about them. After three months on the road he found that he had a vast store of information and several times was able to direct someone a little closer to the person he was looking for. And just as he was asked, he asked. But it wasn't until he had passed through Nashville, Tennessee, did he find someone who thought she knew Mandy. It was an old woman, who reminded him of Aunt Kate, walking down the road with a bundle on her head. Like many others, she didn't know where she was going but, "Where ain't as important as the going, son," she said, laughing. "You know when you let a chicken out of a coop, it don't have the slightest idea where it's going. Might run out in the woods and get eaten by a fox first thing. But all the chickens know is to get away from the coop."

He asked her about Mandy and gave a description of her.

The old lady nodded. "She got some children?"

Jake nodded.

"And she dark skin, you say? Like you is?"

"That's right," he said, getting excited.

"Well, if it's the same Mandy, she live on Mr. Jim

Jenkenson's place on the other side of Pulaski. When you gets in the vicinity, son, you just ask somebody to direct you to Mr. Jim Jenkenson's place. Everybody 'round there know where it is. If it's the same Mandy, she be out there."

"How many days walking is that?"

"Three days if you stroll. Two and a half if you walk fast. And a day if you can hitch a ride on somebody's mule cart."

Jake tried not to let himself get too excited. It might be another Mandy. It was a common name. But the old woman said it was outside of Pulaski and that was where Mandy had been sold, too. Still, he kept his feelings inside of him, as if they were a present tied up in a red ribbon which he could open only on Christmas.

It took him two days of fast walking with little sleep to get to Pulaski, and the first person he asked directed him to continue down the road for another two miles. He asked that person if he knew Mandy, and the person nodded and said Mandy had six children. Jake was disappointed. Mandy only had four. He almost didn't go any farther, but since he was so close, he decided to go on. Maybe the person had made a mistake about the number of children she had.

She was walking down the road carrying a bucket of water on her head when he saw her. He knew it was she, the one arm raised over her head, resting lightly against the bucket, the other arm swinging loosely at her side. He had always loved the easy way Mandy had of walking, even with a bucket of water on her head. She never looked like she was working. He started to call out her name, but stopped. It was just possible that it was somebody else. Sometimes every woman he saw looked like Mandy, so he started running to catch up with her.

The woman heard the hurried steps behind her and stopped to look back. Jake saw the soft black face he had loved all of his life and shouted, "It's you! It's you! Mandy!" He ran up to her, tears running down his face. "Oh, thank God. Mandy!"

"Jake? Is that you, Jake?"

"It ain't Abraham Lincoln," he said, laughing.

She gazed at him, uncertain what to do. Then, letting her hand drop from the bucket she screamed, "Jake!" as the bucket tumbled from her head and water splashed both of them. She flung her arms around him, laughing. "Jake, Jake, Jake. It is you, ain't it?"

And with the feel of her arms pressing against his back, Jake felt himself come to life for the first time since he'd last seen her. He buried his face in her neck. "I told you that if anything ever happened, I'd find you. I told you, didn't I?"

"You look just the same," Mandy said, looking at him. "Just the same." She stepped out of his arms and picked up the bucket, laughing. "Look what you made me do. Now I got to go all the way back to the spring and get some more."

"Well, come on. How's Charles and Mary Ann and Caesar and Carl?" he asked, referring to the children.

"Oh, they fine. You probably won't recognize none of 'em. They so big now."

He laughed. "And to think that I almost didn't come out here."

"What you mean?"

"Well, I asked after you in town and a man said he knew of a Mandy who had six children and since we only got four, I just figured it was another Mandy. I almost didn't come, till it occurred to me that he might have made a mistake."

They came to the spring and Mandy bent to fill the bucket.

"Let me do it," Jake said. "You ain't gon' be toting no more water now. And anyway, how come Charles or one of the other children didn't come and get it?"

"They out in the field."

"Well, from now on you ain't gon' be doing no more of that heavy lifting and work like that." Jake filled the bucket. "I never could carry it on my head like you."

"Jake? Set that bucket down." She laughed, looking at him trying to set it on his head.

"I'll carry it," Jake said proudly.

"Set it down," she said, suddenly sad.

He put it on the ground and looked at her. "Anything the matter?"

She nodded. "I ain't your wife no more, Jake," she said sadly, looking at her feet. "That man in town what told you I got six children now was telling the truth. I should've told you back on the road when you brought it up. But I didn't know how to tell you."

"You ain't married to somebody else?"

She nodded and broke into tears. "How was I to know for sure you'd find me, Jake? I could've waited for you until the day I died and you never showed up 'cause you was dead or had done married somebody else."

"Aw, Mandy," he cried, taking her in his arms. "But I told you I'd find you, didn't I? I told you that!"

"I know, Jake, and I wanted to believe you. God knows I did. But a woman gets lonesome, Jake. And Henry was a nice man. The children liked him, too. So we jumped the broom and I prayed that this time the Lord wouldn't let me or him be sold away from each other. And after we was freed, the first thing we done was to go and get married like white folks do, and get a piece of paper so couldn't nobody come and separate us. If I'd known, Jake, I wouldn't have done it. But a woman gets lonesome."

"So do a man," he sobbed. "So do a man."

They held each other tightly for a while. "I just wish I'd known, Jake," she whispered softly, stepping back and wiping her eyes.

"Mandy? You ain't got to stay, do you?" Jake said, getting excited. "Now that I'm here, you can leave and come with me."

Mandy shook her head. "I can't do that, Jake. I swore before God and the preacher to be with Henry until one of us died. And, plus, we got married by the paper, the way the white folks do. And when you get the paper, you married sho' 'nuf. It ain't like jumping the broom. Like we done in slavery time. We ain't slaves no more, Jake. We got to live by the paper now."

"But, Mandy, I love you! I ain't thought about nothing else for seven years but you!"

She started crying again. "I loves you, too, Jake. God knows I do. But Henry's a good man, and I don't love him like I do you, but I guess I love him. I loved him enough to get married by the paper."

Jake shook his head repeatedly, muttering, "No,

no, no, no. It ain't right. First they come and take you away, sell you like you a bale of cotton. They don't ask me how my heart feels about it. Just sell you away. Then you meets somebody you don't love like you love me, but they give you a piece of paper saying you got to be with him, though you love me. It ain't right, Mandy. It just ain't right."

"But that's the way it is, Jake. Wasn't right for us to be slaves all them years neither, but that was the way it was." She picked up the bucket of water and hoisted it to her head. "I—I got to be getting back, Jake. You want to come see the children? I know Henry wouldn't mind. I told him all about you and he say you sound like a very good man, the kind of man he'd like to know. I know you'd like him, too, Jake. Ain't none of this his fault."

"I know that, Mandy. But I reckon not. I don't think I could stand seeing another man happy with you."

She nodded. "I understands."

She started up the path from the spring to the road. Jake didn't move. He raised his head and watched the easy swaying of her body. When she got to the road she turned and looked at him. He could see the tears coming down her face.

"I wish I'd known, Jake."

"God knows, I wished you had too, Mandy," he said, biting his lip and sobbing as he watched her walk down the road and out of sight.

Southern Mansion

by Arna Bontemps

*Oscie comes to realize that when the
Civil War ends, a way of life will die with it
forever. This poem, written almost 100
years after the war ended, presents some
lingering images of that way of life. How
do you think Oscie would react to these
images of the Old South?*

Poplars are standing there still as death
And ghosts of dead men
Meet their ladies walking
Two by two beneath the shade
5   And standing on the marble steps.

There is a sound of music echoing
Through the open door
And in the field there is
Another sound tinkling in the cotton:
10   Chains of bondmen dragging on the ground.

The years go back with an iron clank,
A hand is on the gate,
A dry leaf trembles on the wall.
Ghosts are walking.
15   They have broken roses down
And poplars stand there still as death.

In Honor of David Anderson Brooks, My Father

by Gwendolyn Brooks

Though Oscie's natural father has died before In My Father's House *begins, his presence looms large in the novel. At one point Oscie tells Maria that sometimes "Daddy John" comes to her in her dreams, not saying anything but leaving her with the feeling that he is still "real close" to her. In the following poem, Gwendolyn Brooks remembers her own father.*

July 30, 1883–November 21, 1959

A dryness is upon the house
My father loved and tended.
Beyond his firm and sculptured door
His light and lease have ended.

5   He walks the valleys, now—replies
To sun and wind forever.
No more the cramping chamber's chill,
No more the hindering fever.

Now out upon the wide clean air
10 My father's soul revives,
All innocent of self-interest
And the fear that strikes and strives.

He who was Goodness, Gentleness,
And Dignity is free,
15   Translates to public Love
Old private charity.

She

by Rosa Guy

*As the Civil War begins, Oscie fights a
different kind of battle at home—a battle
of wills with her stepfather, Will McLean.
Such family struggles have taken place in
every age. In the following short story, set
in the present day, the narrator fights a
war against her stepmother.*

"Just where do you think you're going?" she said.

"To the bathroom," I said.

"No, you're not," she said. "Not before you wash
up these dishes."

"This is a matter of urgent necessity," I said. I
hated that even my going to the bathroom had to be
questioned.

"Don't want to hear," she said. "I'm sick and tired
of emergency, emergency every night after dinner.
Get to that sink."

"I'll wash the dishes," Linda said. She got up and
started to clear off the table. I slipped out of the
kitchen. The angry voice followed me down the hall:

"Linda, don't keep letting your sister get away
with everything."

"I don't mind—really, Dorine," Linda said.

"That girl's just too lazy. . . ." I shut the bathroom
door to muffle the sounds of her grievances against
me. She didn't like me. She never had. And I didn't
care. Stepmothers . . . !

Searching the bottom of the hamper for the science
fiction magazine I had hidden beneath the dirty

clothes, I sat on the toilet and began to read to get out of this world—as far from her as I could get.

From the day she had walked into our house she'd been on me. I was lying on my bed reading when she and Daddy pushed into my room without knocking. Our eyes locked. She didn't speak. Neither did I.

I was in a panic. Daddy had forbidden me to read fairy tales. "At twelve years old! You too old," he'd said. He wanted me to read only school books. I hadn't had time to hide the book of fairy tales beneath my mattress as I usually did. I curled up around it, praying to keep his eyes from it.

But Daddy was only showing her the apartment. So she had to turn to inspect my almost bare room. When she looked back at me, her eyes said: What are you doing reading in this miserable room instead of doing something useful around this terrible house? My eyes answered: What's it to you?

They left the room the way they'd come. Abruptly. Hearing their footsteps going toward the kitchen, I got up and followed. Linda was in the kitchen, washing fish for our dinner. When they went in, Linda looked up and smiled.

"What a lovely girl," Dorine said, and the shock of her American accent went through me. What was Daddy doing with an American woman! "She's got to be the prettiest child I ever did see. My name is Dorine," she said.

From the first she had chosen Linda over me. Maybe because Linda was pretty, with her long, thick hair and clear brown eyes and brown velvet skin. I was plain-looking. Or maybe because Linda was two years older—already a teen-ager.

"You're Daddy's friend," Linda said, batting her long black eyelashes the way she always did whenever someone paid her a compliment. "I didn't know Daddy had a lady friend." Daddy gave Linda a quick look and she changed to: "My name is Linda. And that's"—she pointed to where I stood in the doorway—"the baby. Her name is Gogi."

But Dorine had already turned away from Linda to inspect the kitchen. And suddenly I saw our kitchen and the sweat of embarrassment almost drowned me: the sink was leaking and had a pan under it to catch the dirty water; the windowpanes were broken and stuffed with newspapers to keep out winter; the linoleum was worn, showing the soft wood beneath.

And she wore furs. Our mother had never worn furs. Not even when Daddy had had lots of money. People from the tropics didn't think of wearing things like furs. And the way Dorine looked around—nose squinched up, mouth pulled back—judging us, West Indians.

Daddy stood in the middle of the kitchen, quieter than usual—big, broad, handsome in his black overcoat, around his arm the black crepe band of mourning. His hands were deep in the pockets of his gray wool suit. And she hit out at him: "Harry, how can you live like this!"

Linda stopped smiling then. Daddy's eyebrows quivered. My mouth got tight with satisfaction. Daddy had a mean temper. I waited for him to blast her out of our house and out of our lives. She had socked us where we hurt—our pride.

"How you mean?" Daddy had said. "We ain't live so. You see mi restaurant. . . ." So, he had known her while our mother was still alive. ". . . I lose it," he said. "Mi wife dead. I sell mi house, mi furniture, mi car. I—I—mi friend let me stay here for a time—but it only for a short time." He was begging! I hated that he stood there begging.

"If it's only one minute, that's one minute too long," she said.

Lifting my head from the science fiction magazine to turn a page, I heard the sounds of pots banging against pans in the kitchen. And I heard Dorine's footsteps in the hall. I waited for the knob to turn on the bathroom door. She sometimes did that. But this time she went on into the living room. A short time later I heard the television playing.

It had been two years since the pointing, the ordering, the arranging and rearranging of our lives had begun. She had forced us to leave our old free apartment and move into her big one with its big rooms, its big kitchen and all those dozens of pots and pans for all things and all occasions. We had to listen to her constant: "Cleanliness is next to godliness," and "A good housekeeper has a place for everything and keeps everything in its place." Like who told her that what we wanted most in life was to be housekeepers? I didn't!

Daddy let her get away with everything. He stayed out most days looking for work. And he spent evenings gambling with his friends. The times he spent at home he spent with her—laughing and joking in their bedroom. She entertained him to keep him there. I'd see her flashing around the house in her peach-colored satin dressing gown, her feet pushed into peached-colored frilly mules, her big white teeth showing all across her face, her gown falling away to expose plump brown knees. Guess that's what he liked—that combination of peach satin and smooth brown skin.

She worked, a singer. Sometimes for weeks she'd

be out on the road. Then she'd come home with her friends and they'd do all that loud American talking and laughing. She sometimes brought us lovely things back from "the road." Blouses, underwear, coats. She won Linda's affection like that and might have won mine if I hadn't heard a man friend say to her one day: "Dorine, it's bad enough you got yourself hooked up with that West Indian. But how did you manage to get in a family way?"

"Big Red," she called him. "I'm in love."

"With all of 'em?" he asked.

"They come with the deal," she said.

"Some deal," he answered.

"You don't need to worry none, Big Red," she said. "They earns their keep."

She saw me standing in the doorway then, and her big eyes stretched out almost to where I stood. Guilty. Her mouth opened. I walked away. I had heard enough. I went right in and told Linda. "That's what she wants us around for," I said. "To be her maids."

"Gogi," Linda said. "She probably didn't mean it that way at all."

"What other way could she mean it?" I asked. Innocent Linda. She never saw the evil in the hearts and minds of people.

But from that day Dorine picked on me. When I vacuumed the hall, she called me to show me specks I could hardly see and made me vacuum over again. When I cleaned my room, she went in and ran her fingers over the woodwork to show me how much dust I had left behind. "That ain't the way we do things around here," she liked to say. "Do it right or don't do it at all." As though I had a choice!

"Trying to work me to death, that's what she's

doing," I complained to Linda.

"But why don't you do things right the first time, Gogi?" Linda said. I could only stare at her. My sister!

We had always been close. Linda hadn't minded doing things for me before Dorine came, as long as I read to her. Linda never had time for things like reading. She knew she was pretty and kept trying to make herself perfect. Linda washed her blouses and underwear by hand. She ironed her clothes to defeat even the thought of a wrinkle. And she had always done mine along with hers, just to have me read to her.

But now our stepmother who had turned our father against us had turned my sister against me! Well, if Linda wanted to be a maid, that was her business. I did enough when I vacuumed the hall and cleaned my room. If Linda had to take Dorine's side against me, then let Dorine read for her. I was satisfied to do my reading to myself—by myself.

Sitting too long on the toilet, I felt the seat cut into my thighs. I got up to unstick myself and leaving the toilet unflushed—not to give away that I had finished—I sat on the closed stool, listening to what ought to have been sounds of glass clinking against glass, of china against china.

The quiet outside the bathroom unsettled me. I usually knew when Linda had finished with the dishes. I always heard when she passed to join Dorine in the living room. They played the television loud, thinking to make me jealous, making me feel unneeded, pretending not to care that I had shut myself from them and that I might go to my room without even a goodnight. But I hadn't heard Linda pass!

The television kept playing. I strained to hear the program to tell the time. It was on too low. Getting up, I thought of going out to see how things were but sat down again. Better to give Linda a little more time. I started another story.

I had only half finished when my concentration snapped. The television had been turned off. I tried to but couldn't get back into the story. Instead I sat listening, hoping to pick up sounds from the silent house. What time was it?

Getting up, I put my ear to the door. No outside sound. Unlocking the door, I cracked it open and peeked out. The hallway was dark! Everybody had gone to bed! How late was it? Taking off my shoes I started tiptoeing down toward my room. Then from the dark behind me I heard: "Ain't no sense in all that creeping. Them dishes waiting ain't got no ears." I spun around. A light went on and there she was, lying on a chaise lounge that had been pulled up to the living room door. "That's right, it's me," she said. "And it's one o'clock in the morning. Which gives you enough time to wash every dish in the sink squeaking clean before one o'clock noon."

Tears popped to my eyes as she marched me down past my room, past the room where Linda slept, into the kitchen. Tears kept washing my cheeks as I washed dishes. She sat inspecting every one, acting as though we were playing games. If we were, I expected it to go on forever. She had tricked me—and she had won.